THE HAUNTING OF BLACKBURN MANOR

BLAKE CROFT   ASHLEY RAVEN
(REVISED EDITION, 2021)

COPYRIGHT © 2019, 2021 BY BLAKE CROFT

BOOK DESCRIPTION

Blackburn Manor hides a terrifying and unnatural secret.

After months on the run from an abusive relationship, Linda Green is ready to slow down and start her life over again. Exhausted from ever-present fear and stress, she yearns for the peace that a fresh start can bring. A fresh start she hopes to find at Blackburn Manor.

The lush green trees and serene nature surrounding the manor feel so calming to her frazzled soul that Linda is ready to take advantage of everything this peaceful oasis has to offer. No internet, no distractions. It's perfect.

Until she sees the faces in the window.

Not one to believe much in the supernatural, Linda shrugs it off as just a feeling. But the longer she's at the manor, the more the feeling of uneasiness grows. From the creepy old neighbor who watches her every move to the moving shadows and unexplained phone calls in the middle of the night, something is just not right.

She can trust no one. Not even herself.

As Linda begins to uncover the history of the place, she is sure that something strange is going on at Blackburn Manor. Something sinister that hides in the shadows, deep within walls cloaked with secrets.

Something that will stop at nothing to keep those secrets hidden.

Praise for **The Haunting of Blackburn Manor***:*

- *"Creepy Haunting! (...) Not the average ghost story."*
- *"Very enjoyable eerie book"*
- *"Underground terror and ghosts aren't the worst part but a *** on the prowl!"*
- *"Wonderful well written plot and story lines that had me engaged from the start. Love the well fleshed out characters and found them believable. Great suspense and action with wonderful world building that adds so much to the story. Such a thrilling read that I couldn't put it down."*
- *"Excellent read. I was totally drawn into this story."*

An Amazon US/UK New Release Bestseller (#1 Ghosts & Haunted Houses - #2 Supernatural, Horror & Occult Suspense).

From supernatural suspense and psychological horror authors Blake Croft and Ashley Raven comes *The Haunting of*

Blackburn Manor. Follow Linda and her sister in this riveting novel about what happens when a woman's search for sanctuary turns into a desperate and terrifying attempt to save her own life.

Don't miss *The Haunting of Blackburn Manor,* a chilling supernatural horror mystery!

FOREWORD

This story is dedicated to you, the reader.

Thank you for taking a chance on us, and for joining us on this journey.

Do you want to keep up to date with all of our latest releases, and **get a free copy of** *The Abandoned House* (exclusive to members of our readers' group)?

Sign up for the no-spam newsletter. Details can be found at the end of the book.

Blake Croft & Ashley Raven

PART I
STRANGE SANCTUARY

PROLOGUE

The old woman sat on her front porch.

Summer was bleeding into winter, and there was a chill in the air. In the gloom of dusk, even the birds had stopped chirping. The only sound punctuating the arrival of night on that empty street was the rhythmic creak of a rocking chair.

The old woman swayed back and forth on a chair almost as old as she was. The carved wood was warped by the elements, and so were her bones, twisted and rusty under her paper-thin skin. Her thick white hair was cut short, and she wore a pale-blue housedress that sagged at the front and stopped at her knees, revealing blue varicose veins running along the length of her spindly legs. A group of cats sat around the porch, their tails flitting about to the rhythm of the creaking chair.

There wasn't much to see on that empty street hedged in by thick woods, but the woman stared with focused contempt and spite across the street at the only other house for a mile. Being a house was the only thing both buildings had in common. It was a nineteenth century manor, its tiled roofs rearing against the sky, and its narrow windows like eyelets peering down on the old woman's small dwelling, as if the house sneered at something so humble in its presence.

The woman's eyes were narrowed, her lips as thin as the edge of a blade. She stared as if waiting for something to happen.

A low thud broke through the peaceful quiet.

The rocking chair stopped.

The cats' tails stood still.

A low feral yowl rose into the night. A cat hissed, back arched, hair standing on end. The old woman licked her lips as she leaned forward expectantly in her chair.

Another thud broke through the thrumming silence. It came from across the street. A final thud and the front door opened. A dog came shambling out, head lolling from side to side. Its golden coat looked less lustrous than it usually did. Drool dangled in ropes from its open mouth. It was followed by a man in his mid-thirties, a look of concern and consternation on his face.

"Jesus, Bud," the man's voice resounded in the wilderness. "If you wanted to go out, you could just scratch the door. No need to break your head against it."

The old woman's body tensed, her gnarled hands clutched the arms of the chair. Her pupils were so dilated they resembled the dead-black eyes of a shark.

The dog whined, its tail stuck firmly between its legs. It turned in circles, emitting pained yelps. The sounds of its nails clicking against hardwood punctuated its distress.

The old woman licked her lips again. The cats were in a frenzy, their raucous cries a cacophony in the still twilight.

The dog stood still, ears cocked, as if it had heard some animal scurrying in the underbrush.

"Hey, Buddy." The young man's brow was creased in worry. "Are you all right? You wanna go for a walk? We can play fetch, huh, what'dya say?" He leaned down and tried to pet the dog but the animal bolted as if shot.

"Buddy!" The man scrambled for the dog's collar, but it was too late.

The golden retriever hurtled off the steep porch.

The crack of breaking bones was ominous and loud in the sudden silence.

"Buddy?" The man ran down the porch steps, nearly losing his balance.

He knelt down by the twitching dog, and held it in his arms. "You're going to be okay," the man said. "You're going to be fine." His voice broke. "You won't die, Buddy. I'll call the vet. You won't die."

The old woman watched the stooped back of the man as he trudged up the porch steps across the street. Her breathing was shallow, and her lips moist. The cats settled around her, their tails twisted around their hind legs.

The woman sat back in her chair.

Her hands relaxed on the arms.

The chair creaked as it began to rock again.

CHAPTER 1

There were eyes in the woods.

Linda sat up straight in the passenger seat of the old Chevy truck. Her backside hurt. Pins and needles pricked her legs as blood rushed to her cramped limbs.

She squinted at the moving tree line as the truck rushed past. The woods were thick but she could make out houses in the distance. The sun reflecting off glass windows looked like winking yellow eyes in the woods.

Linda shivered and tried to shake the morbid thought from her head.

"I think we're finally closing in on the town," said Ashley.

The two sisters had been driving for hours, and it was the first thing one of them had said for some time. Conversation had run out when they'd crossed into Pennsylvania. They were in Blackwood County now.

A small sign appeared to the left. Keystone Pop. 6000 was

painted black against a stark white background. It was a long way from Brooklyn, where they had always lived.

A lone yellow bus stop emerged in the middle of the woods. Two minutes later, the town itself reared out of the tree line. It wasn't a smooth transition from thick wood to subtle clearing and then office buildings and townhouses. Trees bunched up around the edges as if they remembered the past when the whole area had been one undisturbed carpet of green and they would soon take it back.

"It's remote." Ashley said. "I'll give you that. They have one diner, no hotels, and… Oh my God, that's the movie theater?"

It was something out of the 50s. The posters for *Jurassic World* were glued over so many others they jutted out slightly from the wall. A group of gangling young teens leaned against the building.

"At least they have the latest releases." Linda spread her hands.

Ashley glared at her.

They sat in silence as the town passed by. There was another bus stop at the other end of town next to the post office, and a branch of Bank of America. The woods invaded again. They were oppressive, and as the sun set lower in the sky their branches looked like fingers reaching down to grasp the truck.

"What's the name of the owner again?" Ashley asked.

"Evelyn Blackburn," Linda said, folding her arms across her breasts. "She was one of the pioneers of second wave feminism, used to be a professor at Columbia."

Ashley whistled.

"I hope this place is livelier than Keystone. The town seemed to emerge from the tree line like some lost city in the Amazon forest." Ashley slumped low in the driver's seat.

"It wasn't that bad," Linda tucked her hair behind her ears. "The artisan bakery/café looked nice."

"Lin," Ashley blew air out of her cheeks, "they have one café, the motel looked seedy, the movie theater has one screen, and the hospital is twenty minutes away. I wouldn't call that ideal."

"That's not fair," Linda laughed. "It's a seasonal town and predominantly the B&B kind. It'll perk up in a few weeks once school is out."

Ashley pursed her lips in response.

The woods thinned out a little as the road curved to the left. Large, slightly shabby houses sat brooding for half a mile on both sides of the road. Linda spied the American flag hanging wet and limp outside a house in serious need of paint. A forgotten bike lay upturned in a yard dotted with garden gnomes whose cherub-pink cheeks highlighted the evil slant in their ceramic eyes. There weren't any lights on in any of the windows.

"They certainly have good taste in this town." Ashley snorted. "Are those plastic flamingos?"

Linda couldn't help but smile. Yes, the yards were atrocious and wild. She kept an eye out for people, but they didn't see anyone as they passed the handful of homes that were quickly replaced by thick woods.

It was like no one lived there. Linda twisted in her seat to get another look at the forlorn homes.

The empty windows made her uneasy. It was true that she had come this far for some solitude but this was more than she had bargained for. They left the small neighborhood behind but Linda couldn't shake off the uneasy feeling.

"What does Google Maps say? I feel like we should have reached this place half an hour ago," Ashley said.

Linda checked her map. There was only one bar, and the blip that marked their location was still stuck on Keystone. She zoomed in and marked the neighborhood they'd just passed and made some swift calculations.

"Another ten minutes."

"Jeez." Ashley rolled her eyes. "They should have mentioned these things in the employment letter. If half of my wages go towards gas to get to and from town, how is this job worth it?"

Linda didn't take Ashley's complaining to heart. It was usual for her to look at the negatives in any given situation. Their mother had always said they were Yin and Yang, Ashley the negative and Linda the positive balance in the relationship.

"I didn't hear you complain about it last week," Linda gave a wry smile. "Come on, Ash. We both need jobs and I need the counseling."

"I don't see why it had to be in the middle of nowhere." Ashley grumbled but didn't disagree.

Guilt spread through Linda's chest. They were here because of her.

It was true that Ashley had lost her job because of company downsizing, but Linda still felt a little responsible. By the time she had been let go, Linda was completely dependent on her sister for financial and emotional support.

"Sorry," Linda muttered.

"It's not your fault," Ashley sighed, her voice full of regret. "It's that bastard's fault." Her brow darkened, her jaw clenched, and she frowned. Anyone glancing inside the car at that moment would fear the wrath of Ashley.

She was referring, of course, to Linda's ex-fiancé Jackson.

The scars had mended, the bruises had faded, but the psychological damage was far from healed. She had made progress through the lengthy trial, but getting out of bed had been a mammoth task, let alone caring for herself.

Unable to afford psychiatric counseling, Linda had met with abuse survivors at the local library. One of them had mentioned the Blackburn Healing Retreat in Pennsylvania, where you could work to reduce the fees for counseling, and regain some sense of productivity in the world. The founder was Dr. Evelyn Blackburn herself, a psychologist who had retired from the life of academia to start a retreat to help women just like Linda.

"This will be good for us," Ashley said. "I know I'm gloom and doom sometimes, but I have a good feeling about this. Now if only we can get there."

"Oh, look! I can see rooftops." Linda pointed at the horizon.

The road stretched on, the woods sentinels along its edges, but two houses jutted out of the landscape as afterthoughts. There were no other houses nearby, which seemed off to Linda. The twisting ball of anxiety that had rolled about in her stomach since they passed the barren beginnings of Keystone became still. It didn't go away. Linda doubted it ever would, but that's why she was here.

"Wow." Ashley whistled as they drove closer.

Though they were divided by a single road, both houses looked drastically different.

The Blackburn Health Retreat was nothing short of a sprawling manor house. Victorian in design, it contained all the elements of gothic architecture Linda had read about in her H. P. Lovecraft books. An old stone structure, it had moss and ivy creeping up along one wall and a single spire-like tower on the left side with large windows along its length. Linda thought of Rapunzel when she saw it, but the image that kept creeping into her head was the one in her childhood storybook of Dame

Gothel, her hands twisted into a claw as she snatched out the eyes of the prince.

Linda shook her head. *Get a grip. What's with the spooks?*

Ashley turned into the short driveway of Blackburn Manor. Only one other car was parked in the drive.

"God, my legs are killing me." Ashley stopped the engine and stepped out of the car.

Linda stayed inside for a minute longer, looking at the manor. It captivated the imagination, but why was her heart beating madly in her chest? Her breathing was shallow and she felt trepidation trip down her spine.

Not right now, she thought. *I can't have an anxiety attack right now.*

"Come on, Lin," Ashley knocked on her window, making Linda jump. "Let's go introduce ourselves, then we'll deal with the luggage."

Swallowing to moisten her dry throat, Linda stepped out of the car.

As far as the eye could see, there was nothing but an army of trees. This stretch of road continued to curve along a ridge of rocky hills in the distance. The other house was a slipshod structure of wood, dominated by a large porch and narrow front steps.

Linda smoothed her skirt and stretched her aching limbs. Her stomach was still fluttering. The sun was on its way down; shadows were building in the woods that surrounded the property. A screen door squeaked open and shut from behind them.

Linda swiveled around to the house across the street, her scalp prickling with nervous sweat.

An old woman in a loose summer dress and lumpy cardigan stood on the porch, squinting down at them through thick glasses. Her hair was cut short, accentuating her thin neck. A couple of cats were meowing at her feet, with more rushing out of the trees and under the porch. The woman held two large bowls in her hand.

Linda smiled and waved. The woman scowled, placed the bowls on the porch, and huffed back inside. Cold fingers dribbled down Linda's back. She flashed hot and cold, her skin peppered with goosebumps.

"Neighborly," Ashley commented. "Come on, Lin, let's get inside."

Suddenly Linda didn't want to go inside. The front doors were large and imposing. The windows were dark eyes staring down at her. Ashley had already climbed the steep stone steps to the front door. Linda wanted to scream at her to turn away.

Stop this, she scolded herself. *You're not going to jeopardize such an amazing opportunity because of some stupid trigger you don't even recognize at the moment. Calm down, breathe in and out. Take it one step at a time.*

Using the calming techniques she'd picked up at group meetings, Linda took shaky breaths and climbed the steps, her hand tracing the railing, feeling the rough sun-warmed stone beneath her fingers.

Ashley rang the bell. It gonged through the manor, deep and ominous. All calm abandoned Linda.

"Are you okay?" Ashley asked. "You look pale."

Something shuffled behind the door. Linda heard footsteps, and a cough. The sound was too familiar. Jackson had coughed like that after a smoke.

"Lin?" Ashley held her arm.

She glanced nervously behind her, the spot between her shoulder blades tingling as if someone was watching her.

It couldn't be possible. He wasn't here. He couldn't be. He was in jail.

Her eyes grew hot and wet. She blinked away the sudden tears. The sun was bleeding out in the sky.

"Linda, is everything alright?"

A lock turned and the door opened.

A blade flashed, catching the last of the dying sun.

Linda screamed.

CHAPTER 2

Linda stepped back so fast in her terror, she trod on Ashley's foot.

Ashley yowled in pain.

A man stood in the doorframe. He was tall, easily a head taller than Linda.

"I'm sorry," he said. "Did I startle you?" He stepped back, staring at Linda as if he'd seen a ghost.

He was well built and classically handsome, his face strong-jawed and clean-shaven, his eyes blue. There was a small cleft in his chin.

"Who are you?" Ashley hopped on one foot.

Linda's heart was beating a tattoo in her throat. She couldn't take her eyes off the knife.

"I'm Stewart," he said, looking slightly puzzled. Then something dawned on him. "Oh, you must be Linda Green." He looked down at the knife in his hand. He quickly hid it behind his back. "I'm sorry, I was just starting dinner."

"We must have the wrong house." Ashley touched Linda's arm. "It must be the one across the street."

"Oh, no," Stewart said. "This is the house."

"Really?" Ashley spat. "And is this how guests are greeted?"

Stewart flushed. Linda just wanted to get back in the car and get away.

"I've apologized for startling you. I don't think I've ever apologized for making dinner before," Stewart said. "Why don't you come inside? You can meet Mom and we can have a bite to eat."

Linda didn't want to go inside. She wanted to get as far away as possible from the knife-wielding man. Her basic instincts had taken over and she was like a deer in the headlights, caught between fight and flight. But Linda's instinct for the longest time had been paralyzing fright.

Ashley must have read her mind. "Don't take this the wrong way, but I hardly think it's smart to walk into a stranger's house like that."

Stewart smiled. It was charming and boyish. He rubbed the back of his neck, a lock of his dark hair falling on his forehead.

"I hardly think we're strangers. I knew your name," he pointed out. "I also know that you're from Brooklyn. I even have your CV on my computer. Do you want me to get the account number it got sent from?"

As he spoke, Linda's anxiety receded to the back of her throat. She was no longer biting it between her teeth. The tenor of his voice was soothing, and the facts he mentioned put him down squarely as someone who knew her situation.

"Where's Dr. Blackburn?" Linda asked.

Stewart turned his face from Ashley to look at her. The

fading light hit his face so his eyes shone a deep blue. If she wasn't careful she could get lost in those depths.

"Dr. Blackburn is my mother," Stewart said. "Would like to meet her?"

"That's why we came." Ashley had her hands folded across her chest. She was not taken in by the man's charm.

"Come on in. I'm sure she'll be happy to see you."

Linda and Ashley exchanged glances.

Linda nodded. Ashley rolled her eyes.

Stepping into the front hall was like walking into a cavernous womb. The walls were covered in green wallpaper and imposing paintings in gilded frames. A teakwood staircase spiraled up to the second floor, its surface dark with age. The furniture was an antiquarian's dream come true; the ceilings were high with intricate plaster moldings.

It was a little disconcerting. Linda had expected white walls and minimalist interiors to hone a sense of peace and calm. This was more cluttered, and more gothic than she had expected.

Doors lined the long hall. Stewart went to the only one on the left, which was slightly ajar. The interior here was starkly different. It was cozy and looked like it had been furnished by a grandmother. There were crocheted doilies on the tables, hand-embroidered cushions on the chairs, and a patchwork quilt on the back of the sofa.

Linda watched Ashley wrinkle her nose. She swatted at her sister's arm.

"This wing is off limits to employees and clients. This is where Mom and I live. It's another step to ensure clients are relaxed when they stay here." Stewart walked through a narrow hall with built-in stairs that led to the upper floor. Through a narrow arch at the end of the hall they reached a kitchen.

Unlike the front hall, this space was relatively new with modern furnishings. Linda could see a modest table in the middle of the kitchen surrounded by mismatched chairs. Something was bubbling in a saucepan on the stove, and vegetables lay on the draining board ready to be chopped. It smelled lovely.

Stewart didn't stop. He placed his knife next to the vegetables and opened the screen door to the back of the manor.

The back porch was another relic out of some fairy tale. Wide and surrounded by stone colonnades, it reminded her of old castles.

The back lawn was sprawling but it looked like the woods had encroached on it over the years. The woods climbed steadily, cresting the hill beyond. There was a vegetable garden in one corner of the yard and rioting flowers in another. In the middle was a large swathe of grass, and at the very back was a tool shed.

In that circle of green was a wheelchair. On that wheelchair sat a woman in a long cotton nightdress. Her hair was iron gray, her chin wrinkling into her neck. She sat with her arms loosely crossed in front of her. The right index finger scratched at her left arm just below the shoulder. A woman in a nurse's smock stood beside her. She was holding a book from which she had been reading to the old lady.

"That's my mom," Stewart said. "That's Dr. Evelyn Blackburn."

Linda's knees wobbled.

"We were given the impression that she ran this retreat." Ashley turned on Stewart as if he had been responsible for their long drive up here for nothing. "That's why we chose this establishment, because of her expertise in rehabilitation."

"She did." Stewart's face was suddenly stony. "She ran the retreat, but I have always been her assistant. She would deal with the therapy side of the operation, while I managed administration and accounts ensuring minimum interaction with clients."

"You're S. Blackburn?" Ashley pointed a finger at him. "You're the recruiter who hired us. We've been emailing you thinking you were Evelyn's daughter. I really don't know why we'd assumed you were a woman."

He sighed and ran a hand through his hair. "It's not the first time, I'm sorry for the confusion. Evelyn... Mom had a heart attack almost a year ago. It wasn't severe. She was making a quick recovery, but then the second one followed less than twenty-four hours later. She's lucky to still be alive."

Linda looked at the old, thin woman. Her body was slack and weak, but her blue eyes were sharp. They looked right back —direct, questioning, very much alive. They held all the power and knowledge she must have once exuded through every limb. Now it was only one finger that had any mobility.

Scratch

Scratch

Scratch

Evelyn's finger kept moving over her arm.

Stewart walked down the steps toward his mother. She made a gurgling noise. Stewart bent down and smiled. "Look who's here, Mom. These are Linda and Ashley Green." He waved towards Linda. Linda waved back. "This is Cindy May. She's Mom's caregiver."

"Nice to meet you," Cindy said. Her skin was the color of

milky coffee. She looked a little distracted. "They've come to work with us, Evelyn," she said to the wheelchair-bound psychiatrist. "And Linda here is going to make use of your excellent initiative and get counseling from Marissa while she works here. Remember I told you about them?"

Evelyn made a noise in her throat.

"Linda's going to be our landscaper," Stewart said. "She'll get your rose bushes thriving again. And Ashley is going to be handling the books. I'm afraid they're in dire straits since Mom stopped handling them. I've never been good with numbers. Right, Mom?"

Evelyn's hand shook with great intensity.

"She's been really animated today," Cindy smiled. "I'll keep her out here till my shift ends in ten minutes?"

"Okay, you can stay out here for a little while. I'll take her in when dinner's ready." Stewart smiled apologetically. "The doctors suggested I put her in care but I couldn't do that to her. I prefer continuing her work and caring for her."

Ashley's frown dwindled a little. Linda managed to smile a little.

"I know how wary abuse survivors are of any male contact, which is why my tasks were kept administrative, limiting any contact with female renters, but I must clarify that we have male clients too who are housed in a separate wing. If any of this makes you uncomfortable, I'll completely understand if you don't want to continue on. However, we won't be returning your registration fees. It's company policy."

Of course it was.

Blackburn was a private retreat; a fact advertised on their website. They had no affiliations with large medical shelters or state sponsored halfway houses. It was a hands-on experience for victims of abuse to build themselves up with regular counseling as they got back on their feet. Linda had read the reviews of previous guests and all things considered it was worth the fee.

"I don't think that would be necessary," Linda said. Her voice was naturally low and most people slouched low to better hear her, but Stewart didn't.

He smiled and clapped his hands. "Great. Let me show you to your apartments."

Linda had started following him back inside the house when Ashley touched her arm and held her back.

"Are you sure about this?" she whispered. "It isn't exactly how you thought it would be."

"I know," Linda nodded. "But I can't live depending on you forever. I'm ready to try and go into the world again, and the world isn't always what you expect."

On the inside, she wasn't as confident. The past few months had been a harrowing whirlwind. She still felt like she was riding on the tail winds of that storm. Jackson had controlled her life to such a degree she often caught herself suspended between two choices, waiting for him to decide things for her.

All that was going to change now; this was the first step to taking control of her own life. This place might just be the answer to all her problems after all.

CHAPTER 3

They were back in the main hall. Stewart shut the door to his personal wing with a soft click.

"I'll just introduce you to your councilor and housemate," Stewart said with a grin, and guided them through one of the doors.

The living room wasn't dingy, but it lacked the colorful lived-in comfort of Stewart's apartment. More of the green wallpaper was present here; a green sofa was flanked by purple chairs on a scuffed wooden floor. The TV was flat-screen, the only modern accessory in the old-fashioned room. The carpet was red with cream flowers, and the paintings on the walls were generic landscapes and hunting scenes.

It looked like a place people didn't stay long enough in to make their own, but it had a strong personality, enhanced by the gothic interior. Linda had often felt that places, like people, take on the effects of the lives lived inside them. The walls absorb the laughter, the trauma, and the mundane everyday lives of their occupants, until the house is an entity of its own, full of sentient emotion. Efforts had been made to modernize the place a couple of decades ago, but it was like adding a coat of paint to an old car. It didn't really stick.

Stewart walked ahead into the connecting room. From the sound of pots and pans, Linda assumed it was the kitchen. Stewart stepped out of it, followed by a woman with striking red curls. Her skin was pale and there were dark shadows around her eyes. She looked like an adult version of Little Orphan Annie, or a very raggedy Raggedy Ann doll.

"This is Linda," Stewart gestured towards her. "She'll be your new client, and our new gardener."

"Oh, I forgot that was today." Marisa's smile was tight. Linda caught her eye and smiled kindly. Marisa looked away.

"Come." Stewart beckoned Linda and Ashley. "Your rooms are on the upper floor."

"I'll get some of the bags." Ashley took out the keys to the truck and went out the front door.

Linda was left to soak in the aura of the main hall. The true essence of the original structure was encased within the hall. The ceiling wasn't very high but it somehow gave the impression of being vaulted, with plaster moldings decorating the dark corners. A set of steep stairs dominated the space and the line of portraits that stood sentry above them caught the focus as if you were standing before a bench of judges, hoping for mercy.

The stairs were steep and gloomy, the portraits adding to the ominous atmosphere. Linda felt like the eyes were following her as she went deeper inside the house. The landing, however, was refreshing. It had a large window that flooded the floor with twilight. Several doors lined the hall. The walls were covered in feminist posters from the 60s.

The first door on the right led to the bathroom. The old white tiles had turned cream. There was an old claw-footed bathtub and a rust-ringed mirror. The second room was clearly occupied. A messy stack of clothes was on the bed under a poster of Queen. The third and forth rooms were locked.

"Those are for our counselors. They'll be back by next week, a few days before the client load is expected to increase," Stewart explained.

"Why do they work seasonally?" Linda asked. "How can you be sure they'll come back?"

"They've signed contracts, much like you and your sister," Stewart explained. "Think of it as hiring out your specialty machines when you're not using them. They give lectures and help out in other retreats when they aren't working here. Which room would you like to set up in?"

Linda chose the one at the very end, the eighth room.

"Good choice." Stewart grinned. "You get a great view of the street and the hill."

The room wasn't large, nor was it small. It had a single bed, with a bare mattress and pillow. A chair sat in the corner and a floor-length mirror hung beside it. The closet was full of empty hangers.

Linda was observing the depth of the closet when something crashed outside the door. She jumped behind Stewart, who held out a protective arm. Her breathing was ragged. She peered out from under his arm.

Ashley stood in the hall holding her side and gasping. "I did it," she panted. "I got all the boxes."

"You scared me half to death," Linda said.

"Oh?" Ashley wheezed. "I'm sorry." She stumbled into the room and sprawled on her back on the bed. "I'm just going to catch my breath."

Stewart's face was screwed up in concentration. It was obvious he was trying not to laugh. "Come on." He motioned to Linda. "I'll show you the laundry room."

As they climbed down the stairs, Linda ran her hand along the wall to steady herself. It was cold to the touch. Her heart constricted, and then beat really fast. She pulled her finger away. She felt clammy.

"Everything okay?" Stewart asked. He was looking up at her from the bottom step.

"Oh, yes." Linda smiled and joined him down in the main hall. "I was just wondering," she asked, "why do the clients have the option of working to pay their fees? Wouldn't it distract from their counseling?"

"Not really." Stewart flashed her a smile. "It was Mom's idea. As I mentioned before, we wanted to give the victims who came here a sense of independence. That meant their own living space, their own kitchen and laundry, so they would learn to be dependent on themselves. We even have an understanding with the town post office and grocery store to hire our tenants if there are no openings available in house so they can start believing in their own ability to earn for themselves. As far as distracting from counseling, that isn't the case. Lots of people go to therapy while continuing with their regular lives."

He walked her to the living room. Marisa was in the kitchen at the stove stirring something in a saucepan. Her hair was tied up in a messy bun. "Dinner will be ready in another ten minutes," she said over her shoulder.

"Thanks, Marisa." Stewart waved Linda to follow him to a

door in the far wall of the living room. Linda had assumed it was a bathroom but it opened onto a square of pitch black. Stewart extended a hand and flipped a switch. Faint yellow light illuminated a gloomy staircase.

The wooden staircase groaned as they climbed down. The room at the bottom wasn't large but the lack of proper light made it look larger. A series of lights ranged along the ceiling but most of them weren't working, or flickered. The intermittent light didn't reach the shadowy corners.

Small rectangular windows spanned the entire length of one side of the wall but it was night and they provided no illumination. A washer and dryer sat like a sullen old couple by the far wall. An iron was stationed on a stand under the windows. A notch of pitch dark beneath the stairs caught her eye. No light went in there. Linda thought she saw movement within that patch of black. Her hackles rose.

"I've been meaning to get those fixed," Stewart said apologetically. "There's a bad connection in this room; old wiring you know. The fuses blow no matter what bulbs we put in. I'm going to get the wiring checked soon."

Stewart's casual voice tore her away from the contemplation of the darkness under the stairs. He spread his hands taking in the whole room. "And that's the house tour. I can show you the shed tomorrow. Your job mostly entails growing vegetables in the back garden, and there are hiking trails you might enjoy if you're an outdoors person."

"I am," Linda said. "It helps me calm down being out in nature."

"You'll find lots of that," Stewart climbed the rickety steps. Linda followed keeping an eye on the swatches of darkness between the steps.

Stewart reached the landing before her. He switched off the lights.

Linda was in the dark for only a few moments but it had the effect of making her shudder, as if a hundred spiders were crawling up and down her back.

She reached the landing to find Ashley sitting on the sofa while Marisa stood by the kitchen, hands on her hips. Her attitude changed when Stewart showed up. "There you are. I made extra lasagna. I know you like it." She beamed up at him.

"Thank you, Marisa, but not tonight." Stewart's smile was mechanical.

"But I made so much." Marisa pouted. "It'll go to waste otherwise."

"Why don't you share it with our new tenants tonight?" Stewart brightened. "I'm sure they don't have the strength to go buy groceries at this time. I know they'll appreciate it."

"I would," Ashley chimed in. "I'm starving."

Marisa's face was torn between smiling in compliance to what Stewart wanted and scowling at Ashley. Stewart won. "Sure," she shrugged. "It'll be ready in fifteen minutes."

"Great!" Stewart clapped his hands. It seemed to be a habit of his when he was happy. "I'm glad it all worked out. I'll see you in the morning."

He left by the front door. Marisa huffed into the kitchen.

"Better go in to keep an eye on her." Ashley got off the sofa. "She might poison our food." She winked at Linda.

Linda went to select a book from the shelf in the small niche just beyond the staircase in the main hall. It was the main channel to the whole house, like a pipeline connecting the ground floor and upper one, where everything seemed to meet. She could feel the manor breathing, its powerful lungs sucking the warmth and life into the basement and exhaling dusty air that settled on everything, even her soul, making it heavier. She shook her head. Where did she get such thoughts from? She was obviously edgy, tired by the travel and by this change in her life.

Indeed, it was a drastic change. From a bustling city that never slept to a small town that was practically comatose; from sharing a brownstone with her ex-fiancé to living with other girls in a counseling retreat. It was no wonder her insides twisted with nerves and anxiety about the future. Linda could feel it vibrating in her bones, a dull ache in her gut. Her first instinct was to run back to the places and faces she knew. But there was no money in the bank; they were as poor as church mice, and Ashley needed this job just as badly as Linda needed the counseling. The last time she had ignored her instincts, she had ended up face down and bleeding. She wouldn't make the same mistake twice.

I have to make this work. I have to take back control of my life.

She went back into the living room and was about to walk to the kitchen when something moved, seen out of the corner of her eye. She whipped her head around, her eyes large, her heart in her throat.

No one else was in the living room. The curtains were drawn. It hadn't been anyone moving in the street. She walked closer to the living room. If she hadn't been mistaken the movement had been from somewhere along the wall above the sofa.

A large oil painting of a hill hung there. Linda realized it wasn't any hill but the hill across the way from Blackburn Manor. The strokes were gentle and feathery and gave the impression of rippling waves. It was an impressionist rendition of a local landmark. Maybe the light had played tricks, rippling over the paint in such a way.

The frame shuddered.

Linda gasped.

A fat lizard darted out from behind. It scurried to the far side of the wall. Linda stared at it a moment then burst out laughing.

Just a lizard. She had seen the lizard dart inside the frame, just that; nothing sinister.

Sighing with relief, she headed to the window.

It wasn't humid, but it still felt oppressive inside. The open window would allow cool air to pass through and let the lizard out. She pulled back the curtains and stood on tiptoe to unlatch the window. It proved hard at first but she finally managed.

Cool pine scented air swished inside. She breathed it in. She could get used to the fresh air. No park in the city smelled as good as this.

A blood-curdling yowl rose into the night derailing her train of thought.

Linda's hair stood on end.

The animal cry was answered and the night was full of howling cats. At least ten had laid siege to the porch across the road. Linda wondered about the woman who lived there and her unfriendly attitude.

The curtains in the house across the road twitched. Linda stepped back.

The woman was staring right at her, her eyes narrowed, and her mouth curled in a sneer. It was a hateful face, cruel and dangerous.

Linda shut the window and drew the curtains, her heart beating a mile a minute. Her hands began to shake. Her breathing got stuck somewhere along her throat, unable to come up, impossible to go down.

"Dinner is ready, Linda." Ashley placed a hand on her arm. "Are you okay?"

Linda swallowed. Ashley was looking at her intently. It wouldn't do to worry her too much.

"Yes," Linda nodded. "I'm just tired, I guess."

"Eat something and then we can go to bed."

Linda followed Ashley to the kitchen, trying to forget the old woman's face.

The table was set for three with a steaming dish of lasagna and a bowl of salad in the middle. Marisa was popping garlic bread onto a serving plate while Ashley filled a jug with cold water.

"This looks delicious, Marisa," Linda said, taking a seat. "Thank you."

"Stewart invited you to dinner," Marisa said, setting the garlic bread down. "You should thank him, really."

Linda and Ashley shared a look across the table. Ashley shrugged and helped herself to a large slice of lasagna with towering salad on the side, and piled hot garlic bread on top of that. Marisa stared.

"Hungry, aren't we?" she said, arching an eyebrow.

"Famished," Ashley mumbled through a mouth full of pasta.

Linda waited for Marisa to serve herself before she made her plate. The next few minutes were silent except for the tinkle of cutlery against plates. Linda took a sip of cold water and decided to cut the awkward silence.

"It's very quiet here," she said. "Very different from the city."

"That's because it's empty." Marisa shrugged, scooping sauce off her plate with garlic bread. "Once the new season starts, the manor will be full and it won't seem so quiet then."

"Isn't this table too small to fit all the clients then?" Ashley asked, helping herself to more food.

"This isn't the dining room," Marisa snorted. "That's upstairs near the bigger kitchen. This one is for those who want to have something off menu or have midnight cravings."

"How big is this place?" Linda wondered out loud.

"Too big for five people," Marisa said finishing her meal. "But it can fit a couple of dozen people comfortably."

Linda considered this as she nibbled on her food, but the old woman's face from across the street was etched in the back of her mind.

CHAPTER 4

The room had a smell to it.

Linda hadn't noticed it before, when Stewart had given her a tour of the manor, but it was distinctive now. It smelled like stale air mingled with rich, wet earth. It was a subtle odor, not wholly unpleasant, but it was disconcerting every time she got a whiff of it.

"There are bed sheets and extra pillows in the supply closet down the hall," Marisa said, buffing her nails as she leaned on the doorframe. "We can start our first session tomorrow afternoon after I come back from the city. Does that work for you?"

"That works out great," Linda said. "Ashley and I will do our grocery shopping in the morning."

"It's neat that you have a car," Marisa examined a nail. "I have to walk to the bus stop, and though it keeps me fit, it can be a pain in the summer."

"We could take you," Linda offered.

Marisa gave her a look. "I've managed to get myself around before you arrived, you know."

Linda was taken aback. She was having a hard time reading Marisa.

"Have you been here long?" Linda asked, trying to guide the conversation into friendlier waters.

"Only a few weeks," Marisa admitted. "I was here for the last few days of the big clients before everyone left. Incidentally," she smiled ruefully, "the retreat does have a small van to shuttle clients and employees around town but the brakes were faulty so it's been at the mechanics for a few days now. It was kind of you to offer."

Linda still wasn't sure about Marisa's nature, but it wasn't as horrible as she had first thought. She guessed Marisa was also trying to feel them out, hence she was being guarded as well.

"Bathroom times are strictly rotated. You can work out your time with your sister," Marisa pushed lightly off the door. "I need it between eight and nine every morning and six to seven every night. There's another one on the ground floor but it has a leaky faucet and smells so I'd only use it if it's an emergency. The other bathrooms are private and restricted to the most expensive rooms of the paying clients."

"Isn't two hours excessive?" Linda joked.

Marisa looked at her for a few seconds then touched her curls lightly. "These need a lot of work. I can't just pop in and out of a shower; I need to plan a whole crusade. You're lucky you have straight hair. Never get a perm; the maintenance will kill you."

With that last piece of advice she was gone.

The counselor was helpful, and always gave the required information before Linda had even thought to ask, but there was a cold streak to her, and she kept Linda and Ashley at arm's length. Linda wasn't sure if this was the mark of a great counselor, or a really terrible one.

Grabbing a towel from the closet, she picked up her toiletry bag from the chair in the corner, and she made her way down the hall.

Ashley had chosen the room across the hall from Linda's. Her door was wide open and she was sitting in the middle of a mess of half unpacked boxes, blonde hair piled up in a messy bun, writing on a small piece of paper.

"You need the bathroom any time soon?" Linda asked her.

"No," Ashley scratched her cheek, distracted. "I'm making a list of things I need for the room. There's only one shelf for shoes in here."

"I have space in my closet you could use," Linda offered. "I'll be in the bathroom down the hall."

"Don't use up the hot water," Ashley called.

Linda walked down the dimly lit hall. All the doors were closed. It was a cramped space compared to the rooms dedicated to paying clients but Linda didn't mind. At the end of the hall Marisa's door was ajar. Linda heard Marisa speaking in hushed tones inside.

The bathroom was surprisingly cold. Linda frowned. She stepped back out into the hall, and then in again. There was a clear difference in temperatures.

Linda didn't pay it much mind. It was an old house. Old structures were like brooding old men with shifting moods. She turned on the lights and hung her towel on the hooks nailed to the wall beside the sink. Flecks of paint rimmed the sink, and the mirror was old and slightly curved with age. Rust bloomed in one corner.

The bathtub was antique, and that was a nice way to put it. A brown stain ran around the drain, which was clogged with dark red hair. Linda made a face but beggars couldn't be choosers. A soft breeze came from the small frosted-glass window above the tub.

Linda half turned in the small space to shut the door when someone passed quickly by and ran down the stairs. Linda jumped in surprise. She had only caught a glimpse but she knew it wasn't anyone she had met in the house. The girl had long black hair; Marisa's was decidedly red and curly, Cindy had ash-gray highlights in her hair and she didn't live in the house, while Ashley was blonde.

She stepped out of the bathroom to look back down the hall. She could see Marisa pacing her room through the small gap in her door, talking into her phone. Marisa noticed her watching and shut the door firmly.

She probably had a friend over, Linda thought. *Maybe we're not allowed late night visitors, which is why the girl left so quickly.*

She closed the door and the window firmly before she undressed, placed her glasses by the sink, and ran hot water through the showerhead. The pipes rattled and spurted brown water before it cleared.

The shower curtain was white and grimy at the bottom. Linda closed it around the tub for some privacy making sure her naked skin didn't touch it.

As the water sluiced down her back, Linda massaged her neck, her fingers running over the raised scar where the prong of a belt buckle had sliced through her skin. There were several scars along her body, testaments to the various forms of physical torment she had faced over the past six years. They painted an accurate picture of the fractured state of her psyche that she had just begun to gather; sorting through and mending would take longer, but now she was happy just knowing that she was up to the task.

The back of her shoulders prickled. There was a faint sound, scratching at her ears from under the roar of running water. She turned in the shower to face the opposite wall, her eyes squinting to see more clearly. She had the unnerving sensation that someone was watching her.

What was that sound? She couldn't make it out clearly it was so faint, like someone calling her name from a great distance.

Swallowing hard she turned the water down. The water was a thin trickle. The drain sucked it all up noisily. Linda blinked and bent closer to the drain. A family of silverfish scuttled in and out of the drain, their many legs pushing them forward and their bodies writhing repulsively. She blanched and stepped back, her toes curling up.

Linda's hair rose on her arms; she twisted the knob and let the water sluice the insects back in the drain, inching her feet back so they wouldn't come in contact with the disgusting things. Finally the last one was dunked under the force of the water and drained out of sight. Shuddering, Linda shut the water off.

A door closed on the landing, footsteps echoed down the hall, and someone sang a song Linda hadn't heard. Probably Marisa, Linda thought. She placed her hand on the knob again but the feeling of not being alone in the bathroom was too strong.

"Hello? Is anyone there?" She hated the tremble in her voice.

Raising a shaking hand, she slid the shower curtain a little.

The bathroom was empty.

Linda blinked, and squinted, just to make sure.

A skittering rustle, like the feet of many rats across rotten floorboards, came from behind her. She whirled around so fast she lost her balance and had to cling to the moldy curtain to break her fall. Slimy dirt trailed down her thighs. Her heart was beating a choking tattoo in her throat.

Shoving the foul curtain aside, Linda bent down to stare at the small space between the tub and the wall underneath the window. She bobbed in place, afraid of fanged rodents jumping up to bite her. The space was minuscule and dark, but not too small for the agile slinking bodies of rats.

That's just what I need, she thought, shivering, *a rat infestation to keep me up at night.*

There was no sign of any small beady eyes, or shiny whiskers, but Linda's calming shower had turned into a dreadful experience. She washed up quickly, soaping away the mildew.

The pipe rattled again when Linda shut off the water. Steam billowed around her as she got out on the blue bathroom mat. She reached for the towel and hugged it around herself, knotting it over her breasts.

Leaning over the sink she gathered her wet hair and squeezed the excess water out. She rummaged in her toilet bag and brought out a leave-in conditioner. She glanced up at the fogged mirror and ran a hand to clear the condensation off. It revealed her own pale face and someone peering over her shoulder.

The conditioner clattered in the sink. Linda whipped around. When her wet hand reached for her glasses, her towel slipped to the floor. Her skin broke out in goosebumps. The glasses slipped from her fingers, rattling against the tiled floor.

Wisps of steam floated around her. Her hands clawed at the cold sink.

Whimpering, shaking, she fell on her knees and jammed her glasses on her nose. They fogged up almost immediately. She wrenched them off again and squinted to see moderately better.

Nothing was there.

The window was open.

Linda went cold.

She had closed the window. She was sure of it. She had shut it before her shower.

Maybe it was loose, maybe it opened on its own, maybe that was the skittering sound she had heard. There couldn't possibly be anyone out there—could there be?

Linda was suddenly very aware of her nakedness, and just how vulnerable she was. Gathering her towel from the floor, she held it tighter against her chest. She took a cautious step forward and stepped back into the tub. She reached up to hold the windowsill, propped a foot up on the slippery rim of the tub, and pushed herself up. She knew perfectly well how stupid this was but she had to show herself that nothing was out there; just telling herself so wasn't enough.

It was a precarious position which wasn't helped by Linda's terror that she might find someone just outside. Feet slipping on the rim, Linda grasped the wooden ledge, her knuckles white. She leaned forward and looked outside.

It was dark, but a few lights from the downstairs windows illuminated the backyard, and the edge of the woods. There was no tiled ledge beneath the window where someone could climb and sit. It was a sheer wall that dropped neatly down to the ground. The trees were too far away for anyone to make their way up to the second story from there.

She must have been mistaken. It had been a long day and the recent reminder of Jackson didn't help her shattered nerves. She was just imagining things, that was all.

Yet unease nagged at her. She tried to recall what she had seen but no discernible feature came to mind, only a long white oval face framed with dark matted hair hovering over her shoulder. Her poor eyesight without her glasses didn't help.

Linda didn't bother to dress; she had to leave the bathroom. She checked that her towel was firmly attached, she picked up her clothes, and she hurried to the sanctuary of her bedroom.

~

LINDA CLOSED THE DOOR AND CALMED DOWN. SHE SHOOK THE queasy feeling from the bathroom and concentrated on something more pleasant—the room. This was hers: her own space, a room she had rented by applying for a job. This was progress.

She opened the box full of old medical files and her diaries, and stacked them on the shelf at the top of the closet first. The first aid box went there too. There was no dressing table to place her mahogany jewelry box. It had been a gift from her mother and always gave her strength. Reluctantly she stored it in the cupboard.

Next came the clothes. There weren't many. Linda didn't own a single piece that she had bought herself. Some didn't fit properly while others hung off her in loose folds. She put them on the hangers in the closet.

She had no spare shoes.

The rest of the boxes contained the books she had hoarded over the years. She had no place to put them. She would have to buy a bookcase, a side table, a shelf for her jewelry box, a mirror, and maybe a pretty rug.

Linda smiled, but then bit her lip. It was exciting being able to think of such things, knowing she had the power to make it happen. She opened the first box to retrieve her books. She needed to have them out and in her line of sight to completely feel this was her space.

It took four trips to stack the first box's worth of books against the wall. It added a pop of color to the room. She unboxed the rest and was just walking across the room when the book on top teetered and fell to the floor.

Pages flipped and some flew out to different ends of the room.

"Oh, no!" Linda moaned. Sweat peppered her scalp. She dumped the stack in her hands on the bed, heart pounding a war drum against her ears. "He isn't here," she stammered to herself as she retrieved the pages on her hands and knees. "He isn't here. He can't hurt you."

Her ears were cocked to hear heavy footsteps on the stairs, the sound of grinding teeth, and knuckles cracking as a fist was clenched.

She heard nothing.

Taking a shaking breath, Linda forced herself to sit back on her legs. She closed her eyes and breathed deeply the way she had been taught at the support group at the community center back home: once, twice, and again until her heart slowed down to its regular trot. She clenched and released her fingers until they stopped shaking, and the twist of tension in her gut unwound.

Squaring her shoulders, she began to search for the first

page. She gathered most of the pages and placed them on her bed, but she couldn't find the first one.

"Tsk," she clicked her tongue in annoyance and bent down to search under the bed.

There were a few pages down there. She leaned in to retrieve them. Her hand touched something smooth and stiff, flat and rectangular; it felt like a card. She pulled the card out along with the rest of the pages. It was a plain white card slightly yellow with age. Frowning a little she flipped it over.

Her lungs collapsed. All the air had been knocked out of her. Her eyes dilated.

She dropped the card. It fell to the floor and landed against the wall under the window. A couple was framed in wreaths and Christmas baubles. They were sitting in an armchair, the girl on the man's lap. He had his arms around her in such a way that you could only see the face.

The girl was Linda though younger, her cheeks fuller, her hair longer, her eyes sparkling behind her glasses.

The man was older, but only by a few years. He looked lean and hungry, like a wolf out in the winter cold banished from his pack. His eyes were onyx-black like a shark's. His arms snaked around Linda's waist and neck. It looked protective, and it had been in the beginning until those same arms tightened around her like a vise crushing the very life out of her.

What the heck was that picture doing there?

Breathing shakily through her nose, Linda paced her room.

On the brink of tears, she swallowed a rattling sob and rushed towards the card. She knelt down on the floor and picked it up.

She looked at the face of her nightmare, at her ex-fiancé who had started out by protecting her from her father, and ended up beating her within an inch of her life. Jackson Perry was a military man whose father was on the police force, so no one would believe her if she tried to call for help. Jackson had restricted her movements. He hadn't given her an allowance or even let her go to the grocery store to buy food because he was paranoid that she would leave him.

Rage built up in her. A low, guttural cry escaped her lips. She tore the card in two, and then fours, enjoying the sound of ripping paper.

Much calmer now, she stood up and tossed the torn pieces out the window. She suddenly felt drained of all energy. The frightening shower and the assault on her memories had taken a toll.

Deciding to call it a night, Linda slipped in between the sheets, and turned off the lights.

CHAPTER 5

Linda was lying in a dank place.

It was cavernous; sounds of trickling water echoed around. She could smell damp earth and the oxidized odor of pounded rock. She was lying very still. She couldn't move even if she tried. Someone was close by. She could hear their ragged breathing grating on her ears.

"Help," Linda cried. "Please, help me!"

The breathing became louder until it was a whistling moan. The hair on her arms stood on end. Someone was crying in the dark, a painful, desperate keening, that broke Linda's heart and filled it with terror at the same time.

"Where am I? Help me!"

He must have found her. Jackson must have found her and kidnapped her. Now, he would have his revenge.

The quality of the weeping changed. The wail grew deeper. It warbled as if coming from deep under water.

"Help!" Darkness pressed down on her eyes. She couldn't see anything, the gloom was so absolute.

Footsteps echoed in the large space. Her heartbeat became sluggish, matching the halting, squelching steps. The figure drew closer until it stood above Linda.

"Please," she begged. Her fingers clawed at her sides scooping up cold, powdery earth in her palms.

Clothes rustled as the figure moved. Metal scraped against rocks; the clang was loud and echoed around, bouncing off the walls, chasing Linda's whimpered pleas.

It began to rain.

Linda spluttered and spat as cold peppered her face, got into her eyes, and into her mouth. She tasted dirt, and foul earth.

It wasn't rain. Someone was shoveling dirt on her!

Metal scraped in the earth. Soil rained down on her writhing body.

"No!" Linda choked out. Her paralysis intensified. Bits of loose stone struck her face, flames of pain radiated across her body. Her nose and mouth were blocked.

She breathed in dirt.

She was being buried alive.

Her mind was a blazing beacon of red panic. Linda tried to find something, anything to get her out of the grave she was in. Stars burst in front of her vision. Dirt lay heavy on her chest, and limbs.

Open your eyes, the thought thundered through her blind hysteria. *Open them!*

It took an effort to fight against the dirt burying her, and the fear of getting soil in her eyes. She wrenched them open with a feral cry.

Faint sunlight danced on the wooden floor. Her eyes were

burning hot. Books stood against the opposite wall like jagged teeth. Her breath was caught in her throat and her chest was tight with fear. She had to remind herself to breathe.

A dream, she realized, heart still hammering against her throat, the sound drowning out her shallow breathing. *A dream, yet it had felt so real.*

Linda was no stranger to this feeling. As a child she had suffered from sleep paralysis and sleepwalking, but she hadn't experienced those hallucinations in years.

It's probably because of the PTSD, she thought, slowing down her breathing, making it deeper and longer to calm her racing heart. *They said something like this can happen, at the community center. Just calm down. It was just a dream.*

Once her breathing had regulated itself and she was no longer shaking, Linda sat up and reached down to the floor where she had set her glasses. She checked her phone for the time. It was a little past eight in the morning. She groaned. Jackson had never allowed her a phone, and holding it in her hand reminded her that things were changing, and she was getting her life back. She set her phone back down and, to divert her thoughts away from Jackson, she thought about the day ahead.

There was the shed and the back garden that she needed to scope out intimately, and of course her first session with Marisa. Should she mention the dreams and her old sleep disorders? The thought of sharing this information made her queasy but she knew it had to come out if she wanted to get better.

The nightmare stayed with her as she got out of bed and twitched the curtains aside. The world was glowing golden.

The cats had slunk off for the day, and the neighbor's house looked empty.

Shrugging out of her pajamas, Linda pulled on a pair of high-rise jeans and a shapeless white top. She opened her bedroom door a crack and wriggled out into the hall. She tiptoed down to the bathroom and brushed her teeth quickly, glancing over her shoulder at the open window.

"Linda?" Ashley's voice came from down the hall. "Are you up?"

Linda spat out toothpaste. "Yes."

"Stewart wanted a word," Ashley leaned against the doorframe stifling a yawn. "Marisa left early."

"Why does Stewart want to see me?" Linda gargled with some water.

"He needs you to sign the employment contract. I've already signed mine. Hurry it up, would you? I'm starving and I want to get some shopping done before your first session this afternoon."

Linda grabbed her bag from her room before joining Ashley on the front porch. Stewart stood by his car in the driveway. He was dressed in a dark suit. His face brightened at the sight of her.

"Morning." He waved.

"Are you going to a wedding or something?" Ashley asked.

"No such joy," Stewart laughed. "I have to get to the bank. If you could sign this contract, I will be on my way."

Linda took the papers from him. The sight of her name on official-looking documents reminded her she had no means of moving anywhere else, and brought home just how permanent this change was going to be. The house she had lived in for the past years had belonged to Jackson, then she had moved in with

Ashley until she had lost the apartment; Linda realized she'd never really lived in a place that was hers alone. She hesitated at first but then remembered she had no money to her name, and she signed where he pointed.

"Oh, by the way," Linda suddenly remembered. "Are there any rules against late night visitors to the staff quarters?"

Stewart looked puzzled. "I'm not sure what you mean."

"There was someone in the hall last night," Linda tucked her hair behind her ears, not sure how to phrase it. Then a thought struck her. "Who are the other guests in the house? There was a woman chatting with Marisa late in the evening that I didn't meet yet. I didn't get a good look; she left in a hurry."

Stewart shook his head, a small frown creasing his brow. "We have no other guests living here at the moment. It was probably a friend visiting Marisa."

"Oh, really?" She was suddenly unsure if she should be talking about this. It felt like snitching and she was sure Marisa wouldn't appreciate being talked about behind her back.

Stewart rubbed the back of his neck. "I'm glad you told me. We don't have a strict policy but we don't encourage… er… that kind of activity. I'll have a word with Marisa."

"I didn't mean to get her in trouble," Linda wrung her hands.

"No, no," Stewart laughed. "It's not that serious. Don't worry about it." He rummaged in his pocket and produced a set of keys. "These are to the shed in the back. It has some heavy tools so we keep it under lock and key in case one of the clients has a depressive episode."

"I thought you were going to give me a tour," Linda laughed, taking the keys.

"It's not that big," Stewart chuckled. "And I'm sure you know your way around a tool shed. I just don't want you waiting on me to start."

"Okay. Thanks."

"We should get going." Ashley said. "I need food to function properly." She stalked off to the truck.

"Of course." Stewart unlocked his own car. "There are three diners in town, but I'd recommend Yoder's. It's run by an Amish family, and the food is carefully prepared. Their shepherd's pie is to die for."

Ashley closed her truck's door loudly.

"Thanks." Linda smiled, and waved him goodbye. "Don't mind Ash. She's not a morning person." She sprinted over to the car and slid into the passenger seat.

Ashley waited for Stewart to pull away from the driveway. As soon as he drove off, she pressed the pedal and reversed at such speed their truck crossed the road and ended up in the cat lady's driveway.

"Careful!" Linda cried.

Ashley hit the brakes. They had just fallen short of knocking the mailbox down. The car stalled. Ashley cursed. "Jesus! I'm sorry. Just really hungry."

Linda sat back in her seat trying to get her breathing under control. A darting motion from the house above her caught her eye. Shadows shifted in the topmost tower window on the Blackburn side of the manor.

Linda froze.

The sun blazed behind the tower.

She wasn't sure what she had seen but it had looked like a tall figure stepping away from the window.

A screen door screeched shrilly behind them but it was nothing to the voice that followed.

"Useless delinquents!"

Linda saw the cat lady in the rearview mirror. Her flowery dress ballooned voluminously around her small frame. She was waving her fist at them. "Destroying my property. I'm going to call the police, you'll see!"

"Oh, keep your shirt on," Ashley growled and drove off.

"I think there's a pizza crust from yesterday here somewhere," Linda joked.

Ashley glared at her.

Linda sat back and thought about the shape she had seen in the window. It could have been Evelyn, only Evelyn was wheelchair-bound and that figure was standing tall. Maybe it was Cindy May, the nurse; or a trick of the light. The sun was exceptionally bright that morning.

Linda removed her glasses and cleaned them on the hem of her shirt.

"Do you sometimes think Mom would have been proud of us?"

"Of course," Ashley said. "She always did say we were the best thing about her marriage."

"Are you still in touch with Dad?"

Ashley's generous lips pursed into a thin line. "He called me on Christmas. Wanted to know how I was doing."

"That's nice."

"Hmmm. Then he told me I was going to hell for dating a girl, and he asked me to join his church where he'd find me a nice boy to date."

"Yeesh," Linda cringed.

"So I told him I'd rather skip the church and see him straight in hell since wife beaters and alcoholics have their own special circle there."

"He called me too," Linda said. "It was after I'd filed criminal charges against Jackson."

"What did he say?" Ashley was staring ahead at the road but there was a steely glint in her eye.

Linda chewed her lower lip. It wasn't easy when the parent who had been neglectful when you needed them the most suddenly wanted to reconnect and save your soul. "That I was making a mistake." Linda's cheeks flushed at the memory. It still made her angry. "That I was doing the same thing Mom did and look how she ended up dying alone."

Their mother had passed away a few years ago, around the time Linda had started seeing Jackson. Twenty pounds heavier and a million times happier, Linda's mother had died in her sleep a free woman.

"Asshole," Ashley grimaced. "He's afraid of living alone without anyone to make miserable. I'm glad I moved out at sixteen. Now he can't turn up at my door when he's drunk on a Tuesday night."

"You know, I think you leaving gave Mom the courage to do so too."

"If I'd known that I would have moved out sooner." Ashley swiped at her eyes. "Our childhood was shit."

Now that Ashley had awakened memories of that terrible period, Linda couldn't avoid thinking of her late childhood. She forced herself to think about the few good times of those days. Mr. Dartmouth came to her mind, with his unusual behavior.

"Lin, are you ok?" asked Ashley. "Sorry, I shouldn't have brought it up. I know you had a hard time dealing with it. What are you thinking about?"

"Do you remember Mr. Dartmouth, our neighbor?"

"Who?"

"You know, the monocled man with the eccentric suits, and the watch on a chain? He had this really nasty walking stick that he would swish around in a menacing way if you were walking ahead of him in the street."

Ashley gave her a sideways glance. "He sounds like a memorable figure, which is why I'm shocked I don't recall him."

"Really?" Linda returned Ashley's shocked gaze.

Ashley shrugged. "Really."

Ashley's phone rang sharp and clear. "Oh, thank God! The service back at that house was atrocious."

"You were expecting a call?" Linda asked.

"Nope. But at least I'm getting them finally."

She answered the call.

The road curved and disappeared around a thick expanse of wood. Ashley sped up as they came to the curve.

"Hello? Morning, Dax," Ashley smiled, her entire body language relaxing. Linda figured Dax was a girl Ashley had recently met. "I was going to call you after breakfast... hello? Hello! God damn it, not again!"

Linda was about to tell Ashley to pull over if she wanted to talk when she noticed a police cruiser behind them in the side mirror. Linda's eyes widened, but her attention was caught by something more harrowing and immediate.

A small van came roaring towards them around the bend. Linda could see the man behind the wheel, his head drawing back stiffly in surprise, eyes wide and dark with fear.

"Ashley! Look out!" Linda screamed.

Ashley swerved just in time to avoid a collision.

The car screeched; the wheels slipped on the asphalt.

Ashley had lost control of the car and it went careering into the woods where it struck a tree head-on. Linda was jolted forward, her hands outstretched to break her fall. Her skull hit the windshield, but didn't break it. Her neck and shoulders were badly jarred from the collision.

"Ash?" Linda's throat hurt. Her voice grazed against her throat like it was being dragged over gravel. "Ashley!"

"I'm okay." Ashley's voice was worse than hers. Linda searched her frantically for any signs of injury but Ashley looked fine. "What about you?"

"I'm fine." Linda didn't feel fine, but physically she felt unharmed.

Ashley groaned and stepped out of the car. Linda joined her. She felt her limbs, and ran a hand through her hair to make sure she wasn't bleeding anywhere she couldn't see. Her fingers came back slick with blood.

She looked up to see that the van was nowhere to be seen. The driver had hightailed it out of there. The police cruiser sped up as if to follow, but then swerved to the curb where it came to a stop. The siren barked twice before it went silent. The lights started whirling like a dervish.

The truck was a wreck. Steam was billowing out of the engine. The bumper had crumpled into a heap of twisted metal.

Ashley kicked a tire and cursed at the top of her lungs. "Great! That's damage I can't afford."

Linda felt faint. The flash of red light, the opening doors, and the police officers coming their way faded as old memories resurfaced of other officers, smartly dressed, telling her not to waste their time with her bullshit. The men in uniform testifying against her in court, their blank stares, their strong jaws clenched in hate and disapproval, narrowed eyes questioning, accusing…

Linda was far away, falling down the rabbit hole of her memories. She was back in the brownstone house, her back against the kitchen counter, her hands flailed to grab something, anything to loosen Jackson's grip on her neck. His face was so close to hers, she could count the open pores on his cheeks and nose, and the small frown lines developing between his brow and the varying shades of onyx in his dark hell-hole eyes.

Her hand struck something hard. It flitted away across the smooth marble surface Linda had polished the other day. Linda reached, her head spinning, stars bursting at the margins of her blurring vision.

One last lunge and she had it in her hand; the smooth, heavy handle of a knife. She slashed at Jackson's face, not caring if she hit him any place in particular, just wanting his bloody hands off her.

He had jerked back, a spray of blood drenching her face. Blood ran down his cheek where the blade had sliced the flesh apart.

Jackson had stood in shock, staring down at his hands, in remorse Linda had hoped. Maybe he had finally come to his senses, but no. He had roared like a raging bull and charged. Linda had screamed in terror and thrust the knife forward.

It had sunk through his abdomen like a hot blade through butter. Blood had gushed over her hand, drenching it in warm iron-scented liquid. Jackson had stared at the hilt, his eyes disbelieving in Linda's ability to harm him, still shining the smug dominance he had over her even though he had a knife inside him.

Rage unlike anything she had known had reared its head and she pulled the blade back, the wound making a wet sucking noise, and she had stabbed him again, and again...

∽

"Linda? You're bleeding," Ashley touched her arm, jerking her out of her reverie. "We should get you to a hospital."

She stumbled back, wrenching her arm out of Ashley's hand. The acrid smell of gasoline and burning rubber assaulted her nose.

"Lin?" Ashley was pale; all color had drained out of her face, leaving her usually pink lips white. "What's wrong?"

"Nothing," Linda shook her head. She felt disoriented.

Sirens wailed a little way off. Light filtered grainy yellow beneath the tree they had struck, heightening how surreal the whole situation was for Linda.

A police car came to a sudden stop near the shoulder of the road. Ashley glared at them. Linda wanted to lie down.

She sat on the grass, head resting on knees trying to blot out the nausea and dizziness.

"Hey, miss?"

The voice was appeasing. Through the gap between her knees, Linda saw navy blue pants kneeling down in front of her. The shoes were highly polished. The man held his own hands, resting his elbows on his thighs. The nails were neatly trimmed.

"Your sister says you were injured in the wreck." His calm, soothing tones helped alleviate her anxiety a little. "It's a good thing we were patrolling the area. Can I have a look? I have a first aid kit in the patrol car."

Linda lifted her head slowly and blinked.

He looked younger than she had expected. His face was oval topped by reddish brown hair. His eyes were clear blue and squinted at her in curiosity. His skin was pale and delicate, the kind that flushed readily and was prone to sunburns. His mouth was his most arresting feature after his frank eyes, small but full and surprisingly pink.

A small tag on his police uniform read S. Wilson.

"Doesn't look too bad," he said. "Can you walk?"

Linda nodded. Pain throbbed in her temples.

She got up with some difficulty. Officer Wilson held her arm to steady her. He smelled of peppermint. He walked her past Ashley, who was explaining what had happened to another officer.

Officer Wilson sat her down on the shoulder of the road next to the patrol car, then left to rummage in the back of the vehicle. Linda's head felt like it was stuffed with cotton.

"Here we are." Officer Wilson sat on his haunches in front of her. Linda could see his biceps flexing under his sleeves. He removed an alcohol swab from its package and lifted up her hair on one side of her head. "Do you mind removing your glasses?"

Linda did as she was told.

"It's a miracle you didn't fly through the windshield," Officer Wilson said. The pads of his fingers were rough but he used them gently as he coaxed her hair back and found the wound. "Ah," he exclaimed finally. "It looks shallow but we'll soon find out."

Linda hissed. Stinging pain bloomed across her forehead.

"Oops, sorry." Officer Wilson leaned back. "Should have warned you it would sting."

"No, I didn't get a look at his license plate. I was too busy trying not to die." Ashley's sarcastic remarks reached through Linda's deafening haze.

"You two are new around here, right?"

He seemed nice and was friendly, but Linda found his uniform triggering her worst instincts.

"You don't talk much," he observed, his clear blue eyes quizzical.

Ashley's conversation must have come to an end because suddenly she was by her side. "Is it bad, Lin? Do you need to go to the hospital?"

"I've had worse," Linda croaked. Tears stung her eyes, but she made an effort not to cry. She stuck her glasses back on her nose to hide her eyes better.

"Oh, honey." Ashley hugged her. "I'm so sorry."

"It's not your fault." Linda gave a watery smile.

Ashley didn't smile back. Her face was a stiff mask of worry.

"I've called the local mechanic, Earl." The other officer was much older, with a graying handlebar mustache dominating his face. His nametag read M. Carter. "He should be here soon with the tow truck."

"Thanks," Ashley said. "Is there any way we can get my sister home? She looks dead on her feet."

"Scott can drop her in the patrol car," Officer Carter offered. "I'll wait with you for the tow truck. Make sure you're well taken care of. Earl tends to cheat the newcomers."

Linda wasn't listening. All she knew was that she didn't want to go anywhere alone with a police officer. She hardly knew him, and she didn't trust him.

"Ashley." She clawed at her sister's hand. "Please, I can't."

Ashley sighed. "Please, Lin. I need to know you're home safe before I can go and get this fixed. Otherwise I'll worry."

Ashley's smile was strained. Linda could tell how shaken she was. She didn't argue. She let herself be led to the patrol car and sat in the back. Her heart was racing a mile a minute but she was helpless, like a drowning man fighting against the tide.

PART II
VOICES IN THE NIGHT

CHAPTER 6

Officer Wilson kept glancing back at her through the rearview mirror.

She wished he would stop. It was grating on her already raw nerves. His uniform made her skin crawl.

"So you're staying at the Blackburn place?" he asked.

Linda closed her eyes, and rested them against the window pretending to be asleep.

Intermittent sunlight pulsed red behind her closed eyelids like the strobe lights of some insane disco.

She had a strong urge to jump out of the moving vehicle and run into the woods. The car swerved around a turn. Linda had no sense of its direction. He could be driving her to a clearing in the woods for all she knew.

Her eyes flew open.

She saw the house looming up ahead.

One of the knots in her stomach unclenched. The cat lady sat on her porch opposite.

The cruiser came to a smooth halt outside. Linda tried the door but it was locked. Officer Wilson stepped out and opened it for her. "Sorry." His grin was sheepish. "Police procedure."

Linda shot out of the car so fast her head whirled.

"Whoa." Officer Wilson steadied her. "Careful."

"I'm fine, thank you." Linda could only manage a whisper.

"This neighborhood's going to the dogs!" The shrill cry came from across the road. The cat lady sat stroking a tabby in her lap. Her jowls quivered. "The Blackburns were a decent family, but now we have criminals living in respectable homes."

"Now, Mrs. Grady," Officer Wilson said. "It's too early in the morning for talk like that. Why don't you step inside where it's cooler?" He shrugged apologetically and guided Linda up the porch stairs. "Grady's old and crabby, but in the past she was one of the best history teachers in the district. Used to bring maps of the area and tell us about the mines under those hills." He pointed towards the hills that crested along the road.

Linda stood on the front porch fumbling for her keys. Stewart had handed them to her the day before, and she'd stowed them in her purse. Her hands shook badly and things slipped out of her fingers. The bag fell on the porch with a crash, vomiting its contents everywhere.

She bent down on all fours trying to scrabble things back in her bag. Officer Wilson helped. He retrieved the keys from where they had landed near Stewart's welcome mat and unlocked the front door.

Linda rushed inside.

Officer Wilson stood in the doorframe. He looked unsure.

"Do you want me to stay with you?"

"No!" It came out louder than she had intended. "No, thank you. I'm fine."

"Is there anyone else in the house who can sit with you until your sister gets back? I mean I know the wound isn't very serious but…"

"You'll only make it worse," she blurted, edging close to the kitchen, as far away from him as possible.

That gave him pause. His face stilled, his frank eyes appraised her. Linda felt like she was under a microscope and the man before her could peel off layers of her skin to observe things that sloshed inside.

"Okay." He scratched his forehead. "Please lock the door behind you."

He moved away slightly, turned back, and faced her again as if about to say something, then thought better of it. He raised a hand in goodbye and left. Linda didn't go any closer to the door but she heard his heavy boots scuffling down the porch steps.

She waited till the engine started again before she ran to the front door and slammed it shut, locking it with a decisive click. Her head spun and her eyes grew heavy. She went into the living room, closed the curtains, and sat down on the sofa to wait for Ashley's return.

∽

WATER DRIPPED SOMEWHERE IN THE DARK. LINDA SHIVERED.

She was standing by the edge of the water. Shards of ice floated on its dark, still surface.

She blinked a few times, but the light was too gloomy to make any sense of where she was. Water splashed up against her feet. Her ears thrummed with the sound of water dripping in a cavernous space.

Behind her there was upturned earth, ahead of her water. She stood where she was, cold and shivering.

Then the song began: a melodious lament that was at once fascinating and terrifying. Linda moved around in the gloom, trying to find the source of the noise, but all she saw were sheer rock walls and a hard slab of rock ceiling. Panic clapped its insane hands on her mind and she began to hyperventilate.

A shrieking bell cut through the song. The ground beneath her began to buck and shake. Losing its firm shape, it disintegrated into soft sand that sucked her toes, ankles, legs, and thighs, pulling her in.

Linda screamed and struggled, but her torso, then her neck, went inside the maw of devouring earth. Dirt was in her mouth, her nose. She blinked the flecks out her eyes, screaming for help, but she was completely devoured.

Her lungs were on fire. She couldn't breathe!

The shrill bell continued.

Her thrashing feet finally found solid ground.

Linda gave a mighty push with her legs. She broke the surface and opened her eyes.

She was lying on the sofa in the living room. Her neck ached and her body was drenched in cold sweat. The telephone was ringing by her side.

Disoriented and a little groggy, Linda stared at the phone not sure what to do with it, her mind still stuck in the nasty dream. By the time she decided to pick it up, the call had gone to the answering machine.

At that moment, she was distracted by the sound of tires crunching on gravel. She rushed to the front window to see if Ashley had come home.

It was Stewart. He parked in his usual spot and got out with a briefcase in one hand. Linda stepped back into the shadows so he wouldn't see her. The accident had jolted any desire to be sociable out of her system. She wished Ashley would hurry up.

The answering machine blinked red. She realized she hadn't heard the message and played it.

The machine clicked.

Wind whistled, stuttering against a microphone so there was feedback and a low thumping. Linda's back muscles knotted at the sound, like a spring being wound tight. A low gurgling took over the whipping wind like the sound of someone speaking under water.

Images of shards of ice on a cold black lake rose in her mind's eye, and she shuddered. She shut the machine off and was considering deleting the message when keys jingled in the lock and Marisa came in.

She was dressed in an expensive suit that hugged her figure in all the right places, and her red curls were tied back in a fashionable bun. But for all her style and grooming, the dark circles under her eyes looked like two purple bruises.

"Oh, great." Marisa dropped her satchel bag on the sofa. "You're home. Do you mind if I take a small rest before we start? I didn't get much sleep last night."

Linda glanced at the carriage clock on top of the TV. It was a little after two in the afternoon. How long had she been asleep? And why hadn't Ashley come home yet?

She got up off the sofa and moved past Marisa to look out the window.

The sun was suspended high in the sky.

Marisa sat down heavily on the sofa and looked at Linda through tired eyes. There were bags under her eyes and she looked like she could fall asleep on her feet given half the chance. "You got hurt?" She pointed at the bandage on Linda's head. "Was it one of the garden tools?"

"Ashley's truck crashed against a tree." Linda turned to face her and rubbed her arm. She was very cold. "She's at the garage getting it fixed."

"Oh, no," Marisa blinked a few times, her face blank. "That must have been hard on you. Do you want to talk about it? I can rest later." She sat forward with great effort.

Linda shrugged. "I've never done this before." She had thought she was ready to lay everything out in front of a stranger and get help but now that the moment was upon her she was tongue-tied and didn't know where to start. Each memory was an embarrassment, each action shameful. It had been different in the support group. Everyone could relate to what she had gone through.

"That's alright." Marisa didn't smile but her tone was soothing. She was slightly detached from the conversation, like she wasn't an active player in it. That disconcerted Linda even more. "We can take it as slow as you like. The objective is to help you. Maybe we can start with something innocuous. Tell me about the accident. What happened?"

Linda didn't want to talk about the accident either. Ashley had been on the phone when it happened. She didn't want her sister to get in trouble if she wasn't already. It'd be a great impression on their employer if Ashley was hauled into court for such a traffic violation within hours of signing her employment contract.

"You got a call while you were away." Linda pointed to the answering machine instead trying to distract Marisa. She had no way of being sure the call was for Marisa since the house was usually occupied by so many people, but she thought if she phrased the statement this way Marisa would lose interest in the accident.

"Oh?" Marisa frowned at the answering machine just as she had looked at Linda, as if it were an interesting insect scuttling around her shoe.

Or silverfish in the drain, the thought came unbidden followed swiftly by the image of silverfish in the tub. She shuddered at the thought.

Marisa played the message.

The eerie whistling, the sudden feedback, and the gurgling noise at the very end. Linda's hair was on end again, and she was clenching her teeth so tight, her jaw was throbbing with pain.

"What the hell is this?" Marisa frowned.

"I was wondering the same thing." Linda sat down beside Marisa. "I thought it might be one of your friends, you know, prank calling or something."

"I'm not friends with juveniles." Marisa rubbed her temples. "God! I feel like my skin is crawling with insects. That was so bizarre. I kind of feel like I've heard this before though, but not sure exactly where."

"I know." Linda nodded vigorously. "I've got goosebumps."

"We have caller ID." Marisa started jabbing buttons on the cordless. "What time did the call come?"

"About five minutes before you came home." Linda tucked her hair behind her ears.

"Okay, let's see." Marisa frowned at the phone. "It's a landline number. Wait, that's weird." She fished her phone out of her coat pocket and swiped the screen. She tapped icons, and swiped some more. "I know the number."

"Who is it?" Linda asked.

"It's from the other side of the house." Marisa's face mirrored Linda's confusion. "The wing Stewart and Evelyn share. But why would Stewart send us this weird message?"

"He wasn't at home when the call came." Linda's eyes widened. "I saw him parking his car in the drive when the message was being recorded."

"You must be mistaken." Marisa shook her head. "How is it possible for a call to come from a house when the person who lives there isn't at home?"

"Evelyn and Cindy May were home," Linda said. "Maybe it was one of them?"

Marisa's brow cleared. "I doubt it, but it might be possible Cindy was trying some other number and got us instead." She tapped a finger on the phone contemplating the situation. "Let's go ask." She got up, suddenly full of energy.

"I'd rather stay here," Linda said. She hadn't said it, but her overriding fear was that an intruder had called from Stewart's apartment, a tall intruder with black eyes and a scar across his nose. She still hadn't forgotten the moving shadow in the tower window. Had Jackson found out where she was? Was he making strange calls from the Blackburn wing to lure her there?

"Why?" Marisa was frowning again, probably judging Linda for being frail—the epitome of a poor, weak, helpless woman. "You know none of this will be easier if you don't choose to be brave. He's still dictating your life with fear. Why are you giving him that control?"

Apart from the narrowed gaze and thin-lipped frown, this was the most direct thing Marisa had said to her since she'd arrived; like she saw Linda, understood her, and wasn't just dismissive of her. "He's in prison," Linda stammered. "I… he—"

"Is no longer the focus of your life," Marisa said. "Where is he, New York? And he's going to, what, fly here? Or teleport? Is he some sort of superhero I don't know about?" Her lips twitched at the corner.

Linda tugged at her hair in agitation, not finding the situation the least bit funny. "You don't know what he's like."

"They're all the same, Linda." Marisa held her shoulders so Linda was forced to look her in the eye. "The only difference is that he knows you are no longer alone and if he comes for you, you have a community that is standing with you. Now come on. Let's get to the bottom of this message."

Linda swallowed and took a moment to consider Marisa's words. Strength flowed from Marisa's touch into her, and she nodded. "Okay."

CHAPTER 7

Marisa led the way out into the main hall. She knocked decisively on Stewart's door, two sharp knocks.

Footsteps echoed behind the door.

Outside, a car engine rumbled down the road. Linda rushed to the hall window to see a police cruiser slow down along the curb. Silver-haired Officer Carter sat in the front, Ashley in the back. Officer Carter stepped out and opened the door for her. Ashley vaulted out of the car, shook Officer Carter's hand vigorously, then rushed up the stairs.

"What's happened?" Ashley asked coming in through the door, slightly breathless. The police cruiser drove off slowly down the road towards the hills. "Why are you out here?"

Just then, Stewart's door swung open. Stewart stood in a casual gray shirt and yoga bottoms. He held a bowl of something mushy in his hands. His feet were bare.

"Is everything all right?" He looked from one face to the other.

Linda saw Evelyn in her wheelchair by the TV. A large bib covered the front of her shirt. They had interrupted her lunch.

"We're so sorry to disturb." Marisa smiled. Stewart blinked. "It's just that we got a call from your apartment a few minutes ago."

"What?" Stewart frowned. "I didn't make any call."

"You were just parking your car when the call came," Linda added.

"Was there anyone else in the house that could have made the call?" Marisa asked. "Cindy maybe?"

Stewart set the bowl down beside his mother's wheelchair. He ran both hands through his hair so it lay artlessly disheveled on his brow. "Mom can't move her arms to scratch her nose let alone call someone, and Cindy just left, but I can ask her tomorrow." Stewart pressed his hand in front of his mouth thinking. "What was the message? Was it a threat? We can report it to the police, if it was."

He was looking directly at Linda. She felt pleasantly uncomfortable under his gaze.

"It wasn't a threat," she said. "It wasn't much of anything."

"You can come and listen." Marisa pointed a thumb towards the door.

Stewart made to follow them. Evelyn moaned, her body trembling with effort.

"I'll be back in a minute, Mom," Stewart said kindly. "This is important."

"I can feed her, if you like," Linda suggested.

Stewart looked grateful.

"You won't mind?" Stewart asked.

Linda shook her head.

"Okay, great. I won't be a minute." He squeezed his mother's arm and followed Marisa and Ashley to the other apartment.

~

Linda tucked her hair behind her ears.

Evelyn was staring at her, her deep blue eyes wide. Her hands were twitching something awful, more so than before. Linda picked up the bowl of pureed carrots and peas and gave her a shaky smile.

"Hi, Evelyn," she said. "I'm Linda. I'm the new tenant."

"Mmmmmmmm mm," Evelyn moaned, trying desperately to communicate.

Linda took a little bit of mush on the spoon and extended it towards the old woman's mouth but she moved her head away. This was odd. Linda had only stayed behind because she thought Evelyn was hungry.

Evelyn twisted her head down on one side, her eyes darting down to her shoulder. She did it again, and again, moaning.

"Are you cold?" Linda asked. "Do you need a shawl?"

Evelyn made a spitting sound. She shook her head and ducked her head again.

It was horrible to see so much life force trapped in a body that wouldn't obey. The scratching finger slowed down, its movement deliberate—a complete opposite to the rest of her inanimate body.

Linda held Evelyn's shoulder to give some comfort, mimicking the strength Marisa had given her by a similar gesture. The trembling hand landed on top of Linda's hand and the fingers began to slowly scratch along her skin.

The nails were trimmed but managed to scrape painfully

along the back of her hand. Linda tried to pull away but with a grunt Evelyn held her hand firm by placing her head on it. Her eyes were wide, and alight with mania.

The finger scratched.

"Please, let go!" Linda tried to pry her hand away without hurting the woman.

Footsteps resounded from across the room. The others were coming back.

Evelyn straightened her head. Linda snatched her throbbing hand away and held it in the other.

"I can't make heads or tails of it." Stewart was shaking his head.

Ashley looked paler than before. "It was oddly haunting."

"Tell me about it." Marisa shivered. "You still don't know who it could have been?"

"No." Stewart spread his hands. "Mom couldn't have done it, I wasn't at home, and I can't think why Cindy would call and leave such a strange message. It could be a faulty connection. It won't be the first time the wiring's snapped or something."

"Oh, well." Marisa shrugged and flashed her widest smile. "Thanks for helping us out, Stew."

"Huh?" Stewart looked distracted. "Oh, no problem. Thanks, Linda, for being here with Mom. I really appreciate it."

"Don't mention it," Linda mumbled. She shuffled past him, not looking at Evelyn, who was pretending to be dozing. She wasn't sure what was going on in Blackburn Manor, but Evelyn wasn't as meek and helpless as she let on.

Linda followed her sister outside to the front porch where Ashley lit a cigarette. Marisa didn't join them.

"The truck?" Linda asked.

"Five days to get fixed, and it's going to cost me. My insurance isn't going to cover all of it," Ashley groaned. "The weekend's just around the corner, and the guy who can fix the engine is going out of town."

"There goes the shopping trip." Linda bit her lip. "There are no cars to rent, and I don't think the town has Uber. It seems to me that there's a number for a cab company taped on the fridge in the kitchen though."

"Not to mention an infrequent bus service." Ashley rubbed her temples. "You wanted isolation, Lin, congratulations—you got it!"

Linda flexed her fingers. The back of her hand where Evelyn had scratched was red and formed a very weird pattern. Linda squinted at it turning her hand this way and that.

Scratched on her skin in jagged overwritten letters was one word.

Kill

CHAPTER 8

"Jesus Christ!" Ashley grabbed Linda's hand and stared down at the red markings. "Who did that?"

"Evelyn," Linda snatched her hand back. "I think she's crazy."

Ashley looked at her strangely. "If we didn't need the jobs I'd suggest we get out of here." She inhaled deeply on the cigarette and blew out a steady stream of smoke.

"We've signed contracts, Ash," Linda said.

"Yeah, and they don't cover medical," Ashley joked. "But seriously, ask Marisa where the first aid kit is and get some ointment on that."

Linda went in to do just that.

The late afternoon light from the main hall windows fell on the main staircase but it still felt encased in shadows. She avoided looking straight at the portraits, especially of the buxom lady in the middle of the row with her hard face and flinty eyes that seemed to bore into your back long after you'd rushed past.

In the upstairs bathroom, Linda cleaned her hands vigorously, eyeing the open bathroom window.

She soaped them twice before cleaning them again.

The marks had faded a little but she still felt foul.

Her face was pale and drawn in the mirror. Light began to fade outside the open bathroom window behind her, as the sun settled into its descent. Linda stared at it, unease tripping down her spine like ice cubes.

She didn't feel safe anymore. First the crazy neighbor Grady, next the shadow in the tower window, then the accident, the strange message, and now Evelyn Blackburn. All of that coupled with the isolation of the manor was enough to break Linda's resolve to stick it out.

If the truck hadn't been in such a bad state she would have urged Ashley to leave within the hour. As it was, they were stuck here for the next few days. She felt an urge to just walk out the door, but the thought of walking miles through dark woods was terrifying.

She dried her hands on a towel and swabbed the scratches with antibacterial-soaked cotton. The smell made her nose wrinkle up in distaste.

Finally she stepped into the tub to close the window. She latched it shut so it wouldn't open on its own, and left the bathroom.

The hall was empty. She glanced up at the outline for the sealed-up attic door. Even the rats were quiet.

Marisa was right. She needed to stop whining and take control of her life. Linda squared her shoulders and decided to sleep on things. She'd decide what to do in the morning.

She took the stairs carefully. For such a large house the main hall wasn't very well lit. A single lamp glowed sentry on the hall table below. The portraits along the wall looked darker and more brooding because of this.

Linda climbed down slowly. The angle of the light made it look like the pictures were moving. She had to stop often and stare at a frame to make sure that the faces in it hadn't tilted her way, that a hand hadn't moved away from a thigh.

She stopped in the middle and stared at the buxom lady. The face was heavy-jawed and bloated, the cheeks florid as if the woman had been constantly feverish in life. There was no beauty in the pinched mouth or the flinty, narrow eyes, but the most striking part of the portrait was the left hand curved on top of a staff, the fingers crooked and hooked, the nails long and sharp like an albino spider, blind and evil, scuttling in the dark.

It was unnerving.

Linda shivered and turned from the portrait.

When she finally reached the landing she hurried through the living room door.

Soft murmuring voices came from the kitchen. Linda gravitated towards them like a ghost does to the living.

The kitchen was brightly lit. Ashley was chopping tomatoes and onions at the table. Marisa stood by the stove, frying potatoes and burger patties.

"How's your hand?" Marisa asked. "Did you find the kit alright?"

"Yes, thanks." Linda sat in a chair opposite her sister. "Just a little sore."

"Evelyn's worse than Grady." Marisa flipped a patty. "I mean don't get me wrong. Grady's bat shit crazy, but she isn't violent like Evelyn."

"Why do you think she scratched that word, though?" Linda asked.

"Lost her marbles," Marisa said. "The patties are done. Fries will take another minute."

"Thanks again for this," Ashley grunted. "What with the crash, I completely forgot to get groceries."

"I'll charge you for the meal," Marisa joked. "You'll find that we're pretty generous with food here at Blackburn. You can give me a list, and I'll ask Stewart to grab groceries when he goes to town next."

"That's very nice of you." The way Ashley said it sounded like she was still suspicious of Marisa.

They sat down to dinner. Marisa and Ashley opened beers. Linda stuck to water.

"I'm really sorry about the session, Linda," Marisa said to initiate conversation. "It just slipped my mind after the events of this afternoon. I'm usually not this unprofessional."

"I was distracted too." Linda shrugged and smiled. "We can start tomorrow morning."

"First thing." Marisa smiled. "So, Ashley." She wiped mustard from her mouth. "How did your day go? It was an unusual day for sure, but what about your first day of work?"

"Stewart showed me the files, the records. I won't be bored, there's plenty to do. Anyway, I don't think those bookkeeping tasks interest any of you."

"Right," said Marisa with a smile. "So, tell me about this boyfriend of yours."

Ashley frowned and chewed furiously. She swallowed with

difficulty. "Dax isn't a man. She's a woman. And we're not official; just casually dating."

Marisa froze with her mouth open about to take a bite of her burger. Tomatoes fell out and fell splat on her plate.

"Diane Xiang." Linda grinned. "Dax for short."

Marisa looked impressed. "Good for you."

"What about you?" Ashley asked. "Only men in your life? Because Linda saw some chick in the hall last night."

"Stewart mentioned that." Marisa gave Linda a look. It was neither reproachful, nor angry. It was hard to read and Linda found this a little frustrating as well as admirable. She wished she could mask her feelings half as well. "I didn't have anyone over last night."

"But I heard you talking to someone, and then I saw them leave." Linda flushed.

"I was on the phone," Marisa said with a nod. "That's what you heard. I even closed the door… It's not important, really." She smiled. "And to answer your question, Ashley, unfortunately, yes," Marisa sighed. "And not many great ones neither, although none of them were abusive. I just have a very low threshold for bullshit and men are nothing if not full of that."

They laughed at that. The mood was light around the table again, but the manor was too quiet around them. Linda could feel its oppressive silence at the fringe of their warm gathering, encroaching fingers inching closer.

"I shouldn't be drinking this stuff." Ashley belched. "I'm already having nightmares."

Linda stopped eating. "What kind of nightmares?"

"Oh, just silly ones." Ashley's tone had an edge to it. "The usual paralysis while someone's hovering above you kind of thing. Linda used to have those all the time as a kid. Next thing

I know, a vault is being closed and I'm stuck in some crypt or something. Creepy." She shrugged in nonchalance but Linda could see that the dreams had disturbed her.

The food became tasteless in Linda's mouth. Marisa had stopped eating too.

"Was there a lake?"

"Was someone crying?"

Linda and Marisa had asked the questions at the same time. Their wide eyes met across the table. Ashley set the beer bottle down with deliberate calm.

"You're both right," she finally said. "Eerily so. It's like…"

"We all had…" Marisa murmured.

"The same dream…" Linda finished the sentence.

The silence of the house was a thick wall around them now. Linda could feel cold fingers dragging down her neck, intensifying the feeling of being exposed and vulnerable. She felt like they were being observed. Linda glanced outside the kitchen windows, but there was nothing but the night out there. Trees rustled in the wind in the distance.

"That can't be possible," Marisa snorted. She took a tentative sip of her beer. "Can it?"

"It could be like synchronized periods," Ashley suggested but she seemed doubtful. "I guess."

"We haven't lived together long enough for that." Marisa shook her head.

"Have you had this nightmare before or just now?" Linda asked.

"I've had something like them before; three weeks ago when I'd just started, the house was full of clients and other counselors," Marisa rubbed the back of her neck, a faraway look in her eye. "But this one was intense, a bit too real.

There was a woman." She swallowed audibly. "I couldn't see her face. Her dark hair kept coming in front of it, but she was young and beautiful. I couldn't look away. Then, she starts to get old before my eyes." Marisa's eyes unfocused and her mouth slightly parted. "Her skin wrinkles until she turns to dust. Then, her bones cave in on themselves until she's a heap at my feet." Shaking her head, suddenly her eyes cleared and she pushed her plate away. "I'm bushed. I'm going to go to bed."

"I'll clean up," Linda said, picking up the plates and taking them to the sink.

Marisa trudged up the stairs.

Ashley yawned, and stretched her arms. "You need help?"

"No, I'm fine." Linda shook her head. "You guys made the meal, so it's only fair that I clean up."

"I think I'll call it a night too. Weird thing about the dreams though." Ashley frowned. "If I wasn't into practical logic, I'd think we were being hypnotized or something. But at least we've found some common ground with your counselor."

Linda chuckled, but there was no humor in it. The similarity of the dreams had really disturbed her. Ashley was very practical; she had been the first to discredit the existence of Santa Claus, and abhorred creationist beliefs. Linda was more inclined to believe that supernatural elements worked in the world around them, things science had no explanation for.

And Ashley had been right about another thing. Linda had suffered from night terrors and sleep paralysis when she was younger. It had started around the same time their father had started drinking to excess, coming home drunk and angry. Details from her late childhood sprang to her mind.

The fights and hate between her parents. The doors slamming. The glasses crashing into the wall. The screams. The cries. Then the beatings.

Then the therapy she'd been through in her early teen years at Dr. King's office. She remembered that the desk was made of the finest wood. There was an antique lamp on it right next to a stack of yellowed papers. The outdated phone never rang when Linda was there, and the heavy curtains kept out all the sun and kept in the smell of leather mixed with the smell of the dust on everything. This was where Linda and her mother put a name to the hallucinations Linda experienced when these fights started.

Dr. King had diagnosed her with PTSD and acute anxiety, and he explained to them that Linda suffered from deep sleep paralysis and strange imaginary friends. That's what the doctor had called the hallucinations she suffered from, as a side effect of her stressful life at home due to the hatred between her parents. He explained that it was not unusual, especially in such a situation. Ashley and her mom were relieved to hear that.

Linda was surprised her sister had mentioned her old issues. Ashley was very pragmatic, and she hated the time when Linda suffered from this episode. Luckily it ended when the fights between her parents stopped with the departure of Linda and her mom, proving the doctor right. Linda and Ashley had never talked about it since.

Her hands wiped the plates dry as her mind flitted back to the imaginary friends her mind created to protect herself from this terrifying period of her childhood.

There had been the man in the old-fashioned clothes who walked around with a walking stick, jabbing it at people's feet but tripping no one no matter how hard he tried. Obviously, Ashley didn't remember him.

And the young girl by the pond in the park that no one, except Linda, could see.

Both disappeared permanently when her mother took her far from her father, and her life relaxed.

Shuddering, Linda shoved that memory to the back of her mind. Ashley's pragmatism was safe ground to walk on. Those people had all been figments of her overly stressed imagination.

Setting the dishes to air dry on a rack, she wiped her hands on a kitchen towel. She shut the lights off in the kitchen, and was about to leave when a movement outside the window caught her off guard.

It was an inky blot superimposed on the darkness of night. It shifted along the garden path listlessly as if lost.

Throat as dry as sandpaper, Linda squinted hard at the shape but she couldn't make out any defining features. It was like a wedge of black drifting this way and that. Then, as if it had sensed Linda's attention, the shape stopped. Linda gasped and stepped back. She couldn't explain it but she knew whoever it was, was looking directly at her.

She was rooted to the ground. The figure now moved with singular purpose towards the back porch as if Linda had given it a guiding light. Fear licked her spine. Jackson had escaped prison and found her, she should have known he would, and now he was going to teach her a lesson for betraying him.

The figure rushed up the stairs.

It was on the back porch now.

Fingers scrabbling at the wall, Linda found the light switch and flipped it.

Light flooded the kitchen, and the back porch through the window.

It was empty.

Linda took in a few rattled breaths. Her head was throbbing, and her eyes felt heavy.

Taking a hesitant step towards the backdoor that lead out of the kitchen and onto the back porch, Linda grabbed a saucepan from the utility rack by the stove. The heavy weight of it felt comforting in her hand.

Fingers trembling, she opened the door.

Pale light flooded the back porch, her own shadow long and dark as it spilled across the porch and the garden.

There was no one there; no footprints on the dirt path.

Shutting the door quickly, Linda placed the saucepan back and promptly shut off the lights.

She rushed through the living room and the dark main hall, and up the stairs that glowed a pale gray from the lights on the landing. The faces in the portraits looked creepier in the half light. The buxom woman seemed to have grown larger in the dark, the paint of her eyes picking out the light from the front windows and shining with an internal venom.

That's silly, Linda thought. *It's just a painting.*

This was different from what she had experienced in her childhood, but it wasn't the first time she had hallucinated figures in the dark. Immediately after Jackson's arrest, she had broken down in her home, screaming and hysterical, because she had seen Jackson outside her window. She had moved to Ashley's apartment after that.

Her PTSD was back in full swing. The accident had jarred her, and brought back traumatic memories. Linda felt defeated, as if she had made no progress at all. She had been near crazy with terror back when the hallucinations had been a regular feature. She hadn't known what was real and what was a product of her anxious mind.

Linda didn't want to go back to being the terrified girl she had been. She never wanted to experience the uncertainty or doubt her own senses again. She hoped the sessions with Marisa would prevent any serious hallucinations going forward.

But what if this time it wasn't PTSD?

They all had experienced the same dream; it wasn't isolated to her trauma.

Ashley's and Marisa's doors were ajar. Not wanting to worry them, she stepped into the bathroom to calm down a little. She turned on the faucet, and raised her glasses on her head. She splashed water on her face, the cool liquid taking the heat out of her skin. Her headache felt a little better.

She turned for the towel and noticed the window was open.

Linda pulled her glasses down.

Yes, the window she had locked was open again.

Her hands began to tremble.

This wasn't possible. She knew she had locked the window before dinner, hadn't she?

A sharp knock on the door made her jump.

Linda opened the door.

Marisa was dressed in Harry Potter themed pajamas. She looked slightly green.

"Are you going to be long?" she asked. She swayed a little on the spot and had to hold the doorframe to steady herself. "It's just that I feel a little queasy."

"No." Linda glanced back at the window. "I'm done."

"Did you lock the window?" Marisa asked, stumbling past Linda to sit on the rim of the tub.

Linda stared. How had Marisa known about the locked window?

"Yes," she said.

"Please don't do that." Marisa moaned, holding her stomach. "It gets really humid in here, and this weird smell develops. I had to open it a few minutes ago to get some air in here."

"You opened it?" Linda felt palpable relief surge through her, lifting the heavy feeling of doom off her shoulders.

"Of course I did," Marisa snapped, wincing in pain. "Who else would it have been?"

"I hope you feel better soon," Linda said, stepping out of the bathroom.

"It was probably the burgers." Marisa belched. "Damn it! I hate being sick."

Linda didn't reply. She closed the door discreetly, and went down the hall to her bedroom. The feeling that somebody was watching her hadn't entirely left her, but now Linda was worried that it wasn't just a product of her mind.

∽

LINDA'S ROOM WAS EXACTLY AS SHE HAD LEFT IT. THE SIGHT OF the bed made all the exhaustion of the day come crashing down on her. She felt bone-weary. All she wanted to do now was get under the covers and sleep for twelve hours.

"Hey, Lin?" Ashley knocked on her partially closed door. "You up?"

"Yeah," Linda said, still shaken from her mad dash up the stairs. Her nerves were frayed and sensitive.

"I just wanted to check on you." Ashley stood at the door in her lumpy nightshirt and torn pajama bottoms. She held one hand behind her back. Linda knew Ashley felt most comfortable in the most old and tattered clothes she possessed. "None of what happened today must have been easy for you."

"I am a little jumpy," Linda confessed, running a hand though her hair. "The accident was jarring, but the calls were no less disturbing."

"Tell me about it," Ashley groaned. She came to sit beside Linda on the bed. She stared at her lap for a second then sighed, and brought her hand forward. "I found this. I knew it would make you feel better."

It was a small pink pentagon-shaped plastic box with cheap string attached to one end. Linda stared at it with her mouth open. This was just as much of a shock as anything that had happened that day, but it was overwhelmingly pleasant.

"My Polly Pocket!" Linda cried, taking the box from Ashley, who was grinning from ear to ear. "You said Sarah Fuller stole it!"

"I lied." Ashley made a face. "I was jealous."

"Why?" Linda asked. "You asked Mom for skates that Christmas."

"Yeah." Ashley scuffed her toes against the floor. "But I didn't think those stupid pocket-sized doll houses would be so neat, and you wouldn't share."

Linda opened it up to reveal a miniature doll house in one half of the box, and a small garden in the other. Nostalgia, sickly sweet and syrup-thick, choked her throat with tears and twisted her gut with half-pleasure half-pain.

"I lost the doll," Ashley apologized.

Mom, can I please have this one? I won't ever ask for anything again, promise!

She could still remember her mother's broad, tired face... the tired lines that seamed the corners of her eyes and mouth, warring against the desire to gift Linda the world. But the reality of their financial situation weighed heavy on her brow.

"I never wanted this one," Linda said, her voice husky. "I wanted the big purple heart Polly Pocket with the prince's castle and moat and grand staircase. I kept taking Mom to the store to show her which one exactly, and I kept telling her not to forget."

"But she forgot." Ashley placed a hand on Linda's shoulder.

"No," Linda laughed, brushing away her tears. "She remembered. She just couldn't afford it. I realize that now."

"She was a good mother." Ashley rubbed her back.

"The best," Linda agreed. "Thanks, Ashley, for keeping it safe all these years."

"Don't mention it," her sister said. "You should get some rest. Sleep off this horrible day."

Linda nodded, and closed the Polly Pocket. Ashley left, closing the door softly behind her. Linda placed it on top of a pile of books and looked at it as she laid her head down and prepared for a sleep that came so suddenly it was like someone had switched off the lights.

CHAPTER 9

Linda's head rested on a lap.

Someone was singing softly in her ear, their breath tickling the side of her neck. The words eluded her but the tune evoked lush green hills, under dark skies. Her heart constricted in her chest and her eyes filled with tears.

Hands stroked her hair gently.

"Mom?" Linda whispered.

She smelled damp earth, and something else she couldn't put her finger on. Her eyes grew heavy with sleep but a nugget of dread kept her from giving into that need. Something dangled in front of her: a silver chain with a peridot pendant in the shape of a shamrock hanging from its center.

Linda lifted a hand to touch the necklace but it hiked up.

She turned a little to retrieve it, disturbing the lap she was lying in.

Bone white hands stroked her face, and in the depths of a black cowl a pointed white chin was visible.

Linda screamed but the sound was lodged in her throat. She began to choke, willing her limbs to move, to run away, but her body refused to obey. Like she was immersed in quicksand, her limbs fell through the lap to the viscous earth sucking her in face first.

The unreality of it all dawned on her, and she realized she was dreaming. She managed to moan, fracturing the dream, coming back to wakefulness.

She sat up in bed, her head still swimming from the terror of her nightmare. They were getting more bizarre with each night.

A sound kept filtering through the haze, nudging at her ears to grab her attention. She listened carefully. The telephone was ringing downstairs.

She heard a door open on the landing. Footsteps tiptoed down the hall and a pair of feet came to rest outside her door. A muffled knock, and then Ashley's face poked inside. She looked white; heavy bags rested dark beneath her eyes.

"Who do you think's calling at this time of night?" she asked.

"What time is it?" Linda asked.

"About three a.m. I woke because of a stupid dream… what?"

"Me, too." Linda was suddenly very afraid. "Where's Marisa?"

Ashley shrugged.

Linda stepped out of her bed. She didn't waste time putting on her shoes but rushed down the hall and the stairs. The main hall was empty. Ashley followed her looking a bit perplexed with Linda's actions. Linda felt the same; she couldn't explain why she was in such a hurry but she knew she needed to find Marisa before… before what?

She found her standing in the middle of the living room illuminated by the grainy streetlamp light filtering through the windows. Her curly hair was messier than usual and her face was sickly yellow. She was staring at the telephone as if she didn't really see it. The phone kept ringing, ringing till it finally went to the answering machine.

"Marisa." Linda gently touched her arm. "Are you okay?"

Marisa didn't respond.

Her eyes were glazed and there was something frozen about the way she stood as if she were still asleep but had been propped up to stand there.

The machine beeped and the message began to record.

Sound surged and then was muffled like a badly tuned radio. The sound of boiling water, bubbles bursting as they reached the surface, then a low hum of music and a haunting voice singing.

Realization hit Linda. Her eyes widened and she stared at Ashley.

"I know that song!" she said. "I heard it in my dreams."

"What?" Ashley looked paler than usual. "How is that possible? You must have heard it somewhere else."

"No." Linda shook her head. "I'm telling you, Ash, I heard it in my dream. Twice now!"

"I didn't." Ashley frowned; she suddenly didn't look very sure. "I mean… no, I didn't."

"If we shared that dream about being buried, maybe we shared this one too," Linda said. "What do you think, Marisa?"

Marisa hadn't moved, she didn't even look like she had heard the message.

"Marisa?"

"I want to know who's calling us." Ashley went to the phone and checked the caller ID. "It's from a cell number this time."

"Marisa?" Linda hadn't been listening. She inched closer to Marisa. The woman's face was in shadow, and her figure was slightly hunched, arms dangling by her side as if they had no life in them. "Marisa, what's happened?"

Linda touched her shoulder and shook it slightly.

Marisa screamed, and lifted her face so it caught the light.

Linda cried out and stepped back.

Staring red-rimmed eyes shone in a face contorted in a terrible grimace. The lips were chapped in places and bitten red in others. Her face was ashen white.

Where only a few seconds ago Marisa had been as good as comatose, she was now a frenzy of activity, hands flailing in front of her face, face stretched in a grimace. A choking wheeze like the huffing of a tired locomotive came from her mouth. She bolted through the living room and into the main hall.

Linda ran after her. Marisa ran pell-mell towards the front door and smashed into it like a terrified bird caught indoors, desperately seeking a way out. Her head hit the wood as her body stood taut. Her hands jerked up and down the frame looking for the handle.

Her moans became deeper, gravelly.

Ashley came to stand beside Linda. Her shaking hand found Linda's and squeezed it.

They tiptoed a little closer. Linda's flesh had turned to ice. Her heart mimicked the sound of Marisa's head hitting the wall.

Thud

Thud

Thud

"Marisa?" Ashley's voice trembled.

Marisa's head snapped to attention. The silence was oppressive, pregnant with malicious intent. Linda suddenly preferred the sound of head on door to this silence.

Marisa's hand found the knob. She turned it, and snatched the door open.

Her slight body was silhouetted against the yellow street-lamp light. Shadowy steam hung about her form, like a gray aura so faint that Linda could only see it if she didn't look directly at it but from the side of her eye.

Marisa walked purposefully towards the end of the small porch, her movements short and jerky, like her limbs were stiff and not entirely under her control.

The front steps were only four feet above the ground but they were steep and the bottom was scattered with gravel. If Marisa didn't stop she could trip...

Marisa's body swayed at the edge, propelled forward, arms by her side.

"Marisa!" Linda cried. "Be careful!"

Marisa leaned forward on the balls of her feet, her upper body suspended in the air, ready to fall...

Her arm shot out and grabbed the banister.

Her body swung, the fall jarred by the arm, and she went crashing into the banister, her feet tripping over themselves.

Marisa screamed.

The faint shadow around her flitted away. Linda watched in horror as it rose in the air and beat down upon Marisa's prone body clinging desperately at the banister to break her fall.

Her fingers lost their grip, her eyes rolled up into her skull, and her mouth lay slack, unconscious.

She tumbled down like a rag doll, injured head crashing against the stone stairs before she came to rest on the gravel path.

By the time Linda reached Marisa, she was a heap on the concrete.

CHAPTER 10

Marisa was still breathing, but just barely. Linda kneeled beside her, eyes flitting over the street and dark woods for any sign of the gray shadow she had seen just minutes before.

Ashley was banging on Stewart's door.

"Stewart!" Ashley screamed. "Marisa's fallen down the porch steps! We need your help!"

Across the street, Grady's window bloomed yellow. Her slightly stooped figure came out on to the porch to investigate what had happened, a shotgun in hand. Linda recoiled at the sight of the gun.

Stewart finally opened the door. Linda saw the disheveled hair, and the blinking, crumpled face as he stared at Ashley as if she was talking gibberish. It was only when he looked past her and down at Marisa's prone body that the situation sank in.

He was suddenly alert.

He sprinted down the steps and was by her side.

"What happened?" he asked.

"We got another message," Linda explained, slightly breathless. "Marisa was all quiet at first, like she was asleep on her feet but then…"

"She went berserk when Linda touched her," Ashley said in a rush. "One minute she was a statue, the next she was this crazy lady who was banging her head against the door, and then nearly pitched herself off the porch like she had a death wish."

Stewart had gone very pale. Two points of red blazed in the apples of his cheeks. There was a spark of recognition in his eyes.

"She's still breathing," Linda said. "I think we should take her to the hospital."

"I don't think that's necessary." Stewart shifted his weight from the balls of his feet to his knees. "There's practically no blood." He turned Marisa over. A large weal scarred her face where gravel had scraped the skin off. It was true, there was very little blood, but Marisa's eyes were thin strips of white underneath her eyelids.

"She's just had a nasty fall." Linda's voice rose an octave. Hysteria bubbled up in her throat. "We have to get help for her!"

"I never said we won't get help." Stewart pinched the bridge of his nose. "I'll call Dr. Humphries from Keystone. If we call an ambulance from Hackridge, it will take twenty minutes to get here. Dr. Humphries will come in ten. Which do you think is a better option?" he snapped.

"I think he's right." Ashley nodded. "We should call a doctor first, and then the ambulance. If Dr. Humphries thinks she should be taken to the hospital, at least we'll already have one on the way."

The compromise sounded fair enough.

Linda sat with Marisa, stroking her arm. She picked pieces of gravel from her hair. Stewart went back into the house to make a call. Ashley sat on a porch step. Grady didn't move from her porch; her gun was still held in a pose of casual violence. Minutes passed, Linda didn't know how many, and with each ticking second Marisa grew paler.

Lights flashed in the distance.

Red and blue.

Linda blinked. Had Stewart called the ambulance? And how had it gotten here so fast?

The vehicle pulled up to the curb.

Linda's breath hitched in her throat.

Officers Wilson and Carter stepped out of their police cruiser. Grady seemed to relax on her porch. She even set her gun down by her rocking chair. Linda felt a flash of hate towards the heartless woman for calling the cops but not an ambulance.

Their boots crunched on the gravel. Linda's body shook.

Officer Wilson bent down to sit on his haunches. He observed the scene, scratched his head, and sighed. He touched Marisa's neck with two fingers. "She's still got a pulse but it's very faint."

Stewart came out of the manor. He looked worse than before. The red and blue lights flashing on his face didn't do him any favors either. There was dirt in his hair, and on the hems of his pajamas. He was holding his cellphone and a blanket in a tight grip.

"Dr. Humphries will be here in five minutes. It's lucky he was already out on a house call." He opened the blanket and covered Marisa, tucking it around her prone form tenderly. His fingers trembled slightly, and Linda could tell he was completely distraught but trying to keep up a brave front.

"What happened exactly?" Officer Wilson asked piercing Linda with his clear blue eyes. He was standing with his back to the street and Linda could see Grady creeping closer over his shoulder. One of her cats padded by her feet. The grainy yellow streetlamp light hit her from behind, leaving her face in sinister shadows. The cat jumped up into Grady's arms and she cradled the feline like it was her baby.

"We got a call that Marisa was pushed down the stairs," Officer Carter added helpfully, his mustache quivering.

"We were asleep," Ashley said. "I woke up in the middle of the night to the phone ringing."

"Do you know what time exactly?" Officer Wilson had taken out a notebook and pencil and was jotting down notes.

"I don't know.," Ashley shrugged. "I guess it was a little after two. We all sleep upstairs, and the phone is in the living room so Linda and I came downstairs. Marisa was already there, but she was in this sleep-state. It's hard to explain."

"Like sleepwalking?" Grady croaked from behind Officer Wilson.

Though her annoyance at Grady's presence was like a physical fire in her belly, these words gave Linda pause.

Ashley glanced at Linda. "Yeah, something like that. Anyway the call goes to answering machine, and it's another weird message."

Officer Wilson frowned. "What do you mean by 'weird' exactly?"

"No one spoke… strange noises… we have the recordings if you want to listen," Ashley snapped. She looked agitated. "Point is, after the call we tried to get Marisa to respond, but she went mad. Started to scream, and ran all over the place until she ran out the door, and didn't stop at the top of the stairs. I'm just glad she didn't break her neck in the fall."

Both police officers looked perplexed. Even Grady looked thunderstruck. She was holding the cat so tight the feline was yowling and scratching at Grady's arm to be released. Linda found her behavior very strange.

Stewart was sitting on the porch step, his face blank. He was in shock and Linda wasn't sure if he was even listening to the conversation.

"Could I hear the messages?" Officer Wilson asked, closing his notebook.

He was looking directly at her. All of them were. The back of her neck prickled, and it felt like even the house behind her was peering at her closely, the entire structure focused on her.

"Of course." Linda led him into the house. The living room was still the same, but it felt different from a few minutes ago. Linda would never be able to disassociate what had happened from this room.

She walked forward and pressed the play button on the answering machine.

"You should sit down," Officer Wilson said, his tone offhand. "You look like you'll fall asleep on your feet."

Linda did as she was told.

The messages began to play.

Linda's eyes grew heavy as the scratch and thud of wind against a microphone came from the machine. The hair on the back of her neck tingled in anticipation of a haunting voice and when the melody started, darkness edged her vision and her head lolled to one side. Her thoughts meandered in that state of gloom.

She could smell rich, sodden earth: the kind of black soil that gave life to trees and flowers.

Soil gave life. It healed.

Maybe they should bury Marisa in fertile earth so it could heal her…

Her limbs were heavy.

A gray specter flitted in and out of her vision, teasing her with its amorphous state.

She needed to sleep.

"Miss Green."

Her eyes snapped open. Scott Wilson was kneeling on the floor in front of her, his hand on her knee. He was shaking it gently.

"I know you're tired, and I'll let you go to bed in a bit," he said. "But I need you to answer just a few questions."

Linda licked her dry lips and nodded. Had she been thinking of burying poor Marisa? What was wrong with her?

"Do you recognize any of these numbers?"

"No." Linda cleared her throat. "I mean I didn't, but Marisa knew this landline number. It was from the adjoining apartment. We thought it might be Cindy, but she left in the afternoon, and Stewart's mother can't move her arms."

His eyes widened. He glanced outside the door, and Linda got to observe his profile. He wasn't strictly handsome, but he had a boyish charm to him.

"And this one?"

"No." Linda shook her head again. "I don't know this one at all."

"Oh." Officer Wilson ran a hand over his mouth. "Okay. I'll look into this number and try to find out who it belongs to. Thank you for your time."

He got up and made to leave. He stopped suddenly at the painting above Linda's head. She glanced at it too. It was full of moving shadows in the dim light.

"I thought I saw…" He glanced at the open door. Linda followed his gaze. A car was coming slowly down the street. "Looks like Dr. Humphries is here." He nodded and left the manor.

Linda followed him and joined Ashley in the front yard. They watched as a middle-aged doctor, broad-shouldered and silver-haired, rushed out of his idling car to inspect Marisa. She looked yellow, and sickly. It didn't look like she was breathing at all.

"This is getting odder by the minute." Ashley sighed beside Linda. "And that Grady woman is getting on my last nerve. I swear I'll start kicking her cats up trees if she doesn't quit the whole creepy cat lady routine. God, I'm tired."

Linda nodded absently. She stretched her arms and stifled a yawn. Her mind was numb with lack of sleep and worry for Marisa.

Her back was like a tightly wound rope. Her shoulders hunched as she watched Dr. Humphries examine Marisa. Tears pricked her eyes, and her body flushed hot and cold.

After what felt like an eternity, Dr. Humphries straightened and stood up.

"Her heartbeat is very faint," he said to Stewart. "Did you call the ambulance?"

"Yes." Stewart's voice was hoarse. "It should be here any minute."

"It was good you didn't move her." Dr. Humphries rubbed his chin. "There isn't much blood, but with this kind of fall I won't be sure of the trauma to her spine until we get her to the hospital."

Linda tore her eyes away from Marisa's prone body. The more she looked at her, the more upsetting it became. Flashes of the flickering shadow around Marisa's body kept rising before her eyes. She scuffed her toes in the grass, the cold earth stinging her skin.

Earth... regenerating soil...

Her eyes grew heavy and she swayed on the spot.

"Whoa." Ashley held her before she could fall. "You okay?"

"We should bury her," Linda mumbled faintly.

"What?" Ashley asked. "I can't hear you."

"You should take her to bed."

"She looks tired."

"This must be upsetting for her."

Linda had no idea who was speaking. Her eyes were so heavy they felt glued shut. She couldn't open them, no matter how hard she tried. Someone guided her to the manor, and helped her up the stairs. Her limbs dragged under the weight of sudden exhaustion.

Somehow, she made it to her bed, where the sleep she had struggled to keep at bay engulfed her.

CHAPTER 11

Linda walked down the passage on trembling legs. The smell of damp earth was strong in her nose, and it covered the roof of her mouth like a slick patina of dirt. All of her senses were overpowered. She saw, smelled, tasted, and felt loamy earth and rock. She could even hear the echoing thrum of it, like she was walking in the veins of some large beast.

It wasn't completely dark, nor was it infused with light. The walls gave off a pearlescent glow. Water dripped steadily down the tunnel, and she could hear the distant murmur of a crowd punctuated by the sound of metal clanging against metal. Linda could make out a few drifting words.

... Oisin... injured... blood... bury him... healing... mother earth...

Where was she? What was happening?

As if they had been waiting for her to think that question, the murmuring voices stopped. Water dripped in malignant silence.

Linda took a step back from the dark mouth of the passage.

An ice-cold draft buffeted her from behind, pushing her forward.

Linda moaned, whirled around.

And screamed.

Men stood in front of her, their eyes hollow, their mouths gashes. There were too many to count. They went on and on as far as the eye could see, choking the passage. Their faces were expressionless. They wore dirty torn pants held up by suspenders, and peaked flat hats and jackets. The man in the front with the large mustache held the body of a young boy. The boy's eyes and nose were caked with mud.

Linda stumbled back and fell. Her feet tried to lift her up, but the ground was soft loamy earth. Her hands clawed at the walls for support, and she lifted herself up.

He's dead.

The voices invaded her even though none of them spoke, their mouths unmoving.

He's cold, and hungry, and DEAD!

Linda cried out.

The mob surged forward.

Linda screamed and fell again, but this time she hit hard wood. She looked around frantically to see where her pursuers were, lifting her hands to protect her face.

Sunlight hit her in the eye, blinding her. She looked around her room, disoriented.

Out of habit, she reached for her glasses and put them on.

It took her a while to realize she wasn't in Brooklyn, but Keystone. She had no memory of coming back to her room last night.

Last night!

Getting up on wobbling knees, Linda left her room. She

stood in the sunlit hall for a moment staring at Marisa's open bedroom door. Magazines were stacked on the bedside table, crocheted dolls lined a shelf above her bed, bras and panties dried on the back of a chair. It felt like a vulgar invasion of Marisa's privacy. Linda shut the door gently.

It was unreal what had happened last night. She sent up a quick prayer for her counselor.

Stumbling back into her room, Linda sat heavily on her bed. She could still smell the damp earth from her dreams.

A dream…

That was all it was, yet it had felt so real.

Taking a deep reassuring breath, Linda took off her glasses and rubbed her tired eyes. They stung with sudden pain.

"Ow," she yelped. She blinked against the grit in her eye, using the sheets to clear the tears streaming down her face. "What the heck?"

She looked down at her palms to see what could have caused the obstruction.

They were covered in dirt.

Black soil was caked under her nails.

Mud streaked her pajamas.

Linda's heart fell into the pit of her stomach. Her breathing became labored. She got up slowly from the bed and gingerly pulled back the sheets.

The covers were full of clods of earth. Worms slithered aimlessly across the expanse of her bed.

Hands trembling, Linda removed the covers steadily.

As long as the bed needed cleaning, Linda wouldn't think about the implications of all that dirt in her sheets. It was a dream. It had to be.

Linda had no memory of what happened after she fainted

last night. It was possible, no, very probable, that she had tracked the dirt inside. She had no shoes on when the call came and Marisa had the sleepwalking attack. Linda had stood in the front yard. She must have fainted in the dirt. Her pajamas must have been coated in the stuff and all of it got on her sheets.

Yes. Of course. That's what happened.

The panic at the back of her mind receded a little, but it didn't vanish completely. Something strange was going on in Blackburn Manor: the figure darting down the stairs on her first night there, the strange phone calls, the dreams; in fact, just the atmosphere about the house was odd.

Maybe we should leave, Linda thought, pulling the pillow covers off. *I'll talk to Ashley about it.*

Once the bed sheets were in a neat heap in the laundry basket by the bedroom door, Linda removed her pajamas and added them to the pile. She wrapped a towel around herself, grabbed her toilet bag, and tiptoed down the hall to the bathroom.

Soft murmuring came from behind Ashley's closed door. Linda heard her name. She ignored it. She needed to shower desperately.

The bathroom was as cold as ever, but Linda's mind was preoccupied with her dream, the dirty mess in her bed, and the implications of the phenomena she had experienced since she had arrived. Day by day, she was convinced something in the manor had reactivated her long-gone hallucinations.

Once the water started sluicing down her back she was both relieved and appalled at the amount of dirt washing down the drain. She had to shampoo twice before the water ran clear.

How much dirt had she gotten on herself just by standing in the front yard?

Stepping gingerly out of the shower, Linda grabbed her towel and promptly washed her face. The water had been cold but refreshing. Goosebumps trailed along her arms as she put on her glasses and stared at herself in the mirror.

Bags hung beneath her eyes, and her skin looked sallow and sickly. Linda pulled the towel tighter around her and left the bathroom.

Ashley's door was wide open, but she wasn't inside.

Once in her room, Linda avoided looking at the bare bed as she pulled on an old T-shirt and a pair of jeans. Each action was precise and efficient. Stuffing her towel in the laundry basket, she picked up the basket with a sense of purpose and went out into the hall.

She stopped on the landing.

Her limbs stood at a standstill allowing the dark thoughts lurking in the back of her mind to surge forward.

Images of Marisa on the steep porch stairs came rushing back to her, and Linda grew weak in the knees. She couldn't shake away Marisa's white desperate knuckles clutching the railing, saving herself from the fall, and the flitting gray shadow rising up in the air like some deformed bird of prey before it crashed down on Marisa's poor shoulders.

Had the gray shadow been the same as the apparition she had seen earlier that night outside the kitchen? Her hallucinations were becoming more and more prevalent and that scared her.

This shadow reminded Linda of the terrifying hallucinations she experienced when she suffered from sleep paralysis years ago, the ghostly things that weighed on her chest. The very idea of it made her shudder; it was so real... but the doctor who treated her had been right: when Linda and her mother moved away, the situation calmed down, and the hallucinations just stopped.

Linda shook her head. She never wanted to go back to being terrorized by her own mind.

What happened here was definitely different: she wasn't the victim of her hallucination, like in her late childhood. This time, the victim was someone else. Marisa. And yet, Linda saw that ghostly bird of prey. Her mind probably just invented it to "explain" why Marisa acted like that. It was another side effect of her PTSD following what Jackson had done to her over the past months.

It came to her suddenly how it was a mercy that Marisa had fallen down the seven porch steps and not this steep dark shaft. Linda was sure she would have broken her neck on these. Her own feet were reluctant to go down the stairs now.

She swallowed and took the first step, then the next, and the next. Tension sat heavy on her shoulders like a vulture, talons digging into her flesh.

"Linda, is that you?"

Ashley's voice from the kitchen eased some of the dread that gripped her insides in a vise.

"Yeah." She took the last few steps down and went to find Ashley.

Cheery sunlight bathed the kitchen as if last night had not happened. A sweet-scented breeze was blowing in through the open windows. Ashley was beating eggs at the counter. She looked just as haggard as Linda felt.

"Morning," Ashley mumbled.

"I'm going to get some laundry done." Linda forced a casual tone. "Do you have any clothes you need to throw in?"

"Mmm," Ashley mumbled, clearly distracted. Linda didn't blame her. She didn't feel quite there herself.

"Any news on Marisa?" Linda asked.

Ashley nodded. "I called the hospital only a few minutes ago. Marisa is finally conscious, but they want to keep her to figure out what really happened. They think it's some kind of sleeping sickness, and maybe she experienced an episode of temporary mania because she was woken from her sleep state." She rubbed the bridge of her nose. "It was a little too complicated for me to understand all of it. I'm just glad she's okay. You're doing laundry?" Ashley finally noticed the basket in Linda's hands.

Linda nodded. She was relieved that Marisa was conscious and might be able to recover soon. She still couldn't get the image of her terrified face out of her mind. Or the sort of shadow that swooped down like a hawk on her shoulders.

"I'll give you a few of my clothes after I shower," Ashley said, interrupting Linda's train of thought.

Linda was crossing the living room to the basement door when something along the side wall caught her eye. The oil painting of the hill seemed different somehow. Setting her basket on the coffee table, Linda peered closer. Green trees and grass rolled up the hill. A few clouds dotted the sky. Everything was the same except…

She couldn't put her finger on it at first, but then it struck her. There was a black blot at the bottom right corner. It was perfectly rounded as if someone had taken a black Sharpie and colored in a section of the painting.

"Hey, Ashley," Linda called over her shoulder. "Was this painting always like this?"

"What?" She sounded annoyed. "What are you talking

about?" Her voice got closer and within seconds, Ashley was standing behind her.

"This black blot," Linda pointed. "I'm not sure, but I think that's new."

Ashley stood arms akimbo, frowning. She clicked her tongue and turned her irritation towards her sister. "I don't know. Does it matter?"

"No." Linda shrugged, feeling foolish to have made a big deal out of nothing. "I was just curious, since the last time I saw the painting that wasn't there."

"Who cares?" Ashley spread her hands.

Linda blinked back sudden tears.

"Oh, God." Ashley sighed. She pinched the bridge of her nose. "I'm sorry. I didn't mean to snap."

"It's okay." Linda tucked her wet hair behind her ear. "This entire trip hasn't been easy, and last night was just…"

"Yeah, and no." Ashley shook her head. "Last night was horrible, but it's not that. I was on the phone with the mechanic and the truck needs a new engine. I don't know how I'm going to keep my head out of water if I'm going to start this job drowning in debt."

"That's terrible news." Linda swallowed her disappointment. She'd hoped to convince Ashley to leave but the truck was in a state and Ashley really needed the job. Yet Linda was afraid. Her hopes of getting better with Marisa's help had taken a serious back seat. There was no knowing when Marisa would be back and how soon she could start counseling again. She made a mental note to ask Stewart what could he propose, and what should she do till the rest of the counselors returned. "Don't worry about the truck. I'll pay for half of it."

Relief crossed Ashley's face. "Thanks, Lin. You don't have to, but I'm so broke I'm not going to refuse your help."

"Don't mention it." Linda smiled. "I'll be in the basement."

"We've only been here a day; how come you have so much to clean?" Ashley asked.

Linda considered telling Ashley about her suspicions and her fears about her sleep paralysis and hallucinations returning but dismissed it quickly. It wasn't the right time. Ashley was already very stressed and she wouldn't believe her any way. She had always thought Linda's claims that she was sensitive to spirits was an attention-seeking tactic, until the doctor had explained what Linda was experiencing in medical terms.

"I got some dirt on the sheets after last night," she said. "I don't want to leave in any stains."

Ashley nodded and went back to the kitchen. Linda opened the basement door and stood at the edge of the stairs. Cold radiated out of the basement doorway, rich with the smell of detergent, whitewash, and mud. Linda leaned forward in the patch of darkness, balancing the basket in one hand while the other reached along the wall, feeling for the light switch.

She imagined her hand finding something else entirely in that notch of black—something cold, clammy, and dead. She shook the thought away. She was acting worse than a child.

Light switch found, she flipped it on and the dark receded to an orange gloom. She took the stairs carefully, very aware of the empty open spaces between the slats. Her ankles felt exposed and vulnerable.

The smell of damp earth intensified as she reached the basement floor. What was it with this house and its smells? It reminded Linda of the nightmare and the congregation of men holding that dead boy, Oisin.

Linda set up operations at the far wall, opposite the stairs and the darkness underneath it. She placed her basket on the floor and sorted out the whites and the colored clothes. While she worked, the back of her neck prickled like someone had splashed the smooth expanse of her skin with ice cold water.

She tried to ignore the pressure building between her shoulder blades. She knew this feeling well. It only manifested when someone was staring at your back with intense malice. Jackson had subjected her to many of those, but this wasn't Jackson; she had a feeling it wasn't even human.

Rubbing the back of her neck, she put the whites in first, shaking the dirt off her sheets as much as she could before adding them to the load.

She closed the lid on the washing machine and started a cycle.

A soft thud from the back of the room made her stop cold.

Her back seized up.

For a moment, she was paralyzed.

Her breath came in small jerks, and she was trembling from head to foot.

Infinitely slowly, she turned, her insides roiling painfully.

The basement was empty, but Linda didn't feel alone.

Serves you right for thinking of that boy, Linda thought.

The sound came again, much clearer than before. A low shuffle and a thud. Linda tried to pinpoint the location of the sound.

It was coming from under the stairs.

The first step was the hardest. The dream was still fresh in her mind. The horde of angry men could be waiting in the dark, their fingers hooked in claws to tear her from limb to limb.

No light illuminated the space under the stairs. It was colder here than it was anywhere else in the basement, and the smell of stagnant water dripped from the walls. Patches of sunlight streamed through the narrow windows along the ceiling, but none penetrated the darkness.

Scrape.

Thud.

A longer scrape.

Thud.

Linda's breath was stuck in her throat. She stumbled forward, her knees trembling. The shadows enveloped her in a frost of cold as she walked beneath the stairs. The wall was slick with moisture. Small beads of ice peppered the surface like murky stars. Linda blinked. She'd seen this somewhere before.

Scrape.

Thud.

She touched the wall. Before she realized what she was doing, her ear was pressed against it, listening.

More sounds reached her.

The scrape and thud sounded like a tool, but now she also heard panting, like someone was breathing hard. The voices were faint. A thin, high sound like mic distortion drowned everything else out. Linda pressed closer trying to get the original sounds back.

The noise cut out.

There was silence.

Linda...

A snatch of whisper; a voice she would recognize anywhere.

"Mom?" Linda whispered.

A sudden booming thundered in rapid succession, gaining in intensity.

Boom

Boom

BOOM

BOOM

Linda cried out and stumbled back. Her heart raced, and bile choked her. She clutched her neck, her hands wet and clammy from the wall.

"Linda?"

She whirled around to face the far wall. Ashley stood near the washing machine, her arms loaded with a few T-shirts and pair of jeans. She looked startled and pale, like she'd seen a ghost.

"What are you doing under the stairs?"

"I thought I heard something." Linda licked her dry lips. "Someone called my name."

"I did." Ashley was looking at her weirdly. "I called you when I was coming down the stairs just now."

Linda stared at her sister, not comprehending for a moment. Then it dawned on her. The voice she'd heard had been Ashley calling her. The boom of thunder was just her sister coming down the stairs.

Placing her hand on her forehead, Linda actually laughed. What was wrong with her?

"I think you should go lie down," Ashley said, dumping her clothes in the basket. "I'll take care of this."

"No, I can handle it," Linda said.

"I insist." Ashley folded her arms across her chest. "You look tired."

"So do you."

"Please don't argue with me," Ashley snapped. "Just… please."

Linda nodded.

She looked back once she'd reached the landing.

Ashley's wet hair trailed down behind her like a dirty mop. Her shoulders were hunched as she sorted through her clothes. Linda couldn't help but feel a little relief to be let out of the basement.

There were a lot of things she did not understand at this point in time, but she was now convinced there was something wrong in Blackburn manor, more than met the eye, and it certainly wasn't a trick of her mind.

PART III
SECRETS IN THE DARK

CHAPTER 12

Linda stood in the living room, observing the painting.
She wasn't mistaken. The blot on the lower right side of the painting seemed to be bigger than before.

"Have you been standing here this whole time?"

Linda turned, albeit reluctantly, to face her sister. Ashley stood by the basement door with a basket of freshly folded laundry in her arms. Linda blinked and looked at the carriage clock on the opposite wall above the TV.

Half past eleven.

"I can't have been standing here for an hour." Linda slapped her forehead. "I swear I just got up here."

Ashley looked concerned. "It's probably stress from last night. Did you get any sleep?"

Linda bit her lip. "A little." Rubbing the back of her neck she decided to share some of her reservations with her sister. "I think it's this place. It's very strange."

"How do you mean?" Ashley tilted her head.

"The weird phone calls," Linda spread her hands. "What happened to Marisa and Evelyn." She clutched her hand involuntarily. "I don't know. It gives me the creeps."

Ashley wasn't stupid. She pursed her lips and smoothed her face into relaxed lines but Linda had seen the flash of annoyance in her eyes.

"Hey." Ashley shrugged, smiling gently. "It's an old manor; it's bound to be creepy. The phone calls could be some teenager in town playing a prank. As far as Marisa is concerned we'll find out what happened to her this afternoon. Don't think about it too much. Let's dig in and get started on some work. It'll take your mind off these things."

Linda knew what she meant by "these things." Ashley had always detested any talk of Linda's hallucinations due to her sleep paralysis, and even more of anything that could be considered supernatural.

"Sure." Linda smiled wearily. "I'm going to go for a walk. I'm collecting stones to use as dividers in the vegetable garden. There's some nice variety beyond the estate."

"Okay." Ashley yawned walking towards the stairs. "I'm going to the main office to look at the books. I should have some idea about the accounts before I get down to bookkeeping."

Linda grabbed a tote bag from the kitchen pantry, folded it up and stuffed it in the pocket of her jacket, and walked out the front door. Clouds had scudded along the sky covering up the harsh sunlight. A wet wind was blowing, slapping her in the face as she climbed down the steps.

She stood a moment at the spot where Marisa had fallen, examining the disturbed gravel, the bits of grass and earth that had been torn up in the front yard. It must have rained sometime in the early dawn because there wasn't any significant disturbance to warrant the amount of dirt in her sheets, but the yard was full of muddy puddles.

Stewart's car was still in the driveway, so he must be home though she hadn't seen him. She didn't blame him after the night they'd had.

Linda walked across the street to stand in front of Grady's house and looked back at Blackburn Manor. It was odd but when she was inside, she couldn't wait to get away. But standing on the outside the house had an almost haunting allure inviting her inside.

She couldn't stay there. It wouldn't work. The thought had been germinating in her mind since Stewart— not his mother— had opened the door. Now a girl was in the hospital and the thought had bloomed into a decision.

Linda was going to leave as soon as Ashley's truck was ready. She didn't know how they'd pay for the truck, or what they'd do about their employment contracts, but she'd convince Ashley to leave.

"Meow." A cat slinked between her legs.

"Hello, little buddy." Linda bent down to pet the cat. It let her pick it up.

She looked back up at the manor.

Someone darted back in the shadows in the front-facing tower window.

Linda wasn't mistaken, not this time. She'd seen a face as clear as day. It had been oval, pale, and surrounded by flowing hair. Someone was up there. Linda stared at the tower windows. The rest of the upper-story windows were curtained shut. Only the tower was unshuttered and allowed a bird's eye view.

"She seems to like you."

Linda whirled around, her grip loosening on the cat. The cat climbed her shoulder and tried to sit on her head. Grady was standing on the top of her porch peering down at her.

"Guess there's no accounting for a cat's taste." Grady shrugged. "They have a penchant for nasty things like dead rats and bugs, so there you go."

Linda's lips pressed together in a disapproving line. "They flock to you like flies to a corpse."

"Ha!" Grady laughed, but there was no humor in her voice. "She speaks. And here I thought only your sister had any gumption. Come along, Tiddles," she said and motioned to the cat. "Don't go wasting your affections on people who won't stick around."

Linda started. How did old miserable Grady know of her plans to leave when she hadn't even told Ashley?

The cat padded back to the porch.

"Read your mind, did I?" Grady crowed. "I know I have, since you've gone as white as a sheet."

"How…"

"No one sticks long in that house." Grady made a sour face at Blackburn Manor. "Not with her in there."

Linda's throat went dry. She licked her lips and glanced back at the tower window where she had seen the darting figure. Had Grady seen it too?

"You mean Marisa?" Linda asked, her hands shaking slightly.

"Of course not Marisa, you dolt," Grady snapped. "She's only been here a few weeks."

"Then who?" Linda snapped. "Why do you insist on speaking in riddles? If you know anything about the house, I would like to know."

Grady's thin mouth got thinner, as she sucked her lips in like she'd licked a particularly sour lemon. Her face darkened and looked more thunderous than the sky. "Why don't you figure it out yourself?" She gathered her cat from the porch and stormed back into her house.

Her screen door slammed shut.

Cursing under her breath, Linda walked back to the other side of the street. A glimmering white flash above her caught her attention, and she looked up. Was it the figure again or just lightning? Linda walked forward and the earth slipped from under her feet.

Linda screamed as her feet parted ways, going in opposite directions in the mud. She fell in a heap on the muddy ground. Every inch of her was covered in the sludge.

"Ugh," Linda groaned and pulled herself up again. Making an effort not to look back at Grady peeking through her curtains and laughing at her, Linda climbed the porch steps and reached in her pocket for her key.

Only there wasn't one. She'd left her key with her purse in her bedroom. She was locked outside.

CHAPTER 13

"Ashley!" Linda banged on the door for the third time. "Goddammit!"

This was just great. She was locked outside looking like a stinking Bog Woman. It was no use banging on the door. Ashley was probably on the second floor office listening to music with headphones on to concentrate on her job, and she couldn't hear her. There was nothing for it.

A light rain began to fall.

Linda sighed, and ran to the back of the house. Linda knew it was Cindy's day off since Stewart was at home, but she had wanted to avoid him. She had seen him at his most vulnerable last night, and she didn't think she was in any frame of mind to comfort him when she herself was so confused about what was going on, and what she wanted to do about the future.

She knocked on the Blackburn backdoor anyway, three sharp raps, and stood back to wait.

Heavy footsteps trudged towards the door, and a few

seconds later Stewart was standing there peering at her from red-rimmed eyes. His face was puffy and red in places. She could see he had attempted to shave, but done it badly. There were spots he'd missed all around his chin and jaw. There were streaks of dirt in his hair and on his clothes.

"Wow," he said, a faint light sparkling behind his tired eyes. "You look like something the cat dragged in."

"You don't look so hot yourself." Linda smiled.

"Oh," Stewart looked at his dirty hands and smiled sheepishly. "I was in the garden shed fixing the light so it'd be easy for you to find your tools. I just got back in a few minutes ago." He ran a hand through his hair.

"I just missed you, huh?" Linda's smile was strained. "May I go through? I've locked myself out."

Stewart's eyes widened. "Oh, of course." He stepped aside to let her in.

Linda took off her mucky shoes outside and stepped into the warm glow of the kitchen, acutely aware of how dirty she was.

"You can clean up a little in here." He led her towards the stairs. "I'll rustle up some towels for you."

"That's okay, I'll just clean up at home. Where's Evelyn?" Linda felt uncomfortable using the facilities in this part of the manor. She couldn't explain why. It felt like an intrusion.

"She's taking a nap right now," Stewart said, climbing the stairs.

The phone rang in the sitting room. Stewart gave Linda an apologetic look and picked it up. Linda shuffled towards the door that would lead her to the main hall, trying not to get dirt anywhere.

"Hello? Oh, hi, Dr. Humphries."

Linda stopped in her tracks. She turned back to face Stewart. He seemed to read the question on her mind and nodded in a way that communicated that he'd let her know about Marisa as soon as he got off the phone.

While she waited, Linda observed her surroundings. She had stopped by the stairs that led to the upper floor of this wing. These stairs were very different from the steep spiral ones in the main hall. Thick gray carpet muffled any footsteps, and framed pictures and thin wooden shelves lined the walls. The shelves housed strange masks and a wooden urn. Linda recognized Stewart in a few pictures, and lots of people she didn't know.

There was one picture in particular that caught her attention. She stopped halfway up the stairs, looking intently at the picture. It was tinged in sepia with age but the house in the background was unmistakably the Blackburn Manor.

A little girl of about four was captured in the act of running in the forefront. Her light hair was tied in two pigtails. Her smile was so wide it forced her eyes to crinkle shut. She was in a fairy costume complete with a set of wings. A tall man in a suit stood behind her, grinning in obvious pride.

That wasn't what had caught her eye. It was the shadowy figure in the tower window staring down at the father and child that had stopped her.

"Thank you so much, Doctor. I'll see you in a while."

Stewart finished the call and joined her at the foot of the stairs.

"Who is that?" she blurted out.

Stewart looked at the picture she was pointing to.

"What?"

In for a penny, in for a pound. There was no going back now.

"The very top floor," Linda explained. "With the large bay windows. It looks like someone lives there." She pointed at the picture.

Stewart frowned as he peered at the picture and chuckled. "That's my mom –when she was a kid – and my granddad. And that," he pointed to the figure in the window, "is my grandma's dressmaker dummy complete with wooden head for her hats."

"A dummy?" Linda was nonplussed.

"Yeah." Stewart laughed. "My grandma used to sew her own dresses. After she died, my mom used the dummy as a Halloween prop. She'd dress it up in old rags or dresses and put makeup or masks on the head to scare anyone driving by. I think it might still be up there."

Linda stared at the picture. The quality was grainy, and she couldn't make out any discernible features. Had she really just seen the side of some rickety old dressmaker's dummy?

Reluctantly, she tore herself away from the picture. "Ashley called the hospital this morning but they didn't give her a clear answer. Has Marisa regained consciousness?"

"She has." He nodded. "Dr. Humphries says she's very lucky she didn't sustain much damage to her back and neck. I'm going to go visit this afternoon."

"Good." Linda tucked her hair behind her ear. "I hope she can come home soon."

"She's a fighter." Stewart ran a hand through his hair. "She's only been here a few weeks, but it feels like I've known her forever." His eyes still gleamed, but now it was because they were filled with unshed tears.

"Hey." Linda touched his arm. "She'll be all right. As you said, she seems to be out of danger."

"Yeah." He cleared his throat and touched the back of her hand signaling his appreciation for her support. "She'll be home soon, hopefully."

Linda nodded, and fished for anything to change the subject. "I saw your collection. What's the mask?"

"Huh? Oh, it's a ghost mask from West Africa." Stewart led her down the stairs. "A friend of mine got it on one of his expeditions in the Sahara."

"How interesting," Linda said, wondering if the mask were contributing to the phenomena in the house. "Is the urn from there as well?"

"No, the urn is from the funeral parlor in Hackridge."

"What?"

"We cremated my dog, Buddy, and they gave us the ashes in that urn." He stopped a few steps above the landing. "Here he is."

Linda looked at the framed picture he was pointing at. A younger-looking Stewart was sitting on a couch while a large golden retriever sat on his lap.

"Cute," Linda said.

"I've never been called that before." He smiled up at her.

Linda blushed.

"I'm just kidding. Come on."

Linda followed him to the door of their apartments. He opened it and she finally had access to the main hall. She felt a little dizzy. When was the last time she had eaten? Did they even have groceries for the four days they were going to have to stay here? There wasn't much left in the pantry.

"Thanks," Linda said, pulling the hem of her skirt down. "I would have been stuck out there for hours."

"No problem," Stewart grinned. "Anything you need just let me know."

"There is, actually," Linda said. "Could you please drop me off in town on your way to Hackridge's hospital this afternoon? I need to buy some groceries."

"Of course, no problem." Stewart nodded. "How will you get back though?"

"I'll find a ride." She smiled.

"Okay." Stewart nodded. His smile was at once shy and sheepish. The air was charged with more than the lingering storm outside. "I'll see you later." He walked to his portion of the house, glancing back to catch her eye.

Linda's stomach fluttered. She bit her lip and stepped back to close the door.

The natural light did not illuminate much of the room for a late spring afternoon; Linda stepped closer to the window to get a look at the weather. The rain had stopped, but the clouds were still dominating the sky. Movement from across the street caught her attention. Grady's face was peering through her front windows like a malevolent moon.

CHAPTER 14

The second floor of the house, where the offices were located, was a mixture of old Gothic features and cheap office furniture. The landing windows weren't stained but the arches were pointed and carved into the wall, which rose to high ceilings. Linda walked through a warren of cubicles to the individual offices in the back.

It was less oppressive than downstairs but still held shadows. The air was dusty and stale.

A metal plaque with "Accounts" etched on it was nailed to the door on the far left.

Linda opened it and peered inside.

There were two desks pushed against either side of the room and three large filing cabinets in the middle like pillared dividers between them.

Ashley wasn't there.

Where could she be? Linda wondered.

She went back downstairs to the staff quarters, the air

getting chillier as she descended. At Ashley's bedroom door she knocked lightly before walking in.

Ashley was sprawled on the bed deep in sleep.

"Ashley." Linda shook her sister gently.

"… skjmbuuh…" Ashley mumbled, swatted at her hand, and snored loudly.

Linda looked around the empty room. Ashley's laundry was lying in a pile on the chair, her duffle bag open littered with paperbacks and assorted toiletries. Linda rummaged in her handbag and pulled out a pen and an old receipt. Scribbling furiously on the back of the receipt she tucked it under Ashley's phone on the floor.

She got up to leave but then kissed her sister's forehead as an afterthought.

After a shower and getting into clean clothes, Linda had eaten a peanut butter and jelly sandwich. Time had ticked by. She tried to follow the news on her mobile phone, but the internet connection was lame, and after a few minutes, she turned on the TV. She had flipped through a few channels, not really concentrating on the screen.

Ashley had slept throughout. Linda had figured her sister must have lain down for a five minutes' nap before going to the office floor but the nap had turned into a solid block of sleep.

A horn blared from the front of the house. Linda increased her pace. She glanced at the painting on her way out the door. The black splotch was still there, taunting her. The horn blared again. She had no time to stop and examine the wretched painting.

Linda grabbed her house keys from the key hook by the door before she left the manor. Stewart was sitting in his car. The clouds hadn't dispersed, but they were less ominous now.

Grady was sitting on her porch, a regular, creepy fixture in their lives.

"Sorry," Linda apologized as she got in the passenger seat. "I was trying to wake Ashley, but she's out like a light."

"Probably exhausted from last night." Stewart backed out of the driveway.

"Hmm." Linda stared intently at the bay windows of the tower.

She looked for any twists of shadow, any hint of light to reveal the dummy and put her mind to rest. The clouds reflected off the glass making it hard to make anything out, but Linda persisted till her eyes watered.

It was as they were pulling away down the road that she saw it. A still form standing in the gloom of the attic, a plumed hat sitting on its head at a jaunty angle. There were no arms, or appendages, and the form seemed absolutely still, disturbingly so.

Maybe that's what she had seen. Curiously enough, Linda felt far from relieved.

"Has your family always owned the manor or did they buy it?" Linda asked, settling in for the fifteen-minute journey.

"My ancestor Arthur Blackburn bought the land a little after the War of Independence. He was a famous man around here. I learned all about him from Mrs. Grady across the street."

"I'll bet she was a real Gorgon at school."

"Actually, she was one of the best teachers we had until she retired."

Linda held her breath as they passed the intersection where Ashley's car had crashed against a tree. Even though it had happened yesterday, it felt like years ago.

"You're kidding me?" she said when they finally turned on the bend. "I find that hard to believe."

"Yeah, well." Stewart shrugged. "Old age and feeling dispensable isn't the best for developing sunny personalities."

Linda took this in and realized there was a lot of merit in what he said. "So how old is the house?"

"It was constructed in 1792 by Arthur Blackburn. He even owned the mine in the hill along the road from the house. In the 1860s, Samuel Blackburn – one of his descendants and the heir of the domain – amended the manor to stick to the design of the Victorian era. Lots of development and prosperity, until the 1870s when a few miners died. No one's really sure what happened, but after that the mine was abandoned. There was a speakeasy there during Prohibition; it's been empty for as long as I can remember. A mining company tried to make a go of it but the mine's exhausted. It's belonged to Blackwood County for quite a long time, but it's abandoned now."

"Wow." Linda whistled. "That's a very rich history. Don't you feel overwhelmed living in a piece of historical significance?"

"It does get annoying when the tourists prance around the gardens," Stewart joked. "But yes, history has seeped deep into the roots of our house. Sometimes, I can feel it weighing down on me. Imagine all that those walls have seen."

A shudder went down her spine. She couldn't imagine what the walls had seen, but she could very well attribute the gift of sight to the house. There were points in the day when it felt like the very foundations were groaning under an unseen weight, that the house was listening and brooding in silence.

"How come there are no other houses nearby?" Linda asked. "I'm not trying to be nosey. Just curious."

Stewart laughed. "It's a miracle Grady managed to build

her house at all. We suffered as much as anyone during the Depression and the 2008 stock market crash. My grandfather was forced to sell some of the property; the mines for instance and the acres of land across the street from the house. Mom never liked that; she detested Grady and her house, called it an eyesore. She managed to get further building permits stalled so much that others just abandoned the idea of building here."

Linda chewed over that information.

"I like your shirt." Stewart's gentle comment pulled her out of her thoughts.

She looked down at the Calvin and Hobbes print on her shirt and flushed pink. "I know it's a bit geeky." Linda straightened her knee-length shirt over her jeans.

"I like it," Stewart's knuckles brushed her knee as he changed gears. "You looked nice in it."

Linda's fingers trembled. She tucked her hair back a little too aggressively, and knocked her glasses into her lap.

Cursing under her breath, she jammed her glasses back on her nose. Leave it to her to go to pieces at a simple compliment from a man. "Thank you," she managed to mumble. Marisa was right. She needed to man up or settle for everyone walking all over her.

Keystone was a seasonal town. It boasted a population of six thousand all year round that swelled to ten to fifteen thousand during the summer tourist rush. There were bait and tackle shops for the nearby lake, bike and speedboat rentals, and there was also a Starbucks clone. It was a fifteen-minute drive from Keystone to the Blackburn Manor, but it felt like it spanned years. Where the manor was steeped in suspended time, Keystone was heading slowly into the future, trying hard to ignore the history and legacy of a mining town that had faced its share of controversy.

"Thanks for the ride," Linda said when Stewart pulled the car in beside the Big Brown Bag, the local grocery store.

"We should get dinner sometime," Stewart said. "After Marisa comes home and things settle down a bit, I'd love to show you around. The lake this time of year is a must-see."

Linda swallowed her anxiety and smiled brightly. "Sure, we'll plan something."

It took a lot of courage to lie like that when she had no intention of sticking around. Before her violent separation from Jackson, lying was never an option. White lies snowballed into avalanches, and she'd find herself crushed under Jackson's weight as he pummeled her face into the floorboards.

She got out of the car, and waved Stewart goodbye. She bit her lip. She had told Stewart one more lie; groceries were only her second priority, she wanted to get to the library and get some research done on the history of the house and town. The internet connection at the Manor was sketchy and the mobile network abysmal. Obviously, telecom operators had no reason to spend money to have cables or antennas covering such remote areas; the bad weather and the hill behind the house didn't help. She had no way of getting any research done at home.

Unsure of where the library was, Linda thought to get her groceries and ask the clerk at the checkout. She was rummaging in her bag for her shopping list, and she didn't see where she was going. Her foot tripped over the small step in front of the grocery store, and she went flying.

Strong arms grabbed her arms and broke her fall.

"You have to be more careful than that, you know." It was

Officer Wilson, only he wasn't in uniform. He looked much younger in a casual T-shirt and jeans. "I can't always be there to save you."

Linda straightened her shirt. "You've never saved me before, Officer Wilson," she said tetchily. "But thank you."

"Scott, please. I'm off duty." His grin was infectious. They walked inside. "How's Marisa? You get any news?"

"Stewart got a call this morning. She's conscious. He's gone to see when she'll be released." Linda grabbed a shopping cart and rolled it down the cereal aisle.

Scott nodded, and his eyes brightened again. "That's good news. I hate hospitals; never can stick around in them for more than ten minutes. Depress the hell out of me. It's true I haven't saved your life, technically," he said reading the back of a Cheerios box. "But I'm sure it's only a matter of time. You look like the type that needs saving."

Linda bristled at the comment but choose to stay quiet.

"Speaking of type," Scott said, dumping a box of Lucky Charms in his cart. "What type do you think Stewart is?"

"What?" Linda asked, pretending to choose between Captain Crunch and Frosted Flakes.

"I know you haven't known him for long, but what kind of man do you think he is?"

"Why are you so concerned about Stewart?" Linda turned on him, not bothering to hide her annoyance.

"Because he lied," Scott said. "He said that call from his apartment was a fluke, a one-time thing. It isn't."

Linda had stopped pretending to ignore him. "What do you mean?"

"After Marisa was dispatched to the hospital, I went to check the records of both incoming and outgoing calls from your phone. There have been several calls from Stewart's landline number."

"But that could be a coincidence," Linda said. "He must have called a tenant or two for something or other at some point during their stay."

"The calls were at specific times." Scott was looking at her intently, persuading her to see something only he could. "All of them were at three fifteen, both AM and PM, and all the calls lasted one minute fourteen seconds."

Realization dawned and Linda's mouth fell. "The recordings…"

"Are a minute and fourteen seconds each," Scott finished her sentence.

The earth quaked under her feet and she felt her balance shift and tilt this way and that. "Wha…" Linda cleared her dry throat. "You think Stewart knew about the phone calls?"

"Either that, or something very weird is going on in that house."

You don't know the half of it, Linda thought.

"And what about the other number?" Linda asked.

"Registered under a Manuel Costanzo. I called the guy, and he had no memory of calling at that time of night. In fact, his phone data did not corroborate the call. So, I dug deeper." He beamed like the cat that had slurped up all the cream and devoured a canary or two, and was very proud. "The previous registered owner was a Shannon Dorothy. She's a nurse in Hackridge and worked at Blackburn Manor about eight months ago. I tried to get in touch with her but so far no luck."

Linda chewed the inside of her cheek. A lot of her hopes had been riding on finding enough information on the Blackburn Manor to rationalize her suspicions, and to give a framework to her hallucinations, but this was more of a tangled web than she had imagined.

And what of the throng of men she had seen in her dream? The strange song hadn't been in a man's voice, and Marisa had seen a woman too.

And the woman rushing down the stairs the first night she had come…

Maybe Scott was on to the solution of what was wrong with Blackburn Manor.

And then there was the tickling sensation at the back of her throat, a niggling thought that had germinated when she was a little girl but had been quashed by the doctors – she had supernatural sensitivity. As a child it had been a logical explanation for the strange sights she had seen, but that had disturbed her mother more than the diagnosis of night terrors and sleep paralysis. At least the medical conditions had clear and definable names and cures.

Ashley had never believed her, but Linda always thought she heard her mother warning her every time she was headed into danger. This morning, she had thought she'd heard her in the basement, and long before, she had heard her faint warnings before her wedding, before the final day of abuse.

Now that Linda was willing to admit it to herself, she had freaked out because she had heard her mother's voice as clear as day, whispering her name in the basement of Blackburn Manor.

She knew it sounded crazy, and if Ashley ever found out about her belief she would make fun of her. However, it comforted her in the lonely hours before dawn, and that was more than enough for her.

Her mother was trying to warn her about some danger at the manor. Linda was now convinced it had to do with the history of the house. There was something hidden, some catastrophic event that had triggered something terrible still remaining.

She might be wrong to reopen the possibility of her sensitivity to supernatural elements but at this point it would be negligent not to listen to her instincts.

"Is there a library in town?" she asked.

Scott looked startled. Linda wasn't sure if it was her question that had shocked him or the hunk of smelly cheese he was sniffing. "Yes, why?"

"How far back do the archives go?" Linda was already walking towards the exit, grocery cart abandoned.

"I don't know." Scott followed her. "Probably a little before the Civil War. Maybe."

"Great," Linda said. "Could you give me directions?"

"I'll do you one better." Scott grinned, infected by Linda's sense of purpose. "I'll take you there."

Linda followed in Scott's wake, her mind whirring with questions, theories, and a lurking fear of the unknown.

CHAPTER 15

Overstuffed and undermanned, the Keystone Library was a hodgepodge of bestsellers, battered paperbacks, seedy romances, and yellowing classics all moldering in a dusty building in the main square. The air was thick with dust motes and smelled faintly like stale bread, and very old coffee.

A bored young intern pointed out the archive section for Linda; it was even more disorganized than the rest. Nothing was catalogued by year and reel upon reel of microfilm was missing. Dividing the microfilms into halves she bullied a reluctant Scott into scanning them with her for any sign of the house or one of the Blackburns.

Eyes itchy and dry from the dust in the air, Linda was in her element. She pored over *Hackridge Herald* articles in such fine print it made her temples hurt just from looking at it. She had always been a keen student and had looked forward to a career in academia, but life had other plans for her.

Flitting through the *Keystone Chronicle* she stopped suddenly when the name Samuel Blackburn met her eye. She focused the microfilm and began to read.

Mining Magnate Rebuilds
June 28th 1869

The mines along Hill Road have long been the county eyesore, and a hub for miscreants and Irish immigrants. The fate of the mines, universally recognized as the product of a neglectful owner, is set to change. They were recently inherited by Samuel Blackburn, the son of the late Richard Blackburn, who feels a stricter approach to running the mines will not only increase production but also improve labor conduct.

"Indeed, I have approved the construction of new labor barracks right across from the manor," Mr. Blackburn replied to our august reporters' questions. "It is no wonder they act like heathens when the majority of the labor force come from uncivilized un-American societies. It is up to me to teach them how gentlemen behave by keeping a close eye on their activities, and allowing them to observe a gentleman up close."

Linda made a face. She could make a mental picture of Samuel Blackburn. She'd met people like him before, making light of their micro aggressions and getting deeply offended when called out on their prejudices.

There wasn't much more of interest, just an obituary for Samuel Blackburn on the 8th of January 1876.

We regretfully announce the death of
SAMUEL BLACKBURN
of Keystone, Pennsylvania
A small service will be held at the Baptist Church, Hackridge

Linda frowned at the obituary. It was short, barely three

lines. It didn't say how he died or where, nor who had survived him. It didn't even say anything nice about him either, where usually people waxed lyrical about their loved ones.

If his small quote is anything to go by he wasn't a very likable person.

She flipped the page and saw something else that was peculiar.

BLACKBURN MINES FOR SALE
In the heart of Blackwood County

Samuel Blackburn's relatives didn't want to keep the mines. Why?

She glanced up and saw the time. She gasped. It had been over an hour since she had arrived and she still hadn't bought any groceries.

Linda left the archives to find Scott but he was no longer sitting in front of the microfilm machine. A little nervous, Linda walked out on to the main library floor. He was sitting on a desk by the windows; his laptop was open, and his ears were stuffed with earphones.

Linda bristled with irritation. He had said he'd help her but he was watching a movie instead. Typical. You couldn't ever rely on the word of a man.

Linda walked over and stood before him. Scott's eyes were glazed, and he looked like he hadn't slept in days. This was strange because he had been chipper an hour ago. He didn't seem to notice her. She tapped the desk, and waved her hand before his face to get his attention. He was startled and looked at her in a daze, as if he had no idea who she was.

"Did you look at the microfilm?" Linda asked once he'd removed his earphones.

"I couldn't find anything before 1922," he said, shaking his head and wincing. "But there was this really interesting article on the bootlegging business in the Blackburn mines. Nothing specific. No names or anything, just an open letter from a town well-wisher, that type of thing. I think I can find more details in the police files on the operation. I don't think it's related–"

"So you decided to watch a movie," Linda interrupted him and glanced at the screen but it wasn't a video at all. There were squiggly lines across the screen and buttons and switches. Linda thought that was very odd since you couldn't really touch the screen to operate the buttons, but then again the last time she'd been allowed on the computer was in high school.

"What? No." Clarity was coming back into his eyes. "I was just fiddling with the MP3 of the messages you've been receiving."

Shame burnt up Linda's insides. What was wrong with her? Scott didn't have to help her, he didn't even have to bring her here, but he had been nothing but generous with his time. She felt like a jerk.

"MP3?" Linda pulled up a chair.

"They're digital audio files," Scott said, rubbing his right eye. It was red around the corners. "I got it from the phone operator since all calls are recorded."

"Oh." Linda didn't understand a word he was saying but she felt like she owed him the truth after she'd misjudged him so badly. "I'm not very good with the technical stuff so bear with my stupid questions – sorry. Did the files make any sense to you?"

"Not really, but I did get something."

He offered a bud to her, indicating she put it in her ear. The lead was small so it forced her to scoot over closer to him. She could smell his cologne.

"I was tinkering with the audio, trying to see any pitches we were missing or any words. I played it fast first and then slowed it down. I didn't get anything at first, but once it slowed I could pick up something that sounded like words. Well, sort of." He shrugged, frustrated that he couldn't explain it any better, and pressed play.

Nothing happened at first, but then a low moan began that kept extending on and on. Linda glanced at Scott. He cleared his throat and moved his fingers over a pad on the laptop. The sound rushed in her head, as Scott forwarded the track.

"It starts from here," he said.

Linda didn't expect much, but when the audio began again she finally understood what Scott meant.

It was unlike anything she had ever heard, yet so familiar. She couldn't put her finger on where she'd heard it before. It was a haunting sound, an extended woe that evoked images of green hills under rain-heavy clouds, and sheer cliffs dropping into a choppy sea. There were words, they had a shape and enunciation to them, but she had never heard the language before. She wasn't even sure if it was a language.

Linda's skin crawled, and yet it tugged at her heartstrings.

She pulled the earbud out of her ear.

"Strange, huh?" Scott said.

"Hmm," Linda said.

It was strange, even more so because she couldn't fathom what it could have to do with the strange events in the house. The more she dug up, the more confused she got. She had found no answers, only more questions.

"Can I have a copy of that?" she asked.

"Erm." Scott hesitated, seemed to think it, over then shrugged. "Sure. I don't have any USB key on me; I'll see if Katie at the front desk has any spare CDs I can burn this in. I know, this isn't very modern, but we're in quite a small town."

"Thanks," Linda said. "I need to buy groceries." She got up. "I'll meet you here after to pick it up."

"I need groceries too," Scott called over his back. "Just wait a minute."

He sprinted over to the desk. Katie looked bored, and annoyed at being wrenched away from her phone. She made a face, and got up to retrieve a box from a shelf behind her. Scott thanked her and rushed back.

"This will only take a minute. We'll go to the store together," he said.

"What are you doing later?" Linda asked. Scott stopped what he was doing and gave her a look that made her stomach plop down into her spine. "I need a ride back home," she clarified. "I was wondering if you could take me."

"Sure." Without his uniform, Scott Wilson was less intimidating, but his gaze was just as clear and direct as before. Never one for eye contact, Linda couldn't tear her eyes away. "I can ask Stewart about the calls as well. Just a casual chat."

Linda was curious to see how Stewart would react. The calls implied a lot about her employer, none of it good. She was just glad she had decided to leave soon.

CHAPTER 16

Stewart's car was in the driveway. The afternoon was drawing to a close, the sunlight lingering after a day of choppy cloud cover, but lights were on in Stewart's apartment. The other half of the manor was dark. The house looked like the two theater masks made of century-old wood planks, but sawn in half and glued together so the happy and sad faces were one.

Linda shuddered as Scott pulled up to the drive. She got out and hiked the strap of her bag up on her shoulders.

Grady was sitting in a rocking chair on her porch as always.

"Hi, Mrs. G!" Scott called, waving.

"Hmm," was all the greeting he got in return.

Scott gave Linda a meaningful look. Linda shook her head slightly. Scott opened his eyes wide and motioned with his head again.

"Ask her," he mouthed.

Linda rolled her eyes in exasperation. From the little time she had spent with Scott Wilson, she knew that he wouldn't give up till she did as he wanted, so she turned reluctantly towards Grady's house, bracing herself for an assault of caustic words.

"Mrs. Grady?" Linda's voice was hoarse. She cleared her throat and made an effort to be polite. "Mrs. Grady, Scott tells me you used to teach high school history. I was interested in finding out more about the mining operation. I heard it was abandoned after a mining accident, but couldn't find any details at the library so–"

Mrs. Grady snorted with laughter. "I'm surprised you can read. Oh, this is a hoot!" The old woman got up from her rocking chair. "Junior school dropouts wanting to learn about the mines."

The screen door slammed shut behind her, but Linda could still hear the old woman's laughter from inside her house. Face as red as a beet, she glared at Scott, who looked ashamed.

He opened the trunk. Linda joined him to get her grocery bags, still seething from her encounter with Grady.

"Let me help," Scott said, leaning forward.

"I can do it myself," Linda said, stepping in.

Their heads knocked together.

"Ow." Scott rubbed his forehead. He looked at her with sudden realization and extended his other hand to rub her head as well.

"What are you doing?" Linda snapped.

"It must hurt." Scott explained, shrugging.

"I've had worse," Linda brushed his hand away. Now he was looking at her strangely.

"Was he a cop?" Scott asked. "Your ex. I'm just guessing because you weren't this frank with me when I was in uniform."

They both leaned forward at the same time again. Linda held up a hand. "Wait." She picked up the two heaviest bags and handed them to him. "You can take those." She grabbed the rest and they walked towards the house.

Linda chewed on the inside of her lip contemplating her answer to his question. She didn't have to answer at all if she didn't want to, but she didn't see the point of hiding things that could easily be found out in one phone call to a police precinct in Brooklyn.

Bending to put her groceries down, Linda let her hair cover her face as she spoke. "Yes, he was a cop, as was his father and his grandfather and so on." She fished in her bag for her keys, ignoring her hair tickling her nose. "Some of the worst times were after he came home from a tough day, or just a dull day. I stopped caring about his motivations after a while."

She straightened up and unlocked the front door. She had no strength to look at him, or the pity in his clear blue eyes.

"He sounds like a real bastard," Scott said cheerfully.

Linda turned on him with rage at his flippant response, but was shocked to see the same thing mirrored in Scott. His jaw was clenched tight behind his casual smile, and his eyes were dark like a tempestuous sea.

Scott shrugged. "There are some nasty people on the force. I'll be the first to admit it. But not all of us are like your ex. Trust me on that." His smile was a combination of goofy and sincere. Linda couldn't help but smile back.

They entered the apartment. Linda had only been gone a few hours, but the air was stale and musty, like it hadn't been inhabited in years. She led Scott into the kitchen and put the bags down on the kitchen table.

"Ashley!" she called up the stairs but got no reply.

Linda was distracted. She put her handbag on the counter. "Could you excuse me a minute? I have to check on my sister."

She didn't wait for a reply. She went to the main hall and climbed the stairs as quickly as she could without sprinting up them, keeping her panic at bay. Bad dreams and soil in her sheets was one thing, but Marisa's fall proved that things could get dangerous really fast and she had left Ashley alone for such a long time. What had she been thinking?

"Ashley?" she called down the hall. The light from the sun was fading fast in here, and the shadows were growing longer.

Ashley's door was ajar.

"Ashley?" Linda knocked on the door and entered.

Ashley was asleep in bed. It wasn't her usual way of sleeping, spread-eagled, snoring, and drooling on the pillows. She was lying perfectly still, her breathing so soft and quiet that Linda had to watch her chest for movement to confirm she was alive.

"Ashley." Linda crossed the room and shook her sister, sudden panic gripping her. "Ashley, wake up!"

It disturbed her that Ashley wasn't startled awake like she normally would be. Instead, Ashley's eyes fluttered like panicked moths in flight, and then opened slowly. Her eyes were still swimming in sleep but she opened her mouth, and cleared her throat.

"Ten more minutes," Ashley said. "Just ten more minutes, then we can go to school."

"You've been asleep all day." Linda sat down on the bed beside her. "Are you feeling all right?" She touched Ashley's forehead. It was cool.

"Just sleepy." Ashley yawned. She sat up groggily in bed and rubbed her eyes. "What time is it?"

"A little after six," Linda said. "I brought groceries."

"How? We don't have a car."

"Stewart dropped me in town on his way to the hospital."

"How is Marisa?" Linda was relieved to see Ashley looked a bit more alert.

"Why don't you come on down and we'll ask Stewart?" Linda got up and walked to the door. "Oh, and Ashley." She turned back to face her sister, who was struggling out of bed. "I need to talk to you about something. Freshen up and we'll talk over dinner."

Ashley's legs got caught in her sheets and she went sprawling on the floor. Linda was about to walk forward to check on her when she bounced up like a spring. "I'm okay. I'll be down in a bit. I need to brush my teeth."

Ashley grabbed a towel and headed towards the bathroom.

Linda went downstairs into the kitchen, where Scott had put away most of the groceries. "Everything okay?" he asked.

"Yeah," Linda said. "She's in the bathroom. We should go ask Stewart about the calls." She felt a sudden urgency to continue with their investigation.

Scott gave her a quizzical look. "You're eager."

"I have a right to know what's going on here. My counselor is in the hospital."

"Fair enough." Scott placed the last apple in the fruit bowl. "Let's go."

He led the way to the Blackburn wing. Linda peeked out the window; Grady was nowhere to be seen. Linda counted that as a small mercy. Scott knocked on Stewart's door. They squirmed in awkward silence.

The door opened a few seconds later.

Stewart was looking fresh and more upbeat than he had earlier in the day. His hair was wet from a recent shower and his eyes were less puffy.

"Hi, Linda," he smiled. "Scott."

"Hi, Stewart." Linda gave him a small wave. "How was Marisa?"

"Great." He clapped his hands, startling her. "She was up when I got to the hospital, and the doctors were finishing up tests. They were optimistic about her health. They think it's a combination of sleep deprivation and a rare sleeping disorder. She's coming back home tonight. I'm going to leave to pick her up in another half hour."

"Really?" Linda was ecstatic. "That's fantastic news!"

"I thought so too." Stewart smiled. "It's put a real spring in my step."

"That's good," Scott interrupted. "Because I have a few questions for you."

Stewart's smile became less glaring, its contours became more guarded and secretive. "Sure," he said. "Go ahead."

"You said that the call that was made from your landline to the phone in the adjacent apartment was not made by you, correct?"

"Yes." Stewart folded his arms on his chest. "We've already discussed this."

"You said you had no knowledge of the phone call."

"I didn't."

"Yet there were several phone calls made from your apartment to the adjacent one over the past eight months."

Stewart's mouth fell open, his eyes widened, and his skin

became paler under his eyes. "That's not possible. I would have known."

"No one else has access to your phone on this side of the house?"

"No," Stewart said. "Just my mom, and she can't reach out for anything since her stroke a year ago. I even asked Cindy May, and she denied using the landline at all. She's only been with us for two months, and she hardly uses the landline unless the network's down." Stewart looked from Scott to Linda, accusation brimming in his eyes. "What exactly am I being accused of here?"

"We're not accusing you of anything." Scott held up his hands. "We're just trying to figure out who made the calls from your apartment."

"Well, it wasn't me," Stewart said. "And the messages made absolutely no sense. Why, is this an investigation? No one's been harmed by the calls. They are a nuisance but they haven't hurt anybody."

Except Marisa, Linda thought but even as the idea crept into her mind she knew that it made no logical sense. How could the messages make her mad? There had to be a better explanation.

Just then Ashley climbed down the main staircase.

"Marisa just called," Ashley said. She looked the worse for wear. Her hair was knotted into a lose bun on the back of her head. She looked paler than usual. Yet, there was a twinkle in her eye, and a small smile on the corner of her lips.

"She says we better come get her or she'll walk back home."

"I'll get going," Stewart said, rubbing the back of his neck. "Unless you want to take me in for questioning."

Scott raised his hand in a show of defense. "I'm just doing my job, man."

Stewart shot him a dirty look then sulked back into his apartment. He was out within minutes, car keys jingling in his hands. Scott watched him leave, then waved goodbye and left in his own car, a thoughtful expression on his face.

Linda stood on the porch with Ashley and watched him leave.

CHAPTER 17

Stewart's car pulled back into the drive at dusk.

Linda followed Ashley down the front porch to greet Marisa.

Stewart stepped out first and came around the car to open Marisa's door.

She was gaunt and there were deep circles under her eyes, but she looked very much the same sassy old Marisa. She even had a snarky smile on her face. The only sign that she'd had a rough tumble down the stairs was the livid red scar on her forehead and the welt on her face.

"Thanks for bringing me home, Stewart," Marisa said. Her voice was slightly hoarse but not weak.

"Anytime," Stewart said. He looked fidgety, and his eyes kept flitting back to his apartment. "I'm so sorry I have to abandon you like this, but I should check on Mom. I've already asked Cindy May to stay past her time."

"Of course," Linda said. She took Marisa's hand and helped her on the porch steps.

Stewart took them two at a time, unlocked his apartment door, and went in.

"I hope you got groceries," Marisa said. "Because I'm starving!"

"It's good to have you back," Linda said.

Things weren't perfect but at least Marisa was unharmed.

Marisa followed Linda and Ashley inside the manor and sat down at the kitchen table while the sisters prepared dinner. Once the meal was ready, they all sat down. The tacos hit the spot.

Even Marisa managed to eat one of them. Due to her sensitivity to sharp lights, only the overhead lamp was on. The rest of the kitchen was in relative darkness. Linda felt like she was eating under a spotlight on some vast stage. The sense of being watched was subtle, but still there.

"It's a nice change to have you two feeding me," Marisa joked.

"Hardy har har." Ashley rolled her eyes. "Are you sure they didn't transplant a new personality into you at that hospital?"

"Please." Marisa shuddered. "I hate hospitals. Needles are a very real fear of mine."

"Thanks for the information," Ashley joked.

Linda sipped her iced tea. The jokes and banter were all good, but there was an underlying tension that they were all avoiding even though all of their conversations kept circling back to last night. The problem was that none of them knew how to broach the subject.

"Speaking of information," she said and cleared her throat. "I did more than just grocery shopping in town today. I did some research on the house."

"Really?" Marisa looked quizzical.

"I never pegged you to be a Nancy Drew." Ashley bit into her third taco.

"I was just curious." Linda shrugged. "Anyway, the house is old."

"Duh."

"What a revelation."

"Stop!" Linda laughed and threw a napkin at her sister. "It goes back to a little after the War of Independence. Apparently they owned the lands where Grady's house is and even the mines in the hill along the way. The laborers' cabins were built beyond the back garden so one of the Blackburns could keep an eye on them and they could learn to be 'civilized' by observing him. I mean, how crazy is that? Your workers aren't miserable enough, so you build their housing close by to make sure they are?"

"No wonder this house is creepy. All those people sending it bad vibes."

"That's not all I learned." Linda sipped on some tea again to moisten her dry lips. "I met Scott."

Ashley raised a brow.

Marisa grinned.

"I mean… Officer Wilson had some curious information."

"You're suddenly on a first name basis with him?" Ashley joked.

"About the calls we've been getting." Linda gave her sister a stern look. "They weren't a one-off. There have been multiple calls throughout the past eight months from Stewart's apartment at exactly three fifteen whether it's day or night."

Ashley stopped eating. Marisa went a whiter shade of pale.

"And the calls last one minute and fourteen seconds exactly."

"Did he find the messages left before?" Marisa asked, her tone slightly breathless.

"No." Linda shook her head. "But he knows who the cell phone number belongs to. She used to be Evelyn's nurse. Shannon Dorothy."

"Why is she still calling?" Marisa wanted to know.

"That's the mystery; the number isn't registered with her any longer, and the man who owns it now didn't make the call."

Confusion enveloped them. They played with the remains of their food deep in thought. Marisa's eyes drooped and she looked like she would fall asleep on her plate. Linda still had a very vague idea of what was going on. Scott's information about Samuel Blackburn and his contemptuous treatment of his workers, his death and the sudden sale of the mine all suggested the darkness stemmed from there; but how did that relate to her hallucinations? She needed to be sure before she could convince Ashley to leave.

"I think we should call it a night," Ashley said. "I'll clean up. Linda, you lock up. Marisa, get some beauty sleep. God knows you need it."

Marisa threw a tortilla at her, good-naturedly.

Linda was rather happy in that moment. Marisa was back safe and sound, and though the calls were still shrouded in mystery at least she was doing something about it. She locked the front door, and made sure the window sash was down and secured as well. When she turned to go back into the kitchen, the painting made her stop. A little less than half of the painting was eclipsed by a black moon with a pale peach center.

"Lin?" Ashley called from the kitchen.

Ashley's call forced her to abandon exploring the painting further. Was it a leaking pipe behind it that was staining the edges? Lost in thought, Linda went to the kitchen, where Ashley was cleaning the dishes at the sink.

"You said you wanted to talk to me after dinner?" Ashley asked.

Linda bit her lips. This wasn't going to be an easy conversation but she'd have to power through. "I think we should find another place to work," she said.

Ashley stopped soaping the dishes. She looked perplexed. "Why? We just got here. I know I was being a jerk whining about how far it is from a major city but we need these jobs. I'm actually worried about losing the day when I should have been going over the books."

"I know we need the money but we can find something that pays a little less while we find better jobs. It's not ideal but…"

"That makes no sense." Ashley frowned. "What is it you're not telling me? You were practically begging to come here."

"I know." Linda tucked her hair behind her ears. "But don't you think too many odd things have happened here since we arrived?"

"Okay, yes." Ashley folded her arms across her chest. "I agree; Marisa's episode threw me off but that's her personal health issue. It doesn't reflect on the rest of the company."

"That's not all that's been happening," Linda closed and opened her fists. "The dreams, the phone calls–"

"Coincidence, and teen pranks." Ashley slashed her hand through the air as if trying to physically dismiss the arguments. "We've discussed this. I don't understand why you're making such an issue of it now."

"I've been seeing things," Linda admitted.

"Like your PTSD hallucination?" Ashley's tone softened and she looked concerned.

"These hallucinations didn't feel like figments of my imagination, though." Linda ran a hand through her hair. "At least I don't think so. They've all been so…" Linda couldn't find the words to define what she felt. "They are just too similar, too interrelated to feel random."

Ashley rubbed her forehead, sighing deeply. She looked like she had aged five years. "I know you're going through a tough time, Lin, but getting up and leaving is not an option right now; maybe in a few months but not right now. You're tired from yesterday. Get your rest. I'm sure you'll feel different in the morning."

Ashley turned back to the sink, her shoulders and back tense as she began to rinse the dirty dishes. Linda had known it would be a lost cause trying to convince Ashley, but she had to give it a try.

Feeling weary and tired, she left Ashley. She didn't glance at the painting in the living room this time. She simply climbed the steps as fast as she could, avoiding looking at the buxom woman's portrait on the stairs even though something about that oil on canvas acted like gravity, pulling your attention towards it, daring you to stare into its depths. A full night of sleep did sound like a good idea.

CHAPTER 18

The bathroom door creaked when it opened. Linda walked to the sink, reaching for her dental floss. She pulled out a short length and began to floss her upper teeth, her mind elsewhere. It was when she finally focused on her reflection that her hands stopped.

In the mirror, she met a familiar stranger. The girl in the mirror looked like her, but somehow different.

Her hair was the same. Her chin was slightly more pointed. Her eyes were round. Then Linda noticed what was wrong. There were no glasses in sight.

She touched her eyes but her fingers were blocked by her spectacles. She blinked; so did her reflection but the reflection was not wearing glasses.

What was going on?

Linda looked around her, a sense of the surreal washing over her. The bathroom tiles gleamed bright. Her head spun. Her vision became foggy for a second. The floor looked like it would come up to meet her. The ceiling swayed. Frost bloomed on the window, and her skin erupted in goose bumps.

She looked back in the mirror. A peridot pendant in the shape of a shamrock hung around her neck there. The reflection could be passed off as Linda's sister or an uncanny likeness but essentially they were different people.

She lifted a hand and touched her cheek. The reflection in the mirror did the same.

She tugged at a lock of hair. Reflection-Linda did likewise.

It hurt. Her scalp prickled in protest.

Linda's agitation grew. How could this imposter be her? She couldn't see without her glasses!

Panicked, Linda pulled at her eyelids, removing eyelashes by their roots.

Blood trickled into the whites of her eyes.

She looked back at the reflection.

It was smiling back at her. The woman approached the mirror.

Linda was startled awake in her bed. She looked around the room. There was no one there.

She was sick and tired of these nightmares. The fear still lingered in the harried beating of her heart, but her eyes were heavy with exhaustion and sleep, and they took over the dread.

On the edge of deep slumber, something wrenched her back from the fall.

A thin scraping sound was coming from the hall. High and sawing at her nerves, it was a lingering whine that burrowed into the back of her head like a weevil in a grain of rice. Linda checked the time on the carriage clock she had pulled out of one of her boxes.

3:15 AM.

An ice cube of terror rolled down her spine.

The curious scrape was joined by a muffled thud.

Linda's toes curled under the covers.

Her shaking fingers dug deeper into the fabric of her covers.

She didn't know what the source of the noise was, but she knew it meant danger and she needed to escape. The stairway was the only way out of the house, though, and the noise was coming from the hall.

Gathering her flighty courage, she stepped out of bed. The floor was cold. Pins and needles broke out across her calves. Her toes wiggled to encourage blood to flow freely. Her knees creaked as she moved. She was very aware of all her limbs as she walked to the door and opened it slightly, her senses heightened in the dark.

She peered down the hall through the small crack.

Yellow light came through the hall window that faced the street, long and rectangular like an elongated coffin. The posters on the wall looked skewed in the angled light. The window at the opposite end of the hall was a black space. The hall was empty.

The muffled thud got louder, the screeching scrape an unending sound.

Linda realized she was clenching her teeth, and her nails were digging into her palms. She was too paralyzed with fear to speak.

Anticipation clanged like a hollow moan in her eardrums, and twisted her gut painfully.

The thudding stopped.

The scraping whine broke off abruptly.

A deeper shadow emerged from the staircase's notch of darkness.

Hair disheveled and completely covering her face, Marisa stood in the edge of darkness as if contemplating the light. Her pajamas hung lose on her body, suggesting she had lost weight in a very short span of time.

She must be sleepwalking again, Linda thought. *We mustn't wake her or else she might have another episode.*

She was about to close the door and get back to bed when the scraping noise began again.

Marisa had begun to walk down the hall, infinitely slow step after infinitely slow step. She hugged the wall closely, so at first Linda didn't see the source of the noise but then Marisa's hair shifted and Linda saw the sharp gleaming point of a kitchen knife scraping gently along the wall.

Heart freezing over and plummeting into her toes, Linda gasped and stepped back as if she had been scalded.

Sleepwalking and hurting yourself was one thing, but Linda didn't like the look of that knife. Her mind raced with options about what to do, and she decided to shut her door and let Marisa find her own way back to bed.

Decision made, Linda walked forward but made the mistake of glancing out in the hall.

Marisa stood in front of Ashley's door, the knife held by her side.

Linda froze. She hoped Ashley's closed door would deter Marisa, and she would walk on, but Marisa extended a hand and turned the knob letting the door creak open.

Marisa rushed inside, knife raised.

Linda cried out and swung her door open.

She was across the hall and inside Ashley's room in less than three seconds, her mind a blazing red siren. Marisa was straddling the bed, her back ramrod straight. One hand pinned something down while the other lifted up and plunged down with aggressive speed and intent. Again, and again.

"Ashley!" Linda screamed, waves of horror crashing inside her. "No!"

Marisa stopped.

Her shoulders straightened and her backbone arched, extending back, contorting her spine into a deep curve.

Linda's hackles rose. Marisa didn't stop, she kept arching her back, a guttural noise accompanying the contortion, until her head touched the mattress and she was looking at Linda, face upside down. Her eyes were wide and gleaming with an insane light; the grin was manic showing all of her teeth.

The bed beyond her was empty, with only the stuffing of a pillow scattered along the headboard.

Ashley was nowhere to be seen.

Linda took a tentative step back, mind racing over all the possible escape routes, but she hadn't counted on Marisa's speed. With an ear-piercing cry Marisa lifted her head off the bed, her spine creaking loudly as it straightened. She bolted off the bed, knife clutched in her hand, and launched herself at Linda.

Stars burst before her eyes as Linda's head struck the wall. Marisa was skin and bones, but her strength was overwhelming because of her burst of energy. Linda struggled to get away as her back slid down the wall. Marisa scrambled, digging her knees into Linda's stomach as they both sank to the floor.

The knife hung above Linda's eyes and all the air went out of her lungs.

This was it. This was how she would die.

She should have known it would always end in violence.

Marisa threw the knife away. It clattered against the baseboard.

Linda could hear her own heart beating rapidly. Her breath was caught in her throat, stuck between relief and fear. Marisa swayed a little, her eyes unfocused.

"Marisa?" Linda whispered tentatively.

Marisa's eyes focused on her, and Linda saw confusion and a terror so deep it wrenched an involuntary cry out of her.

"Linda?" Marisa's hands held the front of Linda's shirt. "Help me," she whimpered. Her voice was hoarse, as if her vocal cords had been scraped with sandpaper.

"It's okay, Marisa," Linda soothed. She ignored the pulsing blackness in her head and touched Marisa's rigid hands. "Just let me go, okay?"

"I…" Marisa seemed unsure, then her face contorted in a grimace, her eyes wide and large. "She's coming, Linda! Run!"

"What do you mean?" Linda scratched at Marisa's fingers, trying to pry them open. "Who's coming? Marisa?"

But Marisa had gone perfectly still. There was an edge to her silence. When she raised her head her hair fell back and her eyes were no longer the vulnerable orbs of someone in great distress, they were slits of calculated malice.

The fingers tightened around her shirt till Linda was sure it would rip. Hands like claws locked around her throat, squeezing tight like a vise.

Linda was taken back to every beating, every instance of being pinned under an aggressor and her own inability to do anything to stop them.

Gasping for breath, Linda rammed a fist into Marisa's arm trying to dislodge her grip. Black spots converged on her vision. Marisa's demonic grin became blurry. Linda's fists pummeled her arm, her face, her torso, every impact weaker than the last.

At least, she knew she wouldn't go out without a fight.

"Aaaah!"

A shrill scream tore through the fog. The hands were dislodged. The knees in her abdomen lifted, and sweet, aching air whistled back inside her burning lungs. Coughing and spluttering, Linda sat up. The darkness in front of her eyes lifted with every rapid blink.

Two figures tussled at the far end of the room. Ashley was struggling against Marisa, who was spitting and cursing. Linda got up on watery legs to help restrain her housemate.

"What's wrong with you?" Ashley snapped. "Get a grip!"

"Ash, watch it!" Linda screamed.

Marisa twisted within Ashley's grip and tore free. She collided with Linda and sent her spinning to a corner before she darted out the door. Ashley ran after her, and Linda followed.

A horrible crunching sound came from the end of the hall. They stood in the hallway hearing Marisa's thudding feet on the stairs. A large bloody crack bloomed on the hall window beside the stairs. Marisa had tried to jump out of it head first.

The whole night had a dreamlike quality to it. Linda followed Ashley in the semi-dark, her back breaking out in goose bumps, very aware of being watched from behind.

They reached the living room but Marisa kept going, down the dark staircase of the basement.

Linda and Ashley paused at the threshold.

"Are you okay?" Ashley whispered. She took out her cell phone from her pocket. "I'm calling the police."

Linda nodded. "Where were you?"

"Smoking in the john." Ashley shuddered. "Do we have to go down there?"

"She might do herself some harm." Linda chewed her bottom lip. Whatever it was that had Marisa in its grip could damage her entirely. Linda dreaded going down in the dark. Marisa could be lying in wait anywhere in the pitch black down there, but it had to be done. Linda owed her this much; she couldn't let her come to harm because she had been too reluctant to tell them about her suspicions.

They moved with caution, communicating with silent signs. Ashley grabbed a heavy book from one of the shelves, and Linda extended her arm in the dark to reach the light switch. Linda scrunched up her eyes against the sting of light after being in the obscurity so long. Her whole body ached and her throat was an aching burn.

Ashley went first.

The wood groaned under her weight.

Linda peered over the banister but there was neither sight nor sound of Marisa.

"Where the hell?" Ashley murmured.

They reached the concrete floor.

The basement was empty.

"I saw her come down here," Ashley hissed. "She can't have vanished in thin air."

"She didn't," Linda whimpered.

She had seen the feet first.

Sticking out of the darkness underneath the stairs like two tiny headstones were Marisa's feet.

Trembling from the cold and fright, Linda gripped Ashley's arm as they inched forward. Little by little, more of Marisa came into view. Her hands were placed neatly on her lap, one over the other. It was unbelievable now the strength they had exuded just a few minutes ago when they were wrapped around Linda's neck.

"Is she... dead?" Linda whispered.

"Her chest isn't moving," Ashley said.

And it wasn't.

Only the barest of light picked out Marisa's face, which was slack-jawed and staring. A thin sheen of sweat covered her lips and brow, but her expressive eyes, that had looked in terror at Linda only a few minutes ago, were now blank and lifeless.

Marisa was dead.

PART IV
LEGEND AND LORE

CHAPTER 19

It was the same scene all over again but so devastatingly different.

Linda stood shivering in the front yard. The night was mild and pleasant, but she was beset by an internal cold. Ashley was standing beside her, a scowl on her face. Stewart was sitting on the porch steps, his face white; he stared off into the distance in disbelief. Officer Carter and Scott were talking to the paramedics who were wheeling a body bag into an ambulance.

"My guess is as good as yours," the female paramedic was saying. "Her vitals were stable this afternoon, and there seemed to be nothing wrong with her. This sudden fatal relapse is beyond my understanding. We'll know for sure after the autopsy."

"I look forward to that report," Officer Carter said. The female paramedic nodded and stepped inside the ambulance to sit beside the body bag containing Marisa's body. Linda still couldn't believe what had just happened. The ambulance door closed. The blue lights flashed once before it pulled away and off down the street.

Scott was busy jotting down notes as he walked towards the manor. Officer Carter was sipping on a coffee, clearly dead on his feet.

"Are you sure you're okay?" Ashley asked.

"Yes." Linda's voice was hoarse at first, but she cleared her throat trying to get the words out of her aching neck. "The paramedic said the bruising will diminish within weeks."

Ashley touched Linda's neck. Linda flinched against the touch. The memory of Marisa's hand strangling the breath out of her was too fresh in her mind.

Guilt also licked her spine.

Marisa was dead.

Linda shuddered again. She could have warned her; told her about the malicious gray shadow, but she knew so little at this point. And would Marisa have believed her if she had? She had hardly believed her own instincts about the supernatural. But there was no hiding from it now. Only she had seen the shadow, the same shadow she had seen twice before. This was no hallucination, even if she was the only one to see it. It was real.

But if the shadow was real then what other things she had been seeing were real? Were they all supernatural or were they all hallucinations?

Her head throbbed as it whirled round and round these thoughts.

"I'm going to ask Milo about my truck," Ashley said. "His brother's the mechanic."

"Okay."

Ashley walked off to confront Officer Carter. Linda slid sideways to intercept Scott.

"Hey," she said.

"Hmm." He didn't look up from his notes. He had been distant and cold since he had arrived. She had given him her statement earlier, and he had noted it all down without so much as looking at her.

Stewart sat up straighter on the porch behind them.

"I forgot to mention one thing," she said, rubbing her palms together to generate heat. "I don't know how relevant this is but the whole thing, Marisa coming up and acting weird, it all started at three fifteen."

Scott stopped scribbling and finally looked at her.

Stewart stood up and joined them. Linda didn't want to discuss this with him within earshot but it didn't look like she had much choice.

"You're sure?" Scott said.

"Yes," she nodded. "I remember looking at the clock when I woke up from my dream. And I would remember the time because we discussed how significant that time is in all of this."

Scott chewed the inside of his mouth, frowning deep in thought. "So what are you suggesting?"

"I don't—"

"Because you can't blame it on some ghost, you know," he snapped.

Linda was taken aback by his acerbic sarcasm. Blood rushed to her cheeks.

He looked a little ashamed. "I mean, yes, your bruises support your claim but... I can't trace Shannon Dorothy. It's like she vanished into thin air six months ago." Scott closed his notebook with a snap.

Any color that had remained in Stewart's face vanished. His skin looked like a waxy mask.

A screen door squeaked open behind them, and Mrs. Grady scuttled onto her porch in all her cantankerous glory.

"What... what are you suggesting?" Stewart said.

"I'm not suggesting anything. I just can't track her down. Her last known place of work was Blackburn Manor; neighbors and close friends hadn't noticed anything suspicious, but one day she just vanished. And yet no missing persons report has been filed," Scott said, seeming to grow taller with every word.

"Are you suggesting I'm responsible for that?" Stewart's voice rose. "Her term ended and she didn't want to renew her contract. That was the end of the story for me."

"But why is her number still calling the house?" Scott asked. He was obviously distressed about this mystery that had no leads and was leading to dead ends. "And Shannon isn't the only one. Tara Walsh, one of the guests, has been reported as missing as well. Her stepfather filed a report in Portland—where she's from—when she didn't answer her phone or emails for over a couple months."

"I can't be expected to make sure everyone gets home." Stewart was almost hysterical. "This isn't a rehabilitation center. People are free to come and go as they please. We only provide counseling and job opportunities to those struggling with mental health issues."

"So you don't know when Tara Walsh left Blackburn Manor?" Scott persisted.

"I don't even remember a Tara Walsh," Stewart protested. "We get so many people and I don't work with any of them. I don't recall anyone with that name."

"Whoa! Everyone calm down," Officer Carter intervened,

coming to stand between Scott and Stewart. Ashley's face looked like a thundercloud behind him. Mrs. Grady had shuffled closer down the street, her face wide and creased with worry lines. "Those phone calls have nothing to do with the tragedy today, Scotty, so why don't we give that a rest. We've got the preliminary report, eh? We should let these poor people get some rest."

"Of course, of course," Mrs. Grady said with derision. "No one in Blackburn Manor has ever done anything wrong. Especially not Evelyn, the Virgin Mary with the burning heart, the bastion of feminism."

Linda's interest was piqued. Did Grady know something about Evelyn Blackburn, or her ancestors, that hadn't been reported in the newspapers at the time?

"You vile, loathsome woman!" Ashley growled through gritted teeth. "Are you so devoid of human compassion? Marisa just died, we have no idea what happened to her, and all you can do is deride an honest working woman and her family?"

"Don't you dare say I have no compassion. I never said a word against poor Marisa," Mrs. Grady snapped back. "You know nothing of Evelyn Blackburn and her hypocrisy."

"You're right," Ashley said, arms akimbo, glowering at the old lady in a nightdress. "I know nothing of Evelyn Blackburn, but I see plenty. And what I see is an invalid woman who opened her house to vulnerable people, no questions asked, and who provided them jobs. Opposite her is a bitter woman, who used to be brilliant at what she did, living alone, and only extending her kindness to cats."

Grady's mouth opened and closed. She looked lost for words.

"I pity you." Ashley hit the last nail in the coffin. "But I will no longer tolerate your bullying." She left Grady mumbling on the street.

"Do you have any more questions?" Ashley snapped at Scott. His eyes widened, clearly startled by her sharp tone. "Are you going to interrogate us further, Officer Wilson, or am I free to go back inside my house?"

"I, uh, no; I mean of course you're free to go." Scott shrugged and waved towards the house, releasing them.

Linda was tired, and she needed rest as well, but she was annoyed with Ashley's outburst. Sure, she had no love lost for Grady and her bitterness, but Grady knew something, and Linda felt bad for Scott. She didn't want to go back in that house; not after Marisa's possession. But Ashley was apparently in no mood to listen to reason and would refuse to leave if Linda brought it up right now; her reaction towards Grady was proof of that. There was only one option left to Linda. She stopped by Scott before following Ashley inside.

"I know this whole investigation is ridiculous and makes no sense," she whispered. "Marisa died; I can't explain how and I'm not even sure her sleep issues were to blame. All I'm asking is that you help me and keep an open mind."

Scott ran his hand through his hair but didn't comment one way or the other. Linda hadn't expected anything more.

"Good. Come on, Ash," Linda said. "I've had enough of tonight."

She trudged into the house. Even though she had known Marisa only a few days, her death was so sudden and bizarre it weighed down on her. The main hall was bathed in shadows. Ashley, clad in white pajama pants and a pale blue shirt, was climbing the stairs slowly. She looked like a ghostly apparition in the gloom.

They couldn't stay here. But Ashley wouldn't want to leave, and Linda couldn't bear the thought of leaving without her sister.

I have to convince her, Linda thought.

"Ash?"

Ashley stopped in the middle of the staircase but did not turn to face her. Her body language was odd—stooped and defeated.

"What did Officer Carter say about the truck?"

Ashley grunted. "Soulless crooks, the entire bunch. I can either wait four more business days, or pay extra to get my truck back in half the time. But I don't have any money left, Lin."

"Maybe you should sell it," Linda suggested.

"What?" Ashley finally turned to face Linda. Pale yellow street light illuminated her face from beneath. She looked haggard and furious. "Why would I do that?"

Linda was treading on thin ice. "You're always complaining that it's a piece of junk."

Ashley closed her eyes and breathed in deeply. "I am not having this conversation with you again." Her tone was measured but there was aggression underneath it.

"Marisa just died, Ashley," Linda burst out. "I don't feel comfortable spending the night in this house."

"She died from previous medical issues," Ashley snapped losing all cool. "Not everything is a *Supernatural* episode, Linda. She died; it's a tragedy. That does not mean we pick up and leave when we have nowhere else to go."

Ashley leaned forward on the banister. "And you know what? You wanted to gain real life experience, get back on your own two feet in the real world; this is as real as it gets. Leaving when things get tough is not always an option."

Ashley started climbing the stairs again, her feet stomping on each stair.

"Ashley." Linda allowed the terror she felt to infuse her voice. "Please."

Ashley didn't stop.

Linda sobbed, standing alone in the gloomy main hall. How was she going to convince Ashley to leave?

Deep in thought, Linda didn't see the open basement door, nor the silently screaming face in the painting on the living room wall. She climbed the stairs, the feeling of despair intensifying with each step.

CHAPTER 20

It was early morning, and Linda felt like a zombie.

Fresh air did little to alleviate how tired she was, but she was grateful for the three hours of dreamless sleep she had gotten after the events of the night.

She sat on the porch steps with a mug of coffee. Her mind kept going back to Marisa's blank stare, how there was no spark of life in her eyes, no will to live, and then she had just passed on.

There had been no defining moment; no twitch of the hand, flailing of the arms or legs, no struggle against that final moment. She had just stopped breathing. Linda shuddered at the memory of the previous night and winced. The bruises around her neck were still vividly red, her voice hoarse.

It felt like every inch of her had been scrubbed so thoroughly that even the suggestion of a breeze hit her like a hailstorm. Her senses were on a hair trigger, ready to go off at the slightest provocation.

She took a sip and stared at the house opposite.

The blinds were drawn in all the windows. Nothing stirred. Linda didn't feel wonderful about what Ashley had said to Mrs. Grady, and she wondered what were the chances Grady would talk to her about Evelyn Blackburn now.

Keys jangled and the front door opened behind her.

Linda sat up straighter. Stewart came out of the manor, satchel bag in one hand and a jacket in the other. His tie was askew and he'd missed closing a button on his shirt.

"Morning." Linda got up.

Stewart was startled so badly he dropped his keys. Linda felt pity for him. Last night hadn't been easy on any of them. "Hi." Stewart ducked to grab his keys. "Sorry. I'm a little jumpy this morning." He looked worse than before. The bags under his eyes looked bruised, and he hadn't bothered shaving.

"I don't blame you." Linda gave him a tight smile. "We're all rattled after last night."

"I'm going to Hackridge to visit a few funeral parlors. Marisa didn't have a big family; just a younger brother who lives in London. He works for some startup company so won't be able to arrange the funeral."

"Marisa deserves to be laid to rest respectfully. I'm glad you're handling it. Incidentally, I was hoping to get a hold of you before you left."

"Sure." He shifted his coat to his other arm and ran a hand through his hair, tousling it over his forehead. He gave her a grin that she suspected he thought was boyish but came across as overeager and slightly inappropriate given the current circumstances.

"There's no good way to say this." Linda tucked a strand of

hair behind her ear. "Is it possible to resign from the job if we've signed the three-month contracts?"

Stewart's face had covered all the muted colors in the rainbow by the time she finished. It ended on a very faded violet. Otherwise his face was still, leaking no emotion at all.

Linda shifted from one foot to the other, hoping he would say something and not be offended.

"I don't understand." Stewart shifted his satchel bag from one hand to the other. "It's only been a few days since you arrived. You've only just started work on the vegetable garden."

"I know," Linda stammered. "I was just wondering, hypothetically, if we didn't like—"

"I'm sorry, but that's not an option," Stewart said briskly. He walked past her all hustle and bustle now like he was the White Rabbit, late for a very important date. "That's why we have these contracts to protect the retreat from flaky employees."

Linda was affronted by his attitude and the words he was using. She had just inquired what the consequences could be; she hadn't given him two weeks' notice.

"What if employees chose to live somewhere else?" Linda asked. She followed him to the edge of the porch and watched him hurrying to his car.

Stewart opened the backdoor of his car and put his suitcase in. "It wouldn't be a problem in Ashley's case because she's a fulltime employee; she can choose to stay wherever she likes. In your case it wouldn't work. You have the privilege of a job because you are also part guest. If you choose to stay away from the retreat we will be forced to give the job to someone else. That's the policy."

Great! Linda thought. *How am I going to convince Ashley now?*

Not only will I lose my income, I'd be asking her to shell out for rent that we can't afford.

"Have a good day," was all he said before he got in and closed the door.

Linda watched, flabbergasted, as he backed out of the drive and drove away.

Breathing heavily to soothe her disappointment, Linda went back inside the manor.

"What am I going to do?" she asked no one in particular, but it felt good to say it aloud. She paced the living room, heart hammering against her ribs.

Linda went to the kitchen to get some water to cool down. Ashley hadn't come down yet; Linda suspected she was still fast asleep.

Linda finished her drink of water and put the glass in the sink to wash later. She had been mildly hungry before she had met Stewart but now her hunger had been replaced with clawing anxiety.

She went back into the living room, toying with the idea of watching some TV to pass the time, but the first thing that caught her eye was the open basement door. She looked at the dark doorway; the darkness stared back.

Linda was sure the door had been closed when she came downstairs, but she acknowledged that she hadn't been paying it much attention, her mind being on other things. Walking slowly, images of Marisa's prone body under the stairs superimposed on her mind's eye, Linda approached the door. She kept her distance and pushed the door closed with the toe of her shoe.

It whined as it swung and shut with a soft click.

The air seemed to clear in an instant and the room looked brighter than before.

Sighing with relief, Linda turned to face the living room, and nearly fell back with a strangled scream, biting her tongue painfully.

A face dominated the painting: a screaming face, contorted in painful lines. Linda had seen the face before, in a fevered dream where there was dirt and soil from floor to ceiling. It had belonged to the dead Irish boy. She even remembered his name, Oisin.

Hands trembling, Linda pressed her throbbing tongue to the roof of her mouth, tasting the salty iron tang of blood. The boy's tormented eyes followed her as she walked to the middle of the living room.

You can't blame it on some ghost, you know.

Linda's scalp prickled with sweat, beads of it covered her upper lip, her armpits were damp, her back felt slick with it; she flashed cold and hot all at once. Was it possible? It couldn't be. There were no such things as ghosts... were there?

But the long gone miners and their miserable lives in a world covered in dirt? She had dreamed of them long before she had known of them. Were they sending her warnings like her mother?

"What are you doing?"

Linda jumped. Ashley stood yawning in the kitchen.

"The painting's changed." Linda said, her voice frail and thin.

"What?" Ashley scratched the back of her head. She walked over to stand beside Linda. She smelled of stale sweat. "What do you mean?"

"Don't you see it?" Linda was incredulous. "It's right there staring at us!"

"It's just a bunch of rocks and trees, Lin." Ashley was irritated.

"You can't see the face?" Trepidation tripped down Linda's spine like ice cubes. "How can you not see it?"

"Forget the face, for God's sake, Linda!" Ashley shouted. "I thought this place would heal you, not make things worse."

Linda's own anger was rising to the surface. She had known Ashley would be upset, but not to the extent that she would lie about the painting.

"I'm not crazy," Linda said, biting her lip. "This isn't PTSD hallucinations or sleep paralysis. I'm telling you Ashley, something beyond our control is happening here—"

Ashley's face went from red to purple in seconds.

"Please spare me that," she said. "Let me put this in words you'll understand." She said slowly, like talking to an infant. "We can't leave. We can't afford to."

"I'm not saying we leave the jobs," Linda begged. "Just not stay here."

"You're insane," Ashley snapped. "I'm already in the hole because of the truck, but you want me to shell out extra money for rent?"

"I'm just asking for a little help," Linda snapped back. "I can't do this on my own."

"Of course you can't." Ashley rolled her eyes.

"What's that supposed to mean?" Every word was hitting Linda on a raw nerve. Their exhaustion and worry was culminating in hysterical rage.

"You know exactly what I mean!" Ashley pointed an accusing finger at her. "Poor little Linda can't do anything to save herself. She *has* to marry Jackson to get away from Dad. She *has* to move to a God-awful remote place. She *has* to take Ashley, because Linda can't friggin' do anything!"

Tears pricked Linda's eyes, but she refused to cry and prove Ashley right. Yes, she had always been the weaker of the two sisters but she had never begged anyone to get her out of her problems.

"I never asked you to come," Linda spat. "You were never at home when we were kids anyway, so why do you care now? Because you needed a job and they were offering it. It was never to support me so don't you sit on that high horse and talk down to me."

Ashley flinched, as if Linda had physically slapped her.

"Oh, I'm sorry, Linda," Ashley's mouth twisted cruelly. "I totally believe you now. Yes," she gasped, looking at the painting. "I do see a face in the painting. A screaming witch is running at us!" She turned towards Linda, her face a mask of mockery. "You've been delusional since you were a baby," Ashley said. "That monocle man with a watch on a chain you recall from our neighborhood? He doesn't exist. You would come home with stories about a young girl in a sailor suit at the pond, and neighbors that only you had ever seen. Just like now with this painting."

Linda turned her astonished eyes to the painting.

The face was gone.

Her world shifted on its axis to become a little skewed.

Was Ashley right? Had she been hallucinating people and events her entire life? What was true? What was false? The distinction between fantasy and reality was shattered into a million pieces she had no energy to pick up and fix.

She had been so sure of a supernatural presence at work

here that going back to the original medical diagnosis had her reeling.

Unthinkable questions hammered at her consciousness that broke down all barriers of what had been real and imaginary in her life. Hearing your childhood and your character defined in terms starkly different from your own understanding of yourself was like looking at a funhouse mirror, only it wasn't a trick mirror, it showed you how people saw you. It was disconcerting and obscene.

Had Jackson really beaten her within an inch of her life with a rolling pin, or had she imagined it all?

Was she the aggressor? Had the knife in Jackson's gut been the last assault of many?

Her head spun. She couldn't breathe.

"Lin." Ashley's voice was crumpled under the weight of her remorse. "I'm sorry. I shouldn't have said any of that." She tried to touch Linda's arm but Linda backed away, not wanting any physical contact with anyone. "Please, just forget I said anything."

"I'm going for a walk," Linda said. She rushed towards the door, ignoring Ashley's cries to come back. She couldn't be in the same room with her at the moment. She grabbed the keys from the hall table.

She opened the front door. The fresh air hit her like a wall. It did wonders for her cluttered mind. She climbed briskly down the porch steps and then began walking rapidly towards the hill, her thoughts as wild as the wind that had picked up suddenly. Clouds raced across the sky. It was a beautiful summer day.

Her father's abusive nature had been the talk of the neighborhood.

She hadn't imagined that. She was a child at the time, so maybe her memory was sketchy, but she had a file full of her mother's old medical reports that documented a litany of bruises, scrapes, and broken bones.

Nor had she imagined Jackson's abuses. There were witnesses to some of the incidents. All of them had come forward during the trial. So she hadn't been imagining that.

Then what had Ashley been talking about?

The monocle man... the girl in the sailor suit...

Linda remembered them all. She had always known they weren't real, in the sense that they weren't alive, but they were harmless: her medically defined sleep-deprived hallucinations.

She stopped suddenly. The road stretched ahead of her into unknown territory; all around her the deep woods watched like silent sentinels hiding secrets. Behind her were the two houses —Blackburn Manor and Grady's house— staring at each other for an eternity, their insanity spilling out to taint everything around them.

What am I doing walking alone? The thought suddenly struck cold fear through her confusion. *The town is miles away!*

She doubled back, thinking to dawdle in the backyard to avoid Ashley. She had just crested the road when she saw Grady standing by her letterbox waiting patiently for someone. Cats milled about her feet, grazing their sleek backs against her calves.

Not in the mood for an old woman's spite, Linda increased her pace.

"Miss Green." Grady's voice was surprisingly polite. "May I please have a word?"

Linda looked up at the house. Ashley was standing by the living room window waiting for her to come back in. Linda felt stuck between a rock and a hard place. Exasperated with her rotten luck, she turned away from Ashley.

"How may I help you, Mrs. Grady?" Linda asked, her tone civil but firm.

"No, Miss Green." Mrs. Grady sighed. "It's I who can help you. Come along."

The old woman carved a way for herself through a sea of cats. Curious and needing an excuse to avoid Ashley, Linda followed her up the short porch steps and inside the house.

CHAPTER 21

To say that Linda had expected a house full of fur balls, scratching posts, and kitty litter boxes would be an understatement. Grady's house was none of those things. It was neatly furnished in muted tones of apple green, brown, and cream. The living room was dominated by a bookshelf perfectly arranged with potted plants situated in nooks and crannies to give it an aesthetic appeal. It looked like the home of an intellectual college professor, not the local crazy cat lady.

Speaking of cats, they all lined up at the door, none daring to come in. It was clear that Grady loved the stray cats, but none were allowed inside her home.

"You have a nice place," Linda said.

"I didn't call you in to exchange niceties." Grady sniffed. "Sit down and listen, that's all you have to do."

Linda felt like a chastised student.

She took a seat at a small round table Grady indicated. It was covered with open books, printouts, and notebooks.

"You asked me about the house yesterday," Grady said, taking a seat opposite. "And then your sister had some astute observations about my less than charitable nature."

Linda made to apologize, but Grady lifted a hand to stop her.

"I told you to listen," Grady said, peering over the half-moon spectacles she had perched on her nose. "I don't want to talk about my dislike of Evelyn, but you deserve to know the basics. She seduced and stole my husband when I was pregnant with my second daughter. Stewart's their half-brother."

"They lived across the street from you?" Linda couldn't believe the nerve. Sympathy for the old woman flooded through her.

"No." Grady sorted through papers. "After she fell pregnant, Evelyn Blackburn changed her tune. No, she wouldn't like to get married. No, she didn't want to keep the baby. It was never her intention to be with Brian for the long term. She just wanted to spite us for making a home on what she thought was Blackburn land. But her parents had had enough of that. They made her have the baby."

"What about your husband?" Linda asked, fingering the whorls of wood on the smooth surface.

"Oh," Grady laughed harshly. "She dumped him like a hot potato. Discovered feminism in college, and never looked back. He came slinking back of course, but I'd already changed the locks. He wasn't welcome. Last I heard, he was in California or some other insufferable place. Here." She slammed an open album in front of Linda. "You won't find this in the archives. I had it especially delivered when I was teaching."

Linda peered at the black and white photographs. A man sat in the foreground, his features bland and forgettable if it weren't for the enormous muttonchops that framed his doughy face. His posture was rigid and pompous. In the background stood a troop of men in peaked flat caps, faces streaked with grime. Their hands were black with dirt, their eyes boring into the lens, pouring out all of their discomforts.

Her body became rigid, and her heart skipped a beat.

Oisin. The dead boy from her nightmare.

The boy stared up at her, his face gaunt and drawn. The mustache man from the dreams stood beside him, equally despondent. She looked carefully. They were all of the faces in the crowd she had seen in her dreams.

"This was the crew working in the mines when Samuel Blackburn took over after his father's death. They were the unfortunates who were killed over the whole Molly Maguire business. Mind you, only a handful were Mollies. The rest were innocent, but it didn't make a difference to Blackburn."

"The what?" Linda's throat was dry.

"Molly Maguires." Grady was in full teacher mode. "They were a secret society of sorts; got their name from a rural secret society in Ireland which dressed as women and pledged allegiance to a mythical woman named Mistress Molly Maguire. Sounds innocent enough but they slowly took over the Workingman's Benevolent Association, a local union, and started instigating violence against mine owners, killing a few. They wanted better representation for the unskilled Irish workers who were more dispensable than the skilled English and Welsh workers. Since they were Mollies, they had no qualms about using aggression and violence to achieve their means. Didn't work out too well for them."

Sighing, Grady pulled a book towards them in which Linda could see the print of an old article. "After the last strike was announced in January 1875, one of the detectives on the case suggested vigilante justice. Some people took the suggestion to heart. Three of the suspected Mollies were shot dead, including one of the Mollies' wives. Some sadist broke into their home and killed her clean dead."

Linda realized she was biting her lip very hard.

"The Blackburns had long suffered from strikes, and news of vigilante justice suited Samuel Blackburn just fine. He had his guards shoot the Irish laborers hindering activity at his mine. None of them died because of their injuries, but Samuel Blackburn offered no medical aid. He had the men dragged into an unused shaft to die." Grady's eyes sparkled with buried indignation. "They say he got really paranoid by the end. He would rave about the miners digging a tunnel under his house to come up through the basement to kill him in his sleep. He died in a sanatorium."

He's cold, and hungry, and DEAD!

Linda shuddered. "I saw him in my dreams," she said. "I saw him dead."

Grady stopped shuffling through papers. "You can't have. No one has access to my private collection."

"But I'm telling you I saw this boy in my dream… I…" Linda hesitated. "I even saw him in a painting in our living room."

Grady's eyes were as large as saucers, and her mouth a thin line. Linda flushed. "I know you think I'm making this up, but I'm not crazy!"

"I never called you that." Grady's voice was barely above a whisper, but it held the gravity of seriousness. She rubbed her mouth and looked down at the table for a long time. Finally, she looked up and Linda saw a hint of concern in her eyes. "Is that the only dream you've had since you moved here?"

"No," Linda said. She plucked on the hem of her shirt, recalling the dreams but dreading to go into too much detail. She didn't want to relive them again. "There have been more. There was one where I was being buried alive, and a lake full of ice. There are many."

"I need to know them all," Grady said.

"I heard a song in my dream that was also one of the strange messages we got one night."

"Do you have a recording of the message?" Grady asked, suddenly very alert.

"Yes," Linda said. "It was all garbled at first but then Scott did something to it on his computer so we could make out the words."

"Do you have it on your phone?" Grady extended a hand in anticipation.

"Scott gave me a CD. I don't know if you can play it."

"Of course I can," Grady said. "I have a CD player. Can you go get it?"

"Now?" Linda asked.

Grady didn't say anything, just gave her a hard stare.

"Okay; I can sprint over and get it for you."

Grady waved her away.

∼

LINDA WAS FULL TO BURSTING. THERE WAS TOO MUCH information coming her way in a very short span of time. But this was proof, wasn't it, that Linda wasn't hallucinating? What she saw were people who had lived at some point in time but had never truly left. Now that she thought about it, this was much worse. When it had just been her dead mother warning her, she had felt comfort. But knowing she was some magnet for supernatural beings was alarming.

You can't blame it on some ghost, you know.

Nobody would believe her anyway, but she knew something very wrong was going on in Blackburn Manor. It had dragged Marisa to the point of such insanity it had killed her. It was tearing her relationship with Ashley to smithereens. Both of them had changed drastically under the pressures of that house.

Marshaling her courage, she rushed down Grady's porch and ran across the street. Riding on that momentum, she took the steps two at a time. But before she could get her keys out of her pocket, Ashley opened the door.

"Thank God," she said. "Linda—"

"I don't have time," Linda snapped. She knew she should have been nicer, but she was in hurry and Ashley's words still stung. She made a beeline for her handbag where she had left it on the sofa, retrieved the CD in its cover, and bolted out the door, ignoring Ashley's stricken face.

As she got further away from the shadow of Blackburn Manor, she felt much better. She felt like someone was watching her. It was probably Ashley, so she didn't look back.

~

GRADY HAD FIXED TWO MUGS OF COFFEE BY THE TIME LINDA GOT back. A sleek silver old-fashioned laptop was open at her table.

"This Molly Maguire thing," Linda asked while Grady placed the CD in its tray. "Have you been inside the mineshaft where it happened?"

"No." Grady peered at her over her glasses. "There's an entrance to the mine in the hill beyond. It's a thirty-minute walk. My daughters and I used to explore it often, and we found some artifacts related to the speakeasy, but never the shaft with the poor murdered miners."

"Could you tell me more about the speakeasy?" Linda's interest was piqued.

"They had to open it where the authorities wouldn't find it. The mines were deep and large enough to accommodate everyone." Grady held up a finger to stem the flow of Linda's new set of questions. She pressed some keys on her laptop.

The keening warble filled the quaint living room. Linda wasn't sure, but it seemed like the sun had suddenly gone behind a cloud. Her eyes felt heavy with sudden sleep.

The message ended, and she snapped back to attention.

Grady's eyes had narrowed to slits in concentration, but she had paled considerably. Linda could tell she was clenching her teeth. Once it ended, Grady replayed the audio. Linda's hands started to tremble. She hadn't had to listen to it twice in a row, and the feeling of heartbreak was overwhelming, like a hook tugging sharply at her guts.

"That's a very mesmerizing tune." Grady nodded, her voice muted. Her words slurred slightly. She played it again but this time she didn't sit still. She got up and walked leisurely to her bookshelf.

Linda watched her trace the spines of her books, her head swaying slowly from side to side looking for something.

The song ended. Linda shook her head to clear it.

"I think I recognized some of the words. I might be wrong, but it's better than nothing."

"You do?" Linda was shocked. "That's great!"

"There it is," she said in whispered triumph. She pulled a heavy tome out of her collection and waddled back to the table.

"Another strange thing about the calls I forgot to mention." Linda tucked a strand of hair behind her ear. "The calls all come from Stewart's part of the house, which is weird. Oh, and the mobile number belonged to one of Evelyn's nurses, Shannon." Linda swallowed. "Scott's been trying to trace her but without luck."

"I knew her." Grady was frowning at the book. "Good-natured girl, blonde, slightly bulky. She was very sweet. Would come over to sit with the cats after her shifts."

"I'm surprised you didn't kick her off your property," Linda said, as her mind registered the small detail of Shannon being blonde.

Grady pierced her with a look. Linda chewed on her bottom lip. "I'm not a monster," Grady said. "I always wondered what happened to her. She didn't seem flighty to me; but one day she was cleaning out the litter box, the next day she'd vanished."

"Did you hear from her again?" Linda asked.

"No."

Linda pressed her lips together. "What do you think Scott meant by the two women disappearing without a trace?" Linda asked.

"Well... I've seen every woman that has gone through the Blackburn house, and I can tell you who was flighty. Shannon wasn't one of them. Tara, on the other hand..." Grady lifted both her eyebrows and gave Linda a meaningful look. "She was trouble on legs. She had a temper. I have no qualms telling you that even I was wary of getting on her wrong side. Reminded me too much of Glenn Close in *Fatal Attraction*. She had the same crazy glint in her eyes."

"Was she the type to run away?" Linda asked, caressing her bruised neck.

"Oh, yes," Grady nodded. "She looked like a twitchy rabbit jumping at shadows, not very different from you. But by the end of her stay, she actually looked quite content. I thought she would stay longer."

Linda sipped her coffee deep in thought.

"Now, these dreams," Grady said. "Have they always been this vivid or are these new?"

"New." Linda shuddered. "They actually started—"

"Once you moved into the house," Grady finished her sentence.

Linda's jaw dropped slightly. "Yes," she said. "How did you know?"

"I'm a very sensible woman," Grady said, folding her hands on top of the table. "Which is why I am a firm believer in the paranormal. I believe in more than just the human experience, yes."

"You believe in ghosts?" Linda was having a hard time wrapping her head around that. Serious, grouchy Grady, the strict high school teacher and historian, believed in ghosts.

Grady shrugged. "I believe in an afterlife, in a soul. I find it ridiculous that a soul that can animate a body for decades will slink off quietly to the afterlife as if it had no will. Yes." She gave Linda a hard glare. "I believe in ghosts."

"So what are you saying?" Linda asked.

"I'm saying the Blackburn house is haunted," Grady said. "You're not the only one who had weird dreams. Shannon mentioned them once or twice. I didn't pay much heed to them back then. I won't make that mistake now."

"What do you think is going on in the house?"

"I think it's perfectly clear what's going on." Grady's tone was tart. "Don't pretend to be stupid. It's unbecoming." She picked up her mug but didn't drink from it. "The spirits of the Irish laborers aren't at rest. They are many in number and that contributes to their strength."

"But why now?" Linda asked. This question had been bothering her for some time now. "From what I've heard of the retreat this is the first time anything like this is happening."

Grady cleared her throat and shifted uncomfortably in her chair. "I hardly think this is the first. Something drove Samuel Blackburn mad. Evelyn was hale and hearty till the sudden stroke, and now Marisa. It might have been amplified because of you, but I don't think it's new phenomenon."

"Amplified?" Linda didn't like the sound of that.

"If no one is listening, we give up talking till we find an audience. The spirits are just the same. You can see them; interact with their presence better than most people. They needed an audience to start talking."

Linda let that sink in.

Everything she had thought she had known about her sleep paralysis and hallucinations was wrong. The gut feeling pinching at her that it went deeper had been true.

She was the reason the spirits were agitated again; the reason Marisa was attacked so ruthlessly till she was possessed and killed. If only she had never come. Marisa's death would always haunt her, no matter where she was.

One question nagged at her still.

"You mentioned one of the wives of the mine workers was killed," Linda said.

"Not on the Blackburn mine. That was three towns over."

Linda frowned. She had seen the miners in a dream, she had seen Oisin's face in the painting, but she had seen a woman too. The voice that sang the songs was a woman's, the dark hair, the woman running down the stairs the first night she arrived, the pendant that hung from a cream-white neck.

If a woman hadn't been killed with the miners, then who had she been seeing in her dreams? She had a sinking suspicion that Shannon hadn't made it out of the house. It was a stretch, and Linda had no proof of this, but maybe Shannon had been sensitive to the phenomenon too and was now part of the Blackburn haunting. It made sense if Shannon's old phone number kept calling the house and leaving eerie messages.

Then there was the girl Tara Walsh. Linda wasn't sure how she might feature in this.

Or maybe these girls suffered from the same visions and nightmares as Linda did, and eventually they just left, too frightened to keep staying there. Among all the people who came here to recover, it made sense. Some of the customers of Blackburn Manor were probably more sensitive than the average.

"Were there any other deaths in Blackburn Manor? Particularly of women?"

"Nothing traumatic." Grady shook her head. "They were only natural deaths by old age or sickness. You suspect a woman is involved? Would make sense, since a woman is singing in the messages."

"You think the miners are haunting it?" Linda thought of her dreams, of the face in the painting, and it made sense if the miners' agitated souls were acting out the way they were.

"Maybe," Grady said. "That place has always held an air of oppression about it."

"But Stewart and Evelyn have lived there most of their lives," Linda said, shaking her head. "Wouldn't they have said something about the bad dreams? And as far as I know, Marisa is the only one that was driven mad by them, so maybe it isn't something as sinister as you suggest, just a very sick girl."

"No, Marisa wasn't the only one who went mad. Stewart had a dog that went mad about eight months ago, around the time his mother was in the hospital."

"What?" Linda was shocked. Stewart had told her the dog had died, but he had made it sound like it had been years ago, and of natural causes.

"It kept barking around their porch then flung itself off the porch steps. Broke its neck."

Visions of Marisa holding the banister for dear life came back to her. Her muscles tensed.

"No wonder he keeps the urn with its ashes in his apartment," she thought aloud. "He must have been devastated."

Grady was looking at her quizzically. "You've been in his apartment?"

Linda flushed. Heat radiated off of her. "I had an accident, and he was helping me out," she stammered. "Nothing happened."

"I didn't say it did." Grady held up her hands. She pinched the bridge of her nose and sighed. "Look, there is much I can tell you about the nature of hauntings and how to prevent them, but I don't think that will help you. The song in the recording can help us. It's Gaelic, the language—I think. I recognized some words. She said *Shaesar* at one point. It's Caesar in old Irish Gaelic so the clues all point to the miners, but I could be wrong. Here." She handed Linda the hardcover book she had retrieved from the shelf. It was black with ornate silver lettering spelling out *Lore of the Land – A Concise History of Irish Folklore, Legends, and Myth*. "I picked this up on a trip to England, where I visited an old friend, a teacher who introduced me to an enlightened amateur ethnologist, one of the authors of the book. It reminded me of the mines. This might hold the information on Irish folklore and their beliefs in the occult that is relevant to us. If the miners are behind the haunting, as I suspect, they are using their Irish heritage and it can give you clues on how to combat it."

"Won't you help?" Linda took the book from her.

"I didn't manage to read all of it, Miss Green," Grady said sharply. "But I'm not the one experiencing the phenomenon, so I don't know which track of exorcism will actually work. You must read the book and give me some insight based on your recent experiences. Then I will help you."

Linda couldn't argue with that logic.

She tucked the book under her arm, and finished her coffee.

"I'll keep you posted," she said, getting up to leave.

"Hmm. And Miss Green," Grady said. "Be careful; and if at all possible leave the manor."

Linda paused, nodded, and then left Grady's house.

CHAPTER 22

The book was heavy and oddly cool in Linda's arms. She hugged it close. The sun was shining brightly and it made her blink a few times. Grady's living room hadn't been dark but it was cool and shaded compared to the raw sunlight in the middle of the road.

Linda stared at her feet. They had stopped moving of their own accord when she had reached the center, like there was an invisible wall ahead of her that she instinctively knew not to walk into.

She could feel the hateful gaze of the house bearing down on her. It was a silly thought. Houses had no souls, no personalities. They had no intent and action. Yet Linda felt fear burn the back of her throat.

Tears prickled her eyes. The sun beat down from directly overhead plunging the porch and windows in shadows. She could hear the wind sighing through the eaves; the red geranium pots suspended from the gallery looked like two burning eyes in the terrible face of the house. Shuddering breaths escaped her, and she realized she was paralyzed. The house had her in its awful snare. It would suck her in.

This house had driven miners to jealous plotting, driven Samuel Blackburn to murder, and then drove him insane from the guilt. Now, a woman was dead, and Linda couldn't convince her sister to leave.

Her stomach rumbled as she walked up the porch steps. She pulled out the key and unlocked the front door. The living room was empty. Linda walked in and let the door close behind her. The air in here was oppressive, warm, and stank of stale things.

Linda walked into the kitchen looking for Ashley, but her sister wasn't there. Her phone was charging on the kitchen counter though, so Linda was sure Ashley was still in the house somewhere.

The fight seemed like it had happened years ago. So much had happened in the hours that had passed that Linda wasn't sure how to go about fixing it. Deciding to wait for Ashley in the kitchen, she placed the book on the table and fixed herself lunch. Linda was anxious to read the book, but she was starving, and she needed to check something important first.

While she ate her peanut butter and apple slice sandwich, she unlocked her phone and opened Facebook. She typed in Shannon Dorothy's name and waited for the sketchy internet to grant her the boon of working.

After a few minutes the links began to open. She tapped the image tab and waited a few more minutes. She sighed at the slow speed. The pictures that finally popped up were of various women but none of them fit the description of Shannon that Grady had given her. Some were older, some younger, but none fit.

Grady had mentioned Shannon was shy, so maybe that was why she hadn't found much online.

She typed in Tara Walsh instead. The fifth profile seemed to fit the right age bracket. The pictures were grainy and of a pretty young girl with chestnut hair, styled fashionably. There was an openness about her face; even through the low-resolution pictures her green eyes sparkled.

"Where did you go?" Linda asked the picture on her phone.

Sighing, she locked her phone and placed it back in her pocket. Fidgeting in her chair, she turned to the book. The print was minuscule and the illustrations were vivid ink sketches. Linda flipped through a few pages, the sheer volume of information she had to go through overwhelming her.

She let out a loud breath and started from the beginning, scanning the first few paragraphs before moving on if they didn't meet some of the criteria of what was happening in the house. She made it through the A's in half an hour. She was inclined to give up on the tedious task when she turned the page titled Baal. She was so shocked she dropped the rest of her sandwich back on its plate.

Words surfaced from her memories. Words that were spoken at this very table.

There was a woman... she was young and beautiful... she starts to get old before my eyes... Her skin wrinkles till she turns to dust, her bones caving in on themselves till she's a heap at my feet... I couldn't look away...

Like Marisa in her dreams, Linda couldn't look away from

the illustration either. The drawing was in ink like most of the illustrations in the book. A woman stood alone under a black star-studded sky, her body covered in a long flowing dress that was torn in places. She was forever captured in the act of metamorphosis: thick hair turning brittle while white chunks fell out of her head, healthy cheeks collapsing over teeth loosening in gums, big beautiful eyes entrenched with wrinkles and bags; one arm was healthy, strong, and firm, the other a wasted stump. Wisps of smoke curled around it and flecks of dust swirled around in an invisible wind.

"Banshee – Bean Sidhe," Linda read the title out loud.

Her throat was suddenly sticky with peanut butter. She poured herself a glass of water. She drank it in painful gulps and refilled the glass. Sitting back down at the table, she pulled the book closer and started reading.

The myth told of a manifestation that came into existence wherever there had been a violent and unfair murder. A banshee was created that exacted vengeance on its aggressor, not discriminating against innocents in its path, attacking everything and everyone with its wrath.

Linda sipped water and read on.

The Banshee is recognized by its wailing lament, a sound equally ensnaring and repulsive. Invisible to the human eye, the Banshee relies on dreams and nightmares, attacking its victims in their sleep so they wake up with no memory of the actual attack but have marks and bruises that mimic those suffered by the deceased—an endless rerun of their tragic demise.

Linda frowned and read the text again. The way the banshee used its powers was curious. Linda touched her own bruised neck, a deep frown marking her brow. The details about the dreams were accurate. Linda's vivid nightmares had started when she had entered the house, not to mention the dirt in her bed after her nightmare of stumbling through the mine shafts. But if what this book said was true, banshees were supposed to be invisible. Linda had seen a gray shadow; this reinforced her gut feeling that she could see more than her eyes did. And why were the markings of the event strangulation marks when the miners had been shot?

This also brought into question who actually was haunting the house. If it were the Irish miners, they wouldn't manifest as a banshee, a ghoul almost exclusively female; maybe the fact that they had been Molly Maguires could point to their return as a banshee. Rubbing her aching head, Linda flipped the page to see how long the chapter on the banshee was. There were ten pages in total and most of them looked like diary entries.

A small script preceded the entries.

The following passages were transcribed directly from the journal of Colin Prim, assigned Regional Governor near Doon, Ireland in 1651. The text has faced no changes only the spellings have been modernized for smooth reading and clearer understanding. The entries have been shortened and edited to include only that which pertains to the subject at hand.

She was about to read on when the sound of something heavy hitting the floor came from the main hall. Linda placed a toothpick between the pages as a bookmark and went to investigate. "Ashley?" she called.

There was no reply.

Linda walked out into the living room. The basement door was open again. Cold terror wafted out of that rectangle of darkness.

"Linda."

Ashley stood at the living room door. Her hair was wet, and she looked much better than she had in days.

"Hey," Linda said quietly.

"Hi." Ashley hooked her thumbs in her jeans pocket. "I'm sorry about earlier."

"Me too." Linda nodded. "I shouldn't have… You're a great sister."

"No." Ashley shook her head, her smile bittersweet. "I'm not. You're right, I was constantly thinking of myself. This place obviously isn't working out for you."

"What are you saying?" Linda asked, cautious not to irritate Ashley again.

"I'm saying we can live in town." Ashley spread her hands. "We can commute to work till something better comes along."

"Ash." Linda swallowed the lump in her throat. "Stewart said I can't keep my job if I don't stay at Blackburn Manor."

Ashley's mouth fell open in shock and dismay but she recovered quickly. "That's okay," she said. "I'm sure you can find something in town. It's not a big deal. Besides, the main reason we came here was for you to get counseling. I see no point in sticking around if that's no longer the case."

"You mean that?" Linda was touched.

"I even packed a bag with basics." Ashley smiled. "We can leave today and get the rest of our stuff later."

Linda laughed with relief. "Thank you." She rushed over to her sister and gave her a warm hug. "Thank you, thank you!"

The further away from the house they were, the safer they would be. Marisa had been fine at the hospital; coming back had been fatal. If Grady was right and Linda's presence had exacerbated the haunting at Blackburn, then it would go back to normal once she left.

"I called Milo," Ashley said, straightening up. "Officer Carter. I told him he needs to give us a ride to the nearest motel since his brother was fleecing me. He said his cousin owns a motel in Keystone. I swear this whole town seems to be run by one family. He's coming in five minutes."

Linda laughed. She felt much lighter now that she knew she was no longer going to live in this oppressive house. She picked up the book from the kitchen and followed Ashley into the main hall.

A single trolley suitcase rested at the foot of the stairs. Linda tucked the book under her arm and ran up the stairs. The buxom woman's portrait had no effect on her. She was too relieved to be leaving to care much about its malevolent pull.

In her room she threw a few clothes and underwear in a large handbag. She was about to leave to get her toothbrush from the bathroom when she spotted the pink pentagon Polly Pocket on top of a stack of books.

She smiled at the sweet memories she associated with the object and she swept it into her handbag. She'd come for the books later.

Once she had finished packing, she joined Ashley in the hall and pulled the roller towards the front door. They had just managed to pull the suitcase down on the gravel when Stewart's car turned into the drive.

"Going somewhere?" he asked as he climbed out of the car.

"Just checking into a motel for the night," Ashley said, her tone casual. "It feels weird sleeping in the house after last night."

Stewart gave her an appraising look; it was very different from his usual cheerful attitude. Linda could see some of Samuel Blackburn in the slant of his eyes and the tightening of his jaw. "I won't be able to guarantee Linda a job if she does not stay for counseling."

Ashley laughed. It was a bitter sound. "After last night I'm going to need some counseling too but unfortunately you don't have any. We'll be back in the morning by eight to start our shifts."

Stewart didn't smile. His neck was red and he looked furious. "More councilors will be arriving in a few days' time," he stammered. "And there is a clause in her contract which penalizes her if she leaves the job before the contract is complete. I could file a lawsuit."

"Frankly, Stewart, you should be glad we're still willing to work here and not filing a suit against the retreat." Ashley's tone was still casual but the threat underneath it was palpable. "One of your counselors tried to strangle my sister, her client, before dying. Either the retreat didn't vet her for mental illness, or some hazardous health risk in your retreat led to her death. I don't know which it is, but if it makes the national papers, it won't be very good for your business."

"Are you threatening me?" Stewart glowered.

A police patrol car pulled up along the curb. Officer Carter sat behind the wheel. Mrs. Grady came out on her front porch, both hands carrying bowls of food for the neighborhood cats.

"Call it what you want," Ashley said. This time the casual tone was gone. She placed a hand on Linda's arm communicating protection. "We'll be at work at eight, and if our employment is terminated, I'll call my lawyer and we'll take you to court. Good night."

Dragging Linda with one hand, and the suitcase with the other, Ashley walked briskly to the police car. Officer Carter didn't get out. He popped the trunk and waited.

Linda waved to Mrs. Grady. "I'll return your book once I've read it."

The old woman nodded.

Linda got in the back with Ashley. Stewart was still staring at them as they pulled away from the curb and drove away.

CHAPTER 23

The Keyring Motel was like most motels. Within its pale brown walls it provided the most rudimentary needs like moderately clean beds, functioning bathrooms, and mindless television. Linda and Ashley ate tomato soup and grilled cheese sandwiches for dinner, discussing why motel owners loved to paint the rooms varying colors of beige.

"I think the paint is cheaper in that color," Ashley suggested, opening the Polly Pocket with one hand and closing it. Linda watched the glimpses of the miniature house within as Ashley continued to fidget with the toy.

"Because it doesn't sell," Linda laughed. "And the guy practically pays them to just take it off his hands."

"It could also be a cult, you know." Ashley sopped up the last of the soup with her sandwich. "Some secret society that wants everyone to be miserable, so they make the suckiest, most depressing motels to kick people when they're already down."

Linda didn't laugh this time. Because unbeknownst to Ashley she had just described Blackburn Manor.

"You know..." Ashley traced the outlines of the pink pentagon. "I can't seem to remember what Mom looked like. I mean I can if I really concentrate, but it doesn't come to me instantly like it used to."

"I know what you mean." Linda touched the back of Ashley's hand. She wondered if the departed feared being forgotten by those they had loved when alive, which is why they returned.

"I think that's why I took it." Ashley twirled the toy on the table. "I wanted a solid reminder of Mom, of my childhood. I had nothing else I could pack when I left."

Linda blinked. She hadn't known the Polly Pocket had meant so much to Ashley. "You know what," she said. "You can keep it. I have other things to remind me of Mom. It's only fair you have this."

"Really?" There were tears in Ashley's eyes. Linda had never seen her tough-as-nails sister so emotional before. She squeezed Ashley's hand in consent.

Ashley grinned at her then got up and cleared the dishes and took them to the tiny sink in the tiny kitchenette area. Linda took a quick trip to the bathroom to brush her teeth. It was small and yellow, with paint stains at the bottom of the mirror above the sink. Linda looked at herself; her skin was pale and stretched, there were black bruises under her eyes from lack of restful sleep.

At least I'll get some rest tonight, she thought, drying her hands on a paper towel and shutting off the lights.

They had opted for a room with twin beds rather than two rooms. It was economical and worked out for the moment.

Linda took the bed closer to the window and opened up the book Grady had given her earlier.

"I'm going to bed." Ashley fell on her bed, arms outstretched. "Set the alarm for six-thirty, will you?"

"Hmmm," Linda said, busy looking for the page she was on. The toothpick she used to bookmark the page had fallen out at some point between the manor and the motel.

Ashley shut off her bedside lamp. The room was half plunged in darkness, Linda's bedside lamp the only halo of light.

By the time Linda was deeply engrossed in the book, Ashley was snoring lightly under the covers. Linda rubbed the bridge of her nose as she read.

24th September 1651

They came back again today, the peasants from Glasha Talann; I suspect they never went home. Their talk is tedious and bores me to death. I allowed their village headman an audience but the man spoke no sense; all gibberish and heathen blabbering about some witch that has taken up residence in their village, infecting the populace with bad dreams.

Cromwell no doubt meant well when he tightened the leash on Ireland's despotic Catholic blasphemers, but they hold on to their archaic beliefs, fairies and witches, as reluctant to let them go as the heretic Charles was of the throne. It makes me wonder if it was truly wise to spare any of their villages or lives.

Mathews has reported that it is indeed true that a woman was hanged in Glasha Talann a fortnight ago for stealing eggs and pheasants from the village pantry. She died instantly, when her neck broke. Now the villagers are convinced the woman is seeking her revenge from beyond the grave.

I fear I will know no peace till I have shown a modicum of effort. I have proposed a day trip to the village tomorrow to scout the area, deem it safe and return to the barracks by nightfall.

25ᵀᴴ SEPTEMBER 1651

We never made it back to the barracks. The Irish have surpassed themselves in their devil worship, seeking the darkness above the light of God's truth.

We arrived well before afternoon. The sun was out and the air balmy but the woods reeked of oppression. I suspect as a representative of the Commonwealth I will never feel entirely safe in this land.

The villagers greeted us with a wild frenzy of happiness. It is unknown for an Irishman to be so happy at the sight of an armed British contingent. The headman began a heated conversation with a woman I assume was his wife. Something she said upset him and he struck her hard, forcing her to her knees.

Upon enquiry I was told by the local priest, no less, that the witch had possessed the headman's daughter who was now living in the hovel the witch had previously occupied. The priest looked like a decent man, even though he is Catholic, and I persuaded him to show me where this hovel was.

I have always maintained that the woods in Ireland have a malignancy about them, a sickness in the very roots that is unlike the wholesome fertility of England's green pastures. Even though the sun shone down on our heads the cool shade of the woods was sinister.

A mile or so from the village is a patch of rotting wood. The trees are twisted in various states of agony, their bark black and blistered from an ancient fire. Bugs crawled in the hollows of these monstrosities but nothing compared to the largest tree in the clearing, an ancient oak with a large hollow in its center eaten away over the years by industrious termites.

Within the hovel sat a peasant girl of no more than ten; her malnourished limbs stuck out from her thin dress. She was sleeping.

At the sight of her, the village headman lost his calm. He charged the hovel, screaming obscenities, his cudgel raised to bash in the head of the poor innocent. At my command my soldiers apprehended him before he could do much harm. The man was chained and made to sit down.

In all this commotion the girl had not stirred. None of the villagers would go near the hovel so it was left to me to crouch down and enter the horrid place. There was a pile of tattered clothes in one corner, amidst small bones and rocks. The girl slept on even as I picked her up and brought her out into the clearing. She was a limp straw doll in my hands and I wondered if she were alive. The tree groaned, no doubt on its last limb. I suspect a strong wind would blow it down and turn it to dust.

The girl had bruises around the neck and wrists, and her lips were blue despite her body being warm. I tried waking her but her sleep was deep. Her chest barely moved and when I felt her wrist I could discern no pulse.

"She is dead," the cry went up amongst the villagers. "We must bury her."

I told them that was nonsense; the girl looked dead, I granted them that, but there was something alive about her nonetheless.

They surged forward to take her. "We will break the curse; we will release her!"

My guards made to stop them but were overwhelmed. It was all I could do to place the girl on my saddle and gallop away.

Night has fallen and I am alone. The girl still sleeps and I suspect she suffers from the sleeping sickness but how an illness only seen in Africa could reach the shores of Ireland is something I cannot explain. Her bruises disturb me and I am now sure that the villagers lied. They had tried to hang the girl, who was probably abused by her father; and they had failed in hiding their village shame.

The night grows long and I must get some rest to continue on back to Doon in the morning. I will issue a request to Nester Brown in Galway for reinforcements. If there is more of this in the villages around Doon, I fear we have no other recourse than to take their lands and force them into hard labor in the colonies as was done in Northern Ireland.

26TH SEPTEMBER 1651

There is much that my faith asks of me, the belief in an unseen God paramount in its instructions. But what of the things that I have seen and heard in these past hours? It expresses belief in them as heretic and tantamount to blasphemy yet how can I deny my eyes and ears?

I was suffering from a nightmare of hanging corpses when my sleep was disturbed by the sound of feet approaching my fireside. I promptly slipped out of the rug with which I had covered myself to retrieve the knife my wife had gifted me before my departure to this God forsaken place.

Out of the sentinel trees came a thin figure dressed in white. The man held up his hands in surrender and I saw by the dying firelight that it was the priest I had met in Glasha Talann. He had no weapons but I did not lower my blade.

"I mean no harm, Master Prim," he said. "I have just come to retrieve the girl."

I told him I would not let his villagers continue their barbaric rituals while I was Governor.

"You do not understand," the man protested. "She is not dead, indeed, but she is no longer herself. The banshee has her now. We must

guide her soul back to her body. We must bury her and destroy the banshee."

"What nonsense," I spat. I made it clear that I thought his Catholic leanings had muddied the waters of his faith, which is why he believed these savage myths.

"On the contrary," he said. "I am not a Catholic priest. I am a Protestant."

This shocked me.

"I only wear my liturgical vesture when I fulfill ecclesiastical tasks, but I am a pastor. Your refusal to let us bury her has endangered her life," he continued. "We could have saved her then but now I fear her soul is too lost for it to ever return. We must end the cycle so the curse does not spread."

There was no moon that night and the woods were choked with shadows. I could see that the man was insane and would do anything to harm the girl. I scouted out escape routes only to realize that the girl had gone.

"What have you done to her?" I demanded.

The man only looked fearful. "She has escaped. All is lost."

At that moment a low keening song rose up from the dark depths of the woods around us. It was ever so faint, yet loud enough to be heard, but I could not determine from whence it came. It was all around us, wrapping us up in its tendril-thin curls.

My mind became hazy; a grey gloom invaded my eyes and they fell heavy. The pastor began to moan in terrible fear. "What have you done!" he cried.

I wasn't sure what he meant by it but in that moment, God forgive me, I felt mortal fear.

CHAPTER 24

The book fell with a deafening thud.

Linda had been startled awake.

She wiped the drool from her chin, and yawned, blinking against the sharp lamplight by her bedside. Her eyes were still heavy with sleep as she leaned over her bed and retrieved the book.

Her stomach groaned. The soup dinner hadn't been enough.

Leaning back on her pillow, Linda flipped through the pages till she got to the chapter she had been on when sleep had claimed her.

Colin Prim had come across as the epitome of the Commonwealth of England's short-lived Puritan regime. He had no patience for the people he governed and his contempt dripped off the page. But his fear of the unknown was palpable as the events in Glasha Talann unfolded.

Linda rubbed her eyes under her glasses. The small text strained them something terrible. Her mind grasped at the straws of the day. From the unexpected face in the painting, and the information Grady had given her, Linda's mind was stuffed with information overload that she needed to dissect and organize before she could make heads or tails of what was going on here.

It was a tangled mess and even she wasn't sure what she was looking for, only that if she cleared the mess, the truth would find her.

She traced a finger down the page to find where she had left off. She was eager to find out what had happened to the Governor and the priest.

Yet as she started reading, her eyelids drooped again as if she were under some strange trance that made it so hard to concentrate because nothing was more important than closing her eyes for just one second.

A loud clattering from down the hall made her eyes fly open.

All vestiges of sleep left her. She was on high alert.

"Ashley?" she called, hoping to hear her sister's voice reassuring her.

Nothing.

It was only then she noticed she was back in her room in Blackburn Manor.

Panic arrested her. She let the book slide down on the bed.

Getting up slowly, Linda tiptoed to the door. The hall was empty and dark, but a faint light shone from under the bathroom door.

Linda stepped out into the hall. Icicles of alarm slid down her spine.

How is this possible? We left! We left this house!

"Ashley? Ashley!" she cried.

Her sister didn't respond.

Hysteria was building in her chest. The events of the previous evening loomed to the forefront of her mind and she couldn't shake the image of Marisa twisted and bent on Ashley's bed, staring at her with that insane grin.

She retreated to her room and grabbed the closest thing to a weapon she owned, her bedside lamp. Removing the shade and holding it tight she ventured back into the dark hall, dread nestling like a heavy rock in her gut.

"Ashley, please," she pleaded. "Answer me."

The bathroom door remained closed. Shadows flitted amongst the light through the crack at the bottom of the bathroom door. Someone was inside.

Linda knocked on the door, hoping whoever was in there would leave, or respond somehow. The shadow underneath the door surged. Linda twisted the knob and pushed the door open.

The bathroom was empty.

The lights were on.

The window was open.

The shower curtains rustled in the wind coming through the window, the hooks skittering lightly against the rail.

Linda took a rattling breath. She put the lamp down in the sink.

If someone had just jumped out the window she needed to see, she needed to make sure.

You're crazy, Linda.

Ashley's words echoed in her mind.

Flexing her toes to get a better grip on the porcelain, Linda pulled herself up so her head was leaning out of the window. Wind howled against her face, making her eyes water. The moon hung low on the horizon and the trees cast long shadows on the back garden. Nothing moved at the base of the house.

How was any of this happening? How had she come back to the house? Did the entity here have such power?

Pulling back, she swung the window closed.

The clear glass glistened under the overhead light and reflected her face for a brief second.

It also showed a figure behind her.

Long dark hair obscured the face, but something silver glittered through the dark tresses along the neck, and thin arms stretched out claw-like hands.

Linda whipped around, her feet losing balance. She screamed and grabbed at the shower curtains, ripping them as she fell in the tub. Her head hit the rim. Pain burst across her mind.

Hands reached down and pinned the curtain down over her head cutting off her air supply.

Linda gasped, her lungs burning in her chest. Her fingers clawed at the hands, her nails dug into cold flesh but the grip never loosened. Stars and black spots burst in front of her eyes. Her head was pounding, her feet stuck awkwardly underneath her.

She was spinning down a dark hole.

Her hands loosened and fell by her side.

She slipped into unconsciousness.

She was suspended in that oily darkness for what felt like an eternity. Like a child in its mother's womb she could hear fragments of the outside world. Someone was coughing. A choking noise was followed by a high whistling moan.

The world was upside down, there was no way to know which side was up. Linda pushed against the darkness; she swam the black pool of her subconscious, fighting against an invisible current to make it to the surface.

Something hard struck her forehead. She looked about in the water to see what it was but now an invisible force was lifting her up and out of the water. She felt lighter, airy.

Sounds became clearer. She could hear the scrabbling of feet on a slick tiled floor. She was rising; a dim red light shone in front of her. Just when she thought her lungs wouldn't be able to hold out any longer she burst through the surface.

Her mouth opened wide to suck in greedy air; her eyes opened next.

Ashley was in front of her, her face blue.

"Ashley?" Linda stammered.

Then she saw her own hands. Wrapped around her sister's throat, squeezing, squeezing, nails grazing tender skin.

Crying out, she pulled her hands away.

Ashley coughed and spluttered. Color drained from her face, suddenly only to return in blotches.

"What happened?" Linda cried, tears streaked down her face in torrents. She looked down at her hands. Blood dripped onto her palms. Horrified, Linda looked to see if she had cut Ashley but there was no bloody gash on her.

She looked around at their surroundings. They were still in the bathroom, but it was the motel bathroom. The shower curtains were in a heaped mess on the tiled floor. Ashley was lying in the tub, while Linda towered over her.

She had seen a figure, a dark-haired figure behind her. It hadn't been Ashley. Then how come now… her sister had taken its place… was she dreaming, was this still a dream?

Linda sobbed and ran her fingers over her face. Something warm and slippery was smeared across her cheek. More blood.

It was only then she realized she was bleeding. There was a cut on her forehead.

Her mind was in chaotic turmoil, unable to distinguish what was happening.

"Ashley," she whimpered. "Ashley, please speak to me."

"What the hell, Linda?" Ashley choked out. "Why the hell did you attack me?"

"I didn't," Linda hiccoughed. "I… I had a dream I was back in Blackburn Manor… I dreamt someone attacked me…"

Ashley struggled up on her feet. "I came to use the bathroom and next thing I know you were behind me and you just went cra…" Ashley broke off. Linda guessed she didn't want to use that word again.

"I can't explain it." Linda's tears were still flowing, but she had stopped weeping. "I saw myself doing all the things you've just said. I have a vivid memory of someone strangling me."

Ashley looked perturbed. "When you were standing by the bathroom door… you reminded me of Marisa," she said, stepping out of the tub. "I had to hit you with the toothbrush stand to try and get you off me," Ashley sounded just as horrified as Linda felt.

Marisa… Linda's heart constricted. Marisa had done exactly these things before… before she'd dropped dead. Was Linda going to suffer the same end? She had thought the haunting was restricted to Blackburn Manor, but she had been wrong. The malevolent spirit followed, it infected you till you were so far gone you no longer had control over the situation. The clock had just started for Linda and if she didn't figure out how to stop the possessions, soon she would go the same way as Marisa and the poor girl in Colin Prim's diary. Hysteria obscured all other thoughts. She had nearly killed her sister.

Ashley had been there for her in her most trying times, and Linda had nearly strangled the life out of her.

More sobs rocked her body. Ashley stared at her, still rubbing her neck. Linda could see that Ashley was horrified and not yet able to register what had happened. A part of Linda was just as skeptical as Ashley, and understood that her sister probably thought she was a dangerous threat. This broke her heart.

"Hey." Ashley swallowed, her voice hoarse. She held Linda's arm. "Now we have matching bruises." She pointed towards her own neck and Linda's, making the first move towards reconciliation.

Linda burst into fresh tears. Not only because of the love her sister had for her, but also because she knew that they had to go back. She needed to figure out how to end this before it consumed her. She didn't want to harm anyone; she didn't want to die.

It hadn't worked for Marisa; it hadn't worked for the Irish peasant girl hundreds of years ago. Chances were it wouldn't for her either. She would have to figure this out and end it before she decided anything else. Because this would end her.

She had a dire need to finish reading the rest of Colin Prim's diary. And she had to go back to Blackburn Manor.

PART V
A CALL FROM THE BEYOND

CHAPTER 25

⚜

A strong wind started blowing through the trees. It carried the stench of putrid flesh; fire and brimstone; a hellish wind from the unwashed mouth of Satan himself.

My horse whinnied and skittered, its eyes rolling back in its head. The priest limped closer to me, standing a little behind me. We watched the shifting darkness, trying to keep our eyes open in the gale.

The song on the wind got louder, the voice getting higher, hysterical like a mad woman. I am afraid to say that it tore at me, forcing me to drop my guard to cower in fear, but the strength of God kept me upright. The priest, long having abandoned his faith for the devilish belief of the pagans, was whimpering on his knees in the grass.

Then the wind stopped as suddenly as it had started. Leaves swayed on to the ground, and my horse screamed. I turned to the beast, intent on beating it for its insolence, when I saw the little girl standing beside it.

Now that she was standing on her two dirty feet I could see that she was barely tall enough to reach my navel. Her spindly legs *sprouted out of her tattered dress, which was too short for her. Her face was hidden in the shadows made by her hair, which had spilled out of her braid and swayed about her shoulders in a wind that was no longer there. Her long fingers were twisted in the horse's mane.*

"Stop it!" I ordered.

The girl laughed, a shrill sound that grated on the ears.

With a mighty twist, she broke the horse's neck.

The priest screamed and fainted.

I held my ground. It shocked me that such a small girl had the strength to twist a horse's neck so; and what I had feared was finally confirmed. She was a witch, possessed by a demon that was lending her its strength.

"In the name of the Father, I invoke you to leave this girl!"

The girl skipped over the dead horse and crept closer. Her movements were stiff and fluid at the same time. I prepared to grab her around the wrists but she was too quick. She jumped like a leaping cat and her hair flew away from her face.

I have seen many terrible things in my life but I pray to God that I will never see a sight like that again.

Her skin was bone white and there were deep purple bruises under her eyes. The bruises on her neck shone red. Her teeth were bared, their pointed ends sharp and pricked with red blood. And her eyes... her eyes were the most terrible of all. Large and staring, they shone bright as new pennies and were filled with such malevolent hate that it turned my bowels to water.

I lifted my knife-wielding hand to strike her but she darted away, and landed on top of the priest. The old man's prone body did not fidget when the girl started to strangle him but it twitched as the air was choked out of him.

"Stop it!" I lunged at her. The priest's eyes began to bulge out of his

skull. With the palm of my hand I used the handle of the knife to knock the girl away. She gave an awful scream and fell back.

The priest spluttered and spat. The girl sat where she had landed; the white pallor was gone, her cheeks were flushed now but her eyes had lost all luster and life. She stared ahead for a minute or so then collapsed like a puppet whose strings have been cut.

We watched the corpse for a long time, only approaching it once dawn light had burst through the night darkness. She was cold and stiff; long dead.

Linda sat at the dining table in the kitchen of Blackburn Manor, trying hard not to fall asleep. A mug of coffee grew cold beside her. She hadn't slept a wink after the incident with Ashley; she didn't trust herself to sleep anymore. They had arrived back at the house by eight in the morning, renting bikes from the motel owner.

She had dreaded coming back. Strangely, she had considered finished lining the markers in the vegetable garden. She told herself that she was supposed to work, but she knew that she was just avoiding entering Blackburn Manor. Standing in front of the manor, dominated by its brooding façade, she had felt like a dwarf in the shadow of a monstrous giant. Every fiber of her being had wanted to run away but there was no choice. She had to figure out if there was any way of ending this.

She read more of Colin Prim's account, how they buried the girl and the priest warned him that the curse had been transferred to them now. Linda bit her lip as she read Prim's dismissal of the claim; he was fairly sure that the demon would not think to possess him.

He had gone back to his garrison only for things to get stranger. He would wake up in the morning to find blood and dirt in his sheets, having no memory of walking across the garrison and mutilating a horse. Then the nightmares went from bad to worse, and he finally accepted that the possession was indeed possible.

The last entry was just ramblings of a sleep-deprived man trying desperately not to succumb to the exhaustion, knowing that this last long sleep would be the predecessor of his end.

Linda sighed and turned the page. She could relate to Prim on a very personal level. The night had not been easy and her eyes were heavy from lack of sleep.

Colin Prim sought help at the village of Glasha Talann where the villagers found the receptacle for the original banshee, the woman hung for her crime of stealing. The hangman's post along with the village headman's daughter's ribbon were burnt to stop the curse. Unfortunately, it wasn't enough to save Colin Prim. He was pronounced dead by exposure to the elements in the report submitted by his senior.

A rattling sigh escaped Linda's lips. She was trembling from a cold that had settled inside her bones. Tracing one finger over the words of Colin Prim's entries, Linda wondered what the final moments of this God-fearing man must have been like, all alone and friendless in the foreign woods so far away from home.

She was about to close the book when she noticed the next heading started a page over; not directly after where Colin Prim's entries finished. Linda turned the page, eyebrows scrunched up with curiosity.

It was more information on the legend of the banshee myth, how it had crossed the Irish seas and variations were found in other cultures. Linda lost more hope as the list went on and on till she reached the very end of the page.

Once a manifestation begins, it is very hard to control if the recep-

tacle is not identified. The more time that passes between the initiation of a curse and the investigation for its source, the more likely it is that it will never be identified. Unfortunately, it is the only resource that is foolproof in ending a banshee and its curse. The receptacle is anything that the deceased placed great value on, or had emotional attachment to. Once the receptacle is destroyed the manifestation can end.

Hope tickled the back of Linda's mind. She chewed her lip in thought and closed the book. She needed to discuss this with Grady.

She glanced at the clock. It was nine fifteen in the morning. Grady would be up. Getting up from the chair, she stretched her limbs. A big yawn escaped her lips and she had to slap her cheeks to keep from falling asleep.

She bit her nails and unbidden thoughts of last night came to her.

She had dreamt of a woman; not the miners, not Samuel Blackburn, but a woman. Maybe Grady was wrong; maybe a woman had been killed in the mines. Then there were Shannon and Tara, and their disappearances. Was it related to the haunting at Blackburn? Had they found out something: a clue, or the identity of the ghost? Did this discovery scare them so much that they left in hurry?

Her head throbbed.

Refusing to wait any longer, she climbed the stairs to check on Ashley and tell her where she was going.

Thunder rumbled outside. Dark billowy clouds hung low in the sky. A storm was brewing.

She was walking down the hall when she heard it, the skittering rustle of rats. It came from the ceiling, the attic that could only be accessed from Stewart's apartment.

He should really look into his rodent problem.

"Ashley?" she called as she approached her door.

The office space was empty. The high ceilings highlighted the cavernous feeling of the house and the stained windows weren't that cheerful this morning. The cheap modern furniture looked like an affront to the surroundings.

Linda frowned. Ashley had said she'd be in the offices looking at the accounts. Linda finally found her in a conference room sprawled in a chair, deep asleep. She was snoring lightly and drool pooled on the desk.

Part of Linda wanted to wake Ashley and let her know she was headed to Grady's house; the other part of her wanted her sister to get some rest. Ashley had experienced enough trauma to last her a lifetime.

She sprinted back down the stairs and retrieved the book from the kitchen. A thought struck her when she reached the front door and she pulled out her cellphone. She dialed the number as she climbed down the porch steps and crossed the street.

"Hello?"

"Hi, Scott. It's Linda Green from Blackburn Manor." Linda spoke very quickly. "I had some questions about the speakeasy you mentioned the other day."

"Sure," Scott said. She heard other voices in the background; she assumed he was at the station. "What do you want to know?"

"Could I get a map of the mines?" Linda asked. "Specifically, where the speakeasy was located."

"Okay." Scott sounded confused. "Why do you need it?"

"Just curious about a few things," Linda said casually. She climbed Grady's porch and knocked. "I thought I'd go exploring the mines."

"Oh." Scott was quiet for a few seconds. "Okay. I could get it to you in half an hour."

"Wow," Linda laughed. "That's quick." Grady's feet shuffled beyond the door.

"There's a reason." Scott didn't laugh. "I was looking at the files on the Blackburn mine myself. If you don't mind, can I come along on the tour? I need to see some things myself."

The door opened and Grady squinted up at her. She waved Linda inside.

"I'd be grateful for company," Linda said into the phone. "See you soon."

"Bye."

Linda tucked the phone back in her jeans pocket as she walked inside Grady's house. She placed the book on the table they had sat at yesterday.

"It won't help if we leave," she told Grady. "The thing latches on somehow and follows you. I nearly strangled Ashley to death last night. The nightmare was vivid; I was back in the house..."

Grady placed a hand on Linda's arm. "Sit." She went into the kitchen and brought a cookie jar. "Eat."

Linda didn't feel like it, but she took an oatmeal raisin one out of politeness.

"What did you find out from the book?"

"It's not completely accurate but most of the things we've experienced are like the banshee lore in the book. There's the lament, the dreams, the excessive sleeping, and then Marisa trying to strangle me when she had a knife." Linda took a bite of cookie absentmindedly. "The lore in the book says that those possessed by this particular wraith only kill in the manner the original banshee was murdered. Marisa never tried to stab me, she even threw the knife away at a crucial moment to strangle me."

Grady rubbed her forefinger along her upper lip, deep in thought. "But the miners…"

"Were shot and left to die. We don't know if they strangled each other as a more merciful end but I doubt it. Plus the banshee is female, and I saw a woman again last night."

"You think it might be Shannon or Tara?" Grady asked, placing another cookie in Linda's hand.

"I did at first," Linda said with a nod. "But you mentioned Shannon was blonde, and Tara was chestnut."

Grady looked surprised, clearly annoyed by the frivolousness of the comment.

"The woman I saw in my dreams is a brunette." She chewed on her cookie thoughtfully. "Did Shannon or Tara wear a green pendant? Shaped like a clover?"

"If they did I never saw it, and Shannon was blonde and Tara had chestnut-colored hair," Grady shook her head. "You said it wasn't completely accurate. What isn't similar?"

"The phone calls for one," Linda brushed the crumbs off the table. "And the miner in the dreams as well as the woman… and the burial…" Linda broke off, the memory of those dreams making her queasy.

"What burial?" Grady asked.

"The first few dreams always ended with someone burying me alive. So none of the deaths is consistent with the haunting. It's very confusing." Linda bit her lip but then smiled hopefully. "There is a way to end it though."

Grady's eyes shone. "How?"

"According to the book the banshee spirit resides in some object, a receptacle of some sort. If that is destroyed, the haunting can end. I'm going down to the mines with Scott to see if I can find something. If you're right and this – thing – is reacting to my sensitivity, then I should be able to find something."

"That's a good idea," Grady agreed. "Let me know what you find, and I'll do some more research on the house. Find this brunette woman you've been seeing."

"Thank you, Mrs. Grady," Linda said. "I was wrong to judge you."

"I gave you reason." Grady waved her hand dismissively. "Go. Let's try to finish this."

Linda nodded, and nabbed another cookie before leaving. Talking to Grady had been a good idea. She was nowhere near the answers she needed, but the talk had cleared her head a little and she was more determined and focused.

The manor stared at her across the street. She didn't want to go back. She sat on Grady's porch steps and waited for Scott to show up.

CHAPTER 26

"Sorry I'm late." Scott locked the doors once Linda was in the passenger seat of his car. "I had to take a personal day and Milo started grilling me about it."

"Milo?" Linda asked buckling herself in.

"Officer Carter." Scott pulled away from the curb. Scott looked worse than Linda had ever seen him. There were dark smudges under his eyes, and he looked paler than usual. Even his lips were colorless. "I'm glad you called, though. I needed an excuse to get out."

The car smelled of trapped sunrays, hot and humid. Linda shifted uncomfortably until Scott rolled the windows down. Once they were on their way, Linda felt a surge of relief that got stronger as the car put distance between the house and them.

"Are the mines very far?" Linda asked, sitting back in her seat.

"No." Scott's eyes were on the road, his face a blank mask.

He was sweating slightly even though the breeze was cool. "Ten minutes, tops. Why are you suddenly so interested in them?"

"Why are you?" Linda asked.

Scott glanced at her, a pained expression on his face. "I just have a gut feeling. In fact, it started that day in the library when we couldn't find anything on the bootlegging, and I said I'd look into police files. Milo says I'm crazy to pursue it, as it's off the books, nothing official."

"What did you find?"

Scott bit his lower lip. There was reluctance in his fidgeting limbs and Linda wasn't entirely sure if he believed in whatever it was he was investigating. She could empathize because during lucid moments of panic she felt the same.

"The mines are a big deal around here," he said, squaring his shoulders. "There are tours and guides to the mine shafts at the south of Keystone. Helen Lord even opened an inn inside her family mines. It's part of the town's annual business. But no one makes it to this part of town, specifically this mine."

The road took a turn. The sun was directly in front of them. Linda shaded her eyes. Scott leaned over and pulled down her visor. Linda suddenly felt hot and cold at the same time. She could see the large gaping mouth of the cave up ahead. Ancient winches and rusting machines stood abandoned outside like fallen sentries at the gates of a ruined castle.

"You're not going to ask why?" Scott asked.

Linda stared at the cavernous opening in the mountain. Jagged rocks, like teeth, lined the ceiling. "I suspect you're going to tell me either way."

Scott cleared his throat. "Yes, well. That's why we're here. This mine has a very nasty history."

"You mean about the Molly Maguires."

"How did you know about that?" Scott asked, his surprise shifting his melancholy mood a little.

"Grady told me about them yesterday," Linda said. "How some of the miners were shot and buried for their association with the outfit, and because Samuel Blackburn was paranoid and believed they were digging a tunnel underneath his house."

"Yeah, the town doesn't like to dwell on that, which is why there wasn't much about the 'accident' in the library or the papers. But here's the kicker," Scott grimaced. "It wasn't paranoia. There actually was a tunnel that opened somewhere beneath the house."

Linda did a double take. "You're kidding."

"I wish I was. I kept going back to old files to figure out if there was a history of the house which could implicate the Blackburn family, and I found these."

He gripped the steering wheel with one hand and leaned back to retrieve something from the backseat. Linda's heart leaped up in her throat.

"Scott, the road!"

"No worries," Scott grunted, straightening back to his former position. He had two thick manila folders in his hand. He deposited them in Linda's lap. "Take a look at the one on top first."

Linda did as he asked. It helped that she didn't have to look at the mine coming closer and closer like some nightmare monstrosity. It was a charge sheet that listed the names of several men and a few women. The date was August 1928, right smack in the heart of Prohibition. Linda could figure what the charges were.

"Are these the bootleggers?" she asked, scanning the names hoping one would ring a bell.

"Not all of them," Scott said. The car crawled to a stop. "The distillery belonged to the Coleman brothers, and the Shaw family financed the whole operation. The ladies you see on there, Lily and Penelope Shaw? They expanded the business beyond county lines because no officer would check the cars they drove."

"Wow." Linda examined the charges. The list was long, but it all came down to the same thing: illegal distillery encourages drunk and disorderly behavior. "But what does this have to do with the secret tunnel?"

"I'm getting to that." Scott opened his car door and let the breeze in. It rustled the papers in Linda's lap. Taking the second file from her, he opened it. Black and white photos, damaged by age, spilled out on the car floor. "God damn it!" Scott bent down to retrieve the photos.

Linda leaned down to retrieve some as well. "Mrs. Grady said she found some distillery artifacts on her trips in the mine."

"Yeah," Scott said, shuffling through pictures, a great frown creasing his forehead. "Small-time stuff. Levers, old bottles with liquor gummed up inside. She showed us in class. But the official location of the speakeasy isn't easy to pinpoint. No one who has ever gone in had said with much confidence where the speakeasy had officially been."

"Again…" Linda said, losing patience. "What does that have to do with the secret tunnel?"

Scott finally stopped shuffling the pictures, a small glow of triumph illuminating his eyes, "Because the tunnel and the speakeasy are one and the same!"

He flipped the picture around and Linda gasped.

It was a grainy black and white, one corner completely white due to exposure. Uniformed men in the background stood together, arms over each other's shoulders, their guns hanging on their hips. In the foreground lay two bodies. Both were tall and dark-haired. Their faces were obscured by flecks of black. She could make out the broken nose of one, and the swollen lips of the other.

They were dead.

But more than the police crowing over their kill, it was where they stood that caught her attention.

It was a cavernous place. The ceiling vaulted up, nearly five stories high. Jagged stalactite teeth zigzagged down, their sharp points picked up in the camera's flash. A black diaphanous pool sat perfectly stagnant beside the subjects of the photo. Behind the congregated men, along the base of the far wall, were unmistakable graves. Linda counted ten mounds. Many had makeshift crosses, one of which was lopsided and threatened to topple over.

An itch ran along her scalp like the tiny prickly feet of spiders.

Linda had seen this place before in her dreams.

CHAPTER 27

Linda hugged herself as they entered the mine. A deep sense of foreboding washed over her and she wanted to turn on her heel and run back home, but Scott pushed forward, the light from his flashlight skimming the walls.

Rusty rail tracks guided their way.

Linda was sure that whatever the source of the haunting was, it was in that cavern Scott had shown her the picture of.

"So you think there is a tunnel that leads underneath the manor?" Linda asked, trying to keep her mind off the scary images of falling somewhere in the shaft and breaking her legs.

"Yes," Scott said. "I read the reports from the bust on the speakeasy. The arresting officers were appalled to find the distillery setup amidst the shallow graves of the poor murdered miners. I wanted to interview some of the officers, but they've all passed away."

Linda followed him closely. The light was receding as they went in deeper, and she couldn't help but feel reality slip with it. Was she walking in the mines or was she back in her stumbling dreams where she was blind even though she could see everything?

"What about the perpetrators? One of the Shaws or Colemans?" Linda asked.

"The Coleman brothers were the two dead boys in the picture I showed you. Out of the Shaws only Lily is left, but she's in an old age home battling dementia." He grunted and kicked a stone out of the way. "None of this would have turned into a bloodbath, if the stupid Hackridge police had stayed out of it."

"What did they do?" Linda could feel eyes boring into her back. She tried to ignore it but it was too strong. As soon as she had entered the mine she had felt it, a shift in the air around her as if the place was suddenly sentient.

"They're the ones in the picture," Scott spat, his anger palpable. Linda was glad for it because it distracted her from the nasty thought of being prey in some big predator's game. "As Milo tells it, most of the patrons came out easy enough, as did the Shaw sisters. They had just negotiated release with the Shaw men when the Hackridge police arrived. They think they're city police, so they have more experience. Heck, I know my town and these people, and I'm more qualified to talk my townsfolk off a ledge or out of a stupid idea."

Linda could tell all this anger towards the city police was coming from a very personal space, but she didn't want to pry.

"Anyway, the Colemans smelled trouble and retreated deeper into the mineshaft where they had their distillery. The city cops threatened, and then opened fire. I can imagine the pandemonium. Sound carries in these shafts, and nearly everyone must have been scared hearing gunshots."

For a second Linda thought she heard the exchange of gunfire and the startled screams of innocent bystanders.

"The scene was cleared. Everyone goes home and the place is cordoned off and kept off limits, so as not to stir up town sentiment about the recent killings and the old ones." Scott stopped walking. They had arrived at a cross tunnel. He consulted a piece of paper and went left. "Everyone stays away, and the mine develops a sinister reputation."

"So what are we doing here, if you already know all this?" Linda asked. Her gut had been squeezed suddenly, her body telling her to walk back while there was still time.

"I want to find the cavern and the secret tunnel," Scott said.

"But no one knows where it is." Linda stepped carefully on the uneven ground. Her motivation to come to the mines was to find the remains of the miners. She still wasn't sure about the Shannon and Tara theory, so her best guess was that a female had been murdered with the miners and buried down here. But that wasn't what Scott was here for. "Why did you want to find the tunnel so badly, Scott?"

"Two girls have disappeared, and one died yesterday." Scott looked back at her.

The flashlight was angled away from his face so it was hidden in shadows, but his eyes were two pinpricks of yellow light. Linda shivered and took a step away.

"It won't prove anything, but if I can find the tunnel, maybe it would give some merit to the theory that the girls sneaked off in the tunnels and got lost. And maybe Marisa experienced all that because someone found access to the house through the tunnel. I don't know." He ran a hand through his hair. "I feel like I'm running in circles, grabbing at loose strings that go nowhere."

"Don't lose faith," Linda responded to his frustration.

He was one of those rare police officers who were dedicated to the job. It was endearing, yet at the same time rang of naivety. Linda had seen the worst of them for nearly a decade, and Scott's sincerity rang false before she had to tell herself otherwise.

"You seem to know where you're going, so that's something," she said.

"It was in a report one of the officers made." Scott consulted his paper again. "He gave detailed instructions about the layout of the mine and which tracks they followed. It's ironic because everyone else in town seemed to know the location of the speakeasy like the back of their hand."

They walked on for a few minutes in silence. There was no sound but the low hum of air moving through the tunnels. Linda turned back to see nothing but darkness behind them. Her bruised throat became tighter as claustrophobia invaded her mind. There were dead bodies up ahead somewhere, and a malevolent spirit tracking them, and no trace of light. It was a veritable tomb, and Linda was walking into the heart of it. The earth pressed down on her. It felt as if a single slipping pebble would trigger an avalanche, burying her in there forever.

"It's just up ahead," Scott whispered. The feeling of eerie anticipation must have hit him too. His breath plumed in the flashlight's beam. "Is it just me or did it just get really cold?"

"It did," Linda gasped. It had felt like being doused with cold water. She shivered, her eyes darting all over the place. Her gut was twisted so tight with tension she could hardly move. She didn't want to see that horrible cavern from her dreams. Nothing nice had ever happened in there, and she had a feeling it would do her more harm than good if she were to set foot in it. "I think we should head back," she stammered. "This place is old, and we have no proper light. We could get in some accident if we're not careful."

The tunnel walls were closer than before, the uneven ground littered with rocks and debris. Water trickled along the walls making it glisten like a large shiny intestine. More than ever Linda felt like she was walking in a monster's gut.

"It's just beyond this shaft," Scott said. He sounded just as spooked, but there was an underlying strength that Linda latched on to. What other choice did she have? She couldn't go back without a flashlight and she really needed to find the source to all this misery if she wanted to survive this nightmare. "Just a bit more... Oh, come on!"

Linda came to a stop behind Scott. His shoulders fell and she could tell without looking at him that he was more disappointed than frustrated.

"I don't understand," he said. "It was supposed to be here."

Linda peeked over his shoulder.

The tunnel opened wider a few feet from where they stood, a natural progression for a small fork. The tracks they had been following diverged in two only they didn't go anywhere. The entrances to the tunnels ahead were buried underneath rocks and silt.

Linda stared at the ceiling where a notch of darkness indicated where the earth had fractured and caused a natural landslide. Broken glass lamps and bits and pieces of metal piping littered the ground.

She felt unimaginable relief. Her twisted gut loosened up a little. "There is no way in." Then guilt and devastation hit her. If there was no way in and that was the source of the haunting then she was doomed.

"Or out," Scott frowned.

Linda didn't know why but that observation sent chills down her spine.

"Let's head back." Scott rubbed his eyes. "I can't take much more of this dark." He turned on his heel and began walking back up the passage they had come from.

"Yes, please," Linda said, walking behind him. If she never had to step into another mine, it would be too soon.

CHAPTER 28

Scott dropped Linda off at Blackburn Manor. She hoisted the book Grady had given her up under her arm, and she waved goodbye to Scott. She went inside noticing that Stewart's car wasn't in the drive. She was glad she hadn't met him.

Stifling a yawn, Linda went into the kitchen. Her stomach rumbled, and she realized she had been up most of the night giving her body caffeine and very little sustenance. Maybe a quick breakfast would make her less drowsy.

She cracked a few eggs in a bowl and whisked them to make a simple omelet. Adding salt and pepper she left the mixture on the counter and headed out to the back garden to grab some fresh tarragon.

The air was fresh, dewy, and promised rain. It was a shame she was too strung up to really enjoy it but just being out of the house was enough to lift her spirits a little. She snapped a few sprigs of tarragon from the communal garden and turned back to the house.

Lightning flashed above the house. Three things happened at once.

Linda stubbed her toe on a rock.

She bit her tongue in surprise.

And she saw a face, clear as day, staring down at her from the tower attic.

Linda winced against the rush of pain and blood in her mouth.

She forced her eyes to remain dry and looked back up at the window. A hand was pressed against the glass and a figure stood a little way back. It was definitely a person, not a tailor's dummy.

Who was Stewart kidding? Who had he been hiding in his attic? Was it one of the girls who had supposedly run away? Or rather who had disappeared? Was he keeping them captive?

She calmed her own running thoughts.

No, it couldn't be. Yes, Stewart was somehow greedy, but that didn't make him some psychopath. She thought of how sweet he had been otherwise, the way he had treated Marisa in her time of need, and his general caregiving of Evelyn.

She was wrong. There was a reasonable explanation. No sooner had the thought crossed her mind than she spotted Cindy May in the kitchen window scraping leftovers into the bin. The handprint was still visible on the attic window. It was not humanly possible for Cindy May to have come down two stories in the blink of an eye.

Linda glanced up at the attic window. There was no one there. According to the book, the monstrosity that attacked through dreams was invisible. Then who was the figure in the attic?

Linda knew that Cindy's shift ended at lunch and from the

looks of it she had just finished feeding Evelyn. There was now a sixty-minute window in which Evelyn would be home alone.

Linda walked onto the back porch and peered into the house until she saw Cindy leaving.

Once she was sure the nurse was gone, she tried the back door. The knob swung easily in her hand and the door opened soundlessly. Linda came inside the Blackburns' kitchen. There were dirty dishes in the sink, and a half-eaten apple on the table. Through the kitchen, she caught a glimpse of the living room. Evelyn sat in her wheelchair in front of the TV. Her back was to the kitchen. Linda recalled the word she had scratched onto the back of her hand.

Kill.

She shuddered.

What did Evelyn know?

The kitchen smelled of soap and lavender, yet the feeling Linda got from her surroundings wasn't warm or sweet. There was a rotting stench underneath that was just beyond the realms of perception, but there was decay here that she hadn't noticed before.

Evelyn's back was firmly towards her, her head resting to the side. Her iron-gray hair was tied in a messy bun, tendrils of hair sticking out in all directions. Her shoulders were covered by a thin shawl, and Linda thought she heard the old woman snore, though the TV was too loud to be sure. Taking confidence that Evelyn was sleeping and wouldn't hear her footsteps, Linda took the stairs between the living room and kitchen. There was no sign of anyone else in the house.

The stairs were gloomy, but gray light from the landing hit the pictures that lined the wall. Linda could feel the tiny faces in the frames follow her progress, and the tribal masks on the shelf ahead were deeply sinister in the half light.

Up on the first floor landing Linda scouted the ceiling for the entrance to the attic, but there was no faint outline, or even a dangling string to pull down the stairs. She opened the first door. It was the bathroom; it had 1990s fittings. She stepped inside and checked the ceiling… nothing. She put the door back exactly as it was, then slowly pivoted to face the room opposite.

It was Stewart's room. The room was fairly large and neatly kept. Framed posters of Slayer and Korn adorned the walls. There was a queen size bed. A desk sat along the opposite wall under shelves stocked with books and various decorative items.

She went inside this weird teenager's bedroom that was inhabited by a man in his mid-thirties. Linda spied another tribal mask with moldy feathers, a Darth Vader action figure, and a Magic Eight Ball. The only personal pictures were of a golden retriever. The window looked over the back garden. Linda closed the curtains firmly. Another empty ceiling, though. There were two other doors on the landing.

Was it possible that the entrance wasn't in the ceiling at all but behind a simple door? Linda opened one door. It was another bedroom, neatly kept but with less furniture. It had a generic nautical print above the bed, and pale blue wallpaper.

She hit the jackpot on the last one.

Dark mahogany stairs climbed up into the pale gloom of the tower. The door to the attic must be up there.

Linda took a deep breath, and she climbed the first step. The temperature was much cooler than it had been on the landing. She placed both hands on the walls beside her and climbed, getting chillier by the minute.

Her head emerged first in the attic.

Linda stood confused on the landing. She had thought the attic and the tower windows were two separate rooms. She scanned the floor, and in the middle there were fragments of a broken skirting rising at least two inches above the floorboards. The wall that had divided the two had been broken down.

It was a huge place. It was also a complete mess.

Broken furniture, boxes of clothes, and assorted knick-knacks littered every surface. There were snow globes, and a few broken toys that looked like they were used by children at the turn of the previous century. An old Navy uniform lay yellowing on top of a chest of drawers. There were plumed hats, and broken tennis rackets. There were clear demarcations of time. It had all been cobbled together to rest in a hodgepodge mess. The tailor's dummy stood sentinel at the front of the attic between two windows so the light caught either side leaving the middle in shadow.

Linda kept an eye out for any hunkered figures hiding behind some of the larger pieces of furniture. She hadn't been mistaken; she had seen a figure in here. Her sleep-deprived mind was already on edge, and now her pluming breath was fogging up her glasses.

Though the furniture was old, the clothes in the boxes were modern. There were quite a lot of them. There were six boxes in total, all full of women's clothes. Some were long modest dresses, but most were shorts, neat blouses with pretty prints, and skirts in every color of the rainbow. How many women had gone through this house to leave so many clothes behind?

Linda shuddered and rubbed her arms. It was exceptionally cold up here, even more so than their bathroom.

She walked slowly towards the windows that looked over the back garden. A small chest of drawers sat below them.

Spider webs were festooned all over the drawer, choked with dust. Linda couldn't see anyone in the attic but the pressure was building in the center of her shoulder blades.

She glanced back, but there was still no one there. Linda removed her glasses with shaking fingers. Her vision blurred instantly. Breathing heavily, she bit her lip to keep from screaming and cleaned her glasses vigorously.

A sudden skittering made her jump.

She jammed her glasses back on her nose, eyes wide and staring at the source of the noise. It had come from the side of the attic that looked onto the back garden.

There was a handprint on the grimy glass exactly where she had seen the figure.

She drew closer to the chest of drawers sitting directly beneath it.

The chest of drawers shuddered.

Linda cried out, jumped back, lost her balance and fell.

Something was squeaking and squealing behind it as if trapped.

Hands shaking, throat as dry as a bone, Linda held the chest of drawers and pulled them a little towards her.

A rat skittered from behind the drawer and zipped past her legs. Linda screamed and jumped out of its way. She bumped into the drawer and it skidded so one side protruded away from the wall.

Something fell and clattered dully against the floor behind it.

Drenched in cold sweat Linda peered cautiously around the drawer.

A square black phone lay on the dusty floor, screen side up.

Linda stared at it.

It was too modern to be part of any of the furniture or knickknacks up in the attic.

Why would someone leave their phone up here?

Linda picked it up.

She hissed and dropped it.

It was ice cold.

Flexing her fingers and frowning in concentration, she picked it up again and transferred it into her back pocket to examine later.

The oppression that had been building up around her became too much. She turned to run, but her vision doubled. She felt great pressure behind her neck as if a hand was pressing down trying to lever her head open and enter her skull.

The room changed before her eyes. Sunshine flitted across the floor but she could see the clouds outside as well. The feeling that someone was stalking her grew until she was shaking like a leaf.

Screaming, Linda held her head, and shook it to get the feeling away. The pressure lifted but only just. Linda didn't wait for it to go bad again.

She tried her best not to run down the stairs but it was impossible not to do so. She closed the door behind her with a quick snap, breathing heavily against the fear that still clawed at the back of her spine.

Down the main stairs she went, mind racing over what had just happened. What had that feeling been? When she had gone into the attic, she had been aware that someone might be in there. But the feeling she had gotten when the pressure had built on her neck was unlike any fear she had known.

The phone offered its own implications to the haunting. It

wasn't the miners; they didn't have access to this kind of technology. Whose was it? Had it belonged to Shannon? Tara? Or to another guest or employee? And why was it in the Blackburn attic?

She reached the lower landing and glanced quickly to see if Evelyn had heard her screams up in the attic. Evelyn's eyes were closed and her breathing was regular. Linda sent up a prayer of thanks and walked into the kitchen, where she stopped dead.

Dirt streaked the linoleum floor.

Oh no. If Stewart sees this, he'll know I was poking around!

Scrambling to the closet in the kitchen, Linda went looking for cleaning supplies. The door jammed and wouldn't come loose. Linda grunted, but the door was closed as if something was forcing it shut.

Linda stepped back. Her breathing was heavy, but calm was stealing over her. Something was playing games.

She tried the door again. This time it opened at her touch.

There were no cleaning supplies in the closet. Linda had found the basement instead. The dirt seemed to follow her; there were muddy stains on the stairs going all the way down to the basement floor.

They weren't her muddy tracks.

CHAPTER 29

The smell of rich earth was oppressive.

It washed over Linda in waves of cold as she tried to navigate the stairs, as if she were walking into an industrial size freezer. Painful goosebumps broke out all over her skin. She knew that she shouldn't be doing this alone, that this was risky. If Stewart came home right now she'd have a lot to explain, but she had to know what was down there. It was like a strange magnetic pull; no matter how much she tried to resist, she was incapable of stopping her limbs from going forward, like the bizarre dreams she'd been having.

Though polished on the outside, the inside of the basement door was dusty, and the ceiling was lined with cobwebs.

Spiders and cold spots; just like the chest up in the attic. There was a manifestation here too; but how many were there in this house? Was it possible she was dealing with a cluster of ghosts? That thought made her feel defeated.

Her hands patted the wall on her right to find a light switch, panic crawling over her insides. She was halfway down when she finally felt the telltale ridge of plastic and flipped it up.

Corrosive orange light scorched her retinas. She winced, shutting her eyes against the assault, but a bright red ball still blazed, as if the light was imprinted on the inside of her eyelid, an echo of trauma.

Blinking them open slowly, Linda looked around her.

The basement windows were boarded shut.

The ugly yellow wallpaper dotted with gray flowers was peeling off in places. It was much larger than the basement in the other apartment and messier still. Unlike the abandoned attic, this place looked like it had been visited often but Linda couldn't see why. There was no washing machine or ironing board, nor any other piece of furniture to show the rooms purpose.

When she looked over the banister, she saw something that made her toes curl in their shoes.

Dirt was everywhere. It was piled up against the wall and scattered all over the floor with bits of broken wood. The way the mess was spread away from the dark crevice underneath the stairs it looked like the darkness had vomited it all out in a fit of fury.

The sense of the bizarre was stronger here than it had been in the other basement. Where she had felt acute unease in the other basement, she had been able to go down and get a few things done in the bad lighting.

This was different. The lighting was better, illuminating all the shadowy corners, but she felt dread in her bones. She didn't want to go down, didn't want to touch the banister lest she fall over. She wanted to get away, but she was too afraid to turn off the light because a certainty was building in her mind that once the room was plunged into darkness, something would come out from beneath the stairs and grab her.

Linda backtracked up the stairs. She didn't want to turn her back on this room but she was now sure where the dirt came from and what the room led to; it had turned her blood to ice. Something, some dreaded force, had pulled her down, coaxing her to come down and explore the source of the dirt. Linda already knew what was down there. The mine shaft was blocked, but there was an entrance here.

Linda knew she should go down and find the source but she didn't want to do it alone. Her hands shook at the thought of it, her breath shook and came out in sputters at the thought of being lost in the dark.

Linda suspected she'd found the entrance she was looking for earlier today.

Once in the warm kitchen, she snatched a long wooden spoon from the sink and leaned inside the basement door to flip the switch. Cobwebs clung to her hair, and her shirt. She squirmed, sucked in air, and bit her teeth down hard to prevent herself from screaming.

Gripping the doorframe, she leaned forward on tiptoe. The edge of the spoon collided with the switch and flipped it down. The basement went pitch black. Linda pulled her arm back so fast she nearly lost her balance. She shut the door as quietly as she could, and placed the spoon back in the sink.

A low hum had been building up since she had come back up from the basement. Linda wanted to leave immediately but the sound kept her rooted in the middle of the kitchen. Where was it coming from? It sounded like a stifled scream: someone gagged and bound desperate to get her attention.

What was going on in this house?

She turned in a slow circle to register where exactly the sound was coming from.

It came from the living room, from the slightly thrumming body of Evelyn Blackburn.

CHAPTER 30

Noise from the television muffled her moan, but not quite enough to erase it completely.

Had Evelyn heard her coming in and going about her house? She must be afraid an intruder had entered her house.

"Dr. Blackburn." Linda went to sit by her. "It's just me. I thought I saw something in your attic window so I went to check." She couldn't bear the idea of leaving the old woman in distress. Plus, it was highly unlikely Evelyn would be able to tell Stewart she had taken a tour of their wing.

She walked closer to the old woman. Evelyn's hair had spilled out of her bun; it was the color of dirty snow and just as wispy. There was a dark stain on Evelyn's dress and Linda wasn't sure what it was. The woman stank. Linda wondered when she had last been bathed.

She placed a hand on her shoulder. "Do you need anything while I'm here?"

A clawed hand grabbed hers in a tight grip. Broken yellow nails scratched her skin.

"Ouch," Linda cried. "It's okay, Dr. Blackburn. It's just me. You don't have to be scared."

Evelyn was still keening in that horrible way; her contorted face was a mask of agony. Her eyes were wet with tears, desperation shone out of them. Her fidgeting fingers jabbed toward the TV cabinet.

Linda looked at the innocuous piece of furniture.

"Do you need me to change the channel?"

The moaning rose an octave higher.

As much as Linda was repulsed by Evelyn Blackburn, she also felt a lot of pity for the woman.

Linda walked over to the TV. An old rerun of *Cheers* was on. The laugh track was distracting and grated on her nerves. She was jumpy. Every sound felt too loud. The TV cabinet was a series of small shelves and drawers leaving enough space in the middle for an old box TV.

There was no remote control.

Linda opened the drawer directly beneath the TV.

Her own face stared up at her.

Time stood still as Linda reached into the drawer and pulled out the pinned documents from the drawer. They were contracts of every employee that had worked at the retreat, and signed disclaimers from guests that had been to the retreat were in another folder.

Hers was at the very top. The small passport-sized picture in the corner stood sentry over all her information. Hands shaking, Linda went through the papers. There were employees from Tennessee, Texas, and as far away as Nevada. Four documents in, Linda met Shannon Dorothy.

She was just as Grady had described. Blonde, slightly overweight, and shy with the hint of a smile on her wide generous mouth. Her eyes were clear cornflower blue and full of doubt and uncertainty.

Linda touched the picture, tracing the line of Shannon's jaw.

What happened to you?

Evelyn began to moan again.

Sighing, Linda opened a few more drawers to find the remote control but found nothing but broken knickknacks, a few paperclips, old bills, some pens, and dead batteries. The last one was too high up for Linda to see within. She had to climb the bottom drawers to be able to peek inside.

The drawer got stuck after only an inch had opened. Linda struggled with it in her awkward position. "You know, I don't think this is where it is, Mrs. Blackburn. I'm sorry."

Evelyn groaned.

Linda was about to step down but the drawer suddenly shot out under her hand as if it had been pushed from the other side. She lost her footing and tumbled down on her bottom. The drawer clattered against the floor. Papers rained down on her head.

"Great!" Linda cried.

She swept up pages and cards, stuffing them willy-nilly in the drawer. A small photo album lay open where it had slid under Evelyn's wheelchair. Going on hands and knees, cursing under her breath, Linda retrieved the album.

Evelyn practically cried out.

It wasn't a coherent sound but her slack face was more alert, her eyes kept darting to the closed album in Linda's hand.

"What?" Linda asked. "Do you want to see the album?"

Evelyn's hand tapped her upper arm twice.

Linda opened the album.

There were pictures of a chestnut-haired girl who looked slightly familiar to Linda.

The girl smiled up at the camera. She was sitting in the back garden of Blackburn Manor, the flowers behind her in full bloom. Something glinted in the hollow of her throat but the picture wasn't clear.

In another picture, the young woman was at the stove in Stewart's apartment stirring a steaming pot. Her head was tilted back, and mouth was open in delight. Linda could hear the laughter in her head.

The last picture was a selfie and taken in Stewart's bedroom. The girl was sitting up in bed, the sheets covering her breasts. Stewart was sleeping beside her. Her smile was less erratic, more natural, her green eyes didn't hold the manic glint.

The implications of that picture rang in Linda's head like warning cymbals. Because it wasn't Stewart's sleeping naked body, or the girl's obvious post-coital happiness that had caught Linda's attention. It was the small peridot pendant shaped like a clover at the girl's throat.

The same peridot she saw in her nightmares.

"What is this?" Linda's voice trembled. She glanced up at Evelyn, whose face was wet with tears. "Who is this?"

Evelyn's moans were now weepy, like a woman holding back her sobs.

Linda looked back at the smiling girl. She had never gotten a good look at the face in her dreams but why was she familiar? Placing the album in Evelyn's lap Linda went back to the drawers and took out the employee contracts. She shuffled through them till she found the girl at the very end of the pile.

Tara Walsh.

She was the other girl Linda talked about with Grady.

She had seen pictures on Facebook but they had been grainy and unclear. No wonder she looked familiar.

Tara was smiling in her picture, if that's what you could call it. All her teeth were on display, her cheeks dented with dimples. A mess of rich chestnut hair framed her heart-shaped face but the roots were dark brunette. Tara's hair was dyed.

Her eyes were the most striking feature.

Categorically green, they were arresting not for their beauty, but the manic desperation prominent in them. Her contract placed her as a client/employee about ten months ago at Blackburn Manor. "What happened to Tara, Dr. Blackburn?" Linda asked, putting the photos back in their sleeve. "Is that what you were trying to tell me?"

Evelyn moaned and swayed but was incapable of speech. Her face was awash with tears. They settled in her wrinkles and shone under the sunlight.

"Evelyn, please," Linda begged. "I need to stop this before it happens to me too. Is it the miners? What did Stewart do?"

Evelyn stopped moaning. Her eyes grew large in fear.

Linda stopped talking.

She'd heard it too.

The sound of an engine coming to a halt in the drive before it was cut out completely.

A car door opened in the silence and shut a few seconds later.

Heavy footsteps trudged up the porch steps.

Stewart Blackburn was home.

CHAPTER 31

Linda froze for a good few seconds till Evelyn groaned: a sharp sound to get her to move.

Linda scrambled up on her feet as quietly as she could and threw the album in the drawer.

The footsteps stopped on the top of the porch.

Linda's palms were slick with sweat.

She tried to wedge the drawer back in with arms extended, hitting the wood at odd angles.

The steps got closer to the door.

Keys jangled.

Linda thought about giving up, just throwing the drawer down and running out of the house.

Snap.

Click.

The drawer found the right angle and slid in.

Keys rattled inside the lock.

The drawer got stuck halfway in.

The lock turned.

Linda gave up on closing the drawer completely; she scooted inside the kitchen and hid behind the wall.

The back door was directly in front of her, but she couldn't risk coming out of her hiding place.

"Hello, Mom." Stewart said cheerfully. "I brought bagels. Too bad you can't have any." He laughed.

Linda placed a hand on her mouth lest he hear her breathing.

Footsteps came down the hall towards the kitchen.

"Mmppmm!" Evelyn groused.

"In a minute," Stewart snapped. "I'm not your serving boy, Mom."

Linda's heart sank to her knees.

Evelyn groaned louder.

"What?" Stewart shouted.

A sharp screech tore the air and ended on a thud.

Linda risked a peek. Body shaking from head to toe she leaned forward a little, hands splayed against the wall.

Stewart had his back to her. He was towering over Evelyn, whose wheelchair had been turned to face the kitchen where Linda was hiding. Stewart's fists were bunched by his side. One hand held a paper bag.

Terror shot up her spine. Heart thudding against her ribs, her body flashed hot and cold.

"I told you to shut up!" Stewart growled. "Your days of lecturing me are over. Look at you," he sneered. "You can't even wipe your own ass anymore. You're filthy."

He jabbed Evelyn in the chest with a meaty finger.

Evelyn glanced down at the finger, seemingly dejected, but when she turned her eyes up again they looked at Linda directly for a fleeting moment but their plea was simple: I have him distracted; run!

Linda didn't need to be told twice.

Inching back, keeping well in the cover of the wall, she tiptoed to the back door. Her arms were stretched behind her to make sure she didn't bump into anything but her eyes were riveted on Stewart's back.

His corded muscles, the height and breadth of him had been reassuring when she had first met him. Now he looked like a juggernaut of pain just waiting to be unleashed.

Her trembling fingers met the doorknob.

She froze.

How was she supposed to open the door without making any noise?

"Mmmmmm! Mmmmmm. MMMMMMMMM!"

Evelyn began to scream.

Linda twisted the knob and swung the door open.

"Shut up, you stupid cow! Someone will hear you," Stewart hissed.

Linda stepped outside and under the cover of Evelyn's muted screams, she shut the door with a soft click. She didn't stick around. She bent down so Stewart wouldn't see her from the kitchen window and tiptoed to her own backdoor and let herself in. It was only then she allowed herself to break down into sobs of uncontrollable fear.

CHAPTER 32

After what felt like ages, Linda wiped her face of tears. Her sleepless night was catching up to her, and the emotional turmoil was too much for her to bear. This was not the time to sit down and cry, no time to show her vulnerability. She didn't know exactly what was going on in this house, but she was in danger. They needed to get out of here as soon as possible. She'd come back later to deal with the haunting.

But how would they leave?

The truck was still in the garage. She had to wake Ashley up, and they would have to walk out of the door in front of Stewart to actually make it out of the house. What if he stopped them? What if he became violent?

Ignoring the whisked eggs on the counter, Linda poured herself a glass of water from the faucet. She drank in slow sips, willing her hysterics to come under control.

She didn't know for sure if Stewart had harmed anyone, nor

did she have any proof that he was guilty of making any of the girls disappear. But the cell phone in the attic, the intimate pictures with Tara, and the clods of earth in the basement... All pointed to more guilt than innocence.

And the peridot pendant in the shape of a clover... Mrs. Grady had been right about a haunting, but it was more than the miners.

Panic threatened to bubble up her throat and consume her again.

She tamped it down.

A plan formed in her head.

She made a beeline for the phone in the living room. She dialed a number anxiously. The dial tone blared in her ears. A soft click and then someone answered.

"Scott! I–" Linda tried to keep the desperation out of her voice.

"Hey, it's Scott. I'm busy right now so leave me a message and I'll get back to you."

Linda bit back her disappointment.

"Scott, please, it's important. I have a lead on Shannon and Tara. I think I even know where we can find them. But I need you to come right now. I think Ashley and I are in danger."

She placed the receiver down and hoped that Scott would hear the message soon. With Scott in the house, Stewart would keep away. It wasn't much in the way of security, but Linda felt better knowing help was on the way.

She pulled out the phone from her pocket. She pressed a few keys, but the screen remained blank. It was a model similar to Ashley's phone, so the charger might work on this one. Linda saw the charger dangling from a socket in the kitchen.

Hooking the device up, she waited to see if anything would

light up to show the phone was charging. A green battery sign showed up on the screen with a large 0%. Linda wondered whose phone it was; probably Shannon's, or Tara's.

She guessed she'd find out soon enough, but there were more important things to do before that.

The walls of the house seemed to close in on her. She couldn't stay there another moment, but she could wait across the street at Grady's house. Once she'd thought of the idea she knew it was the right decision. She could discuss the things she had learned with Grady, and be safe from any influences in the house.

She decided to do just that.

"Ashley?" she called up the stairs.

She took the steps two at a time to reach the landing. Rain began to patter across the roof.

She walked down the office hall to the conference room Ashley had been sleeping in.

Ashley wasn't there.

For a moment Linda was completely possessed by fear for her sister. She had to make an effort to push back the disturbing thoughts that came to mind. Backtracking down the hall and a floor down to the employee rooms Linda found Ashley sleeping in her room.

She sighed with relief, but something about her posture made Linda uneasy.

Ashley was a messy sleeper; always had been. She rejoiced in sleeping on her stomach, tucking a pillow under one of her legs while the other dangled off the bed. Her hands were always in the seven or five o'clock position depending on which side her head was on.

That wasn't how she was sleeping now.

Her back was as straight as a board, both hands resting firmly underneath her breasts. Her pale mouth wasn't slack-jawed or drooling but set primly. She didn't look asleep at all. She looked dead.

"Ashley?" Linda placed a hand on her sister's forehead. It was cool, but not deathly cold. A steady pulse throbbed in her forehead, and Linda could see the minute rise and fall of her chest. "Ashley, wake up!"

She shook her shoulders and prodded her cheek. Ashley's eyelashes fluttered.

"Come on, Ash!" Linda shook her harder. "Wake up, please!"

Ashley opened her eyes. They were alert, without any trace of sleep. Linda was a little taken aback by her sister's frank gaze.

"Come on." Linda got up off the bed. "Scott will be here soon." She didn't know if this was true but she hoped it was. "We have to go to Grady's and wait for him to get here."

She started towards the door.

Ashley snored. Linda stopped in her tracks.

Ashley was sitting up in bed. She was curiously motionless.

She was about to shake Ashley awake when someone knocked on the front door.

Linda licked her dry lips. Had Scott already arrived?

The dark clouds still rumbled in the sky. Linda could see flashes of lightning within the nexus of whirling black. She climbed down the stairs, one hand tracing the wall. Why did she feel like the house had conjured up the sudden terrible weather?

The knocking was urgent now.

Linda strode through the kitchen to the living room.

"Scott, thank God you're here." She opened the door.

"Stewart." Stewart stood outside the doorframe. "I've always been Stewart."

CHAPTER 33

Linda's hands fell limp by her side.
She couldn't think, she couldn't even move her body. She was sure her face betrayed her fear.

Stewart was looking at her quizzically; his muscular form blocked the entire doorframe casting her in deeper shadow.

"You look like you've seen a ghost," he said, walking inside.

Across the street, a curtain twitched, and Linda was heartened that Mrs. Grady had seen Stewart enter the living room.

"Hey," Stewart called. "Are you waiting for someone?"

"Yes, actually," Linda said. She willed herself to move and closed the door.

"Scott, right?" Stewart grinned.

"Do you need anything?" She was cold and distant, hoping he'd take a hint and go away.

Stewart laughed. It wasn't jovial or good-humored. The laugh was high, and edged with steel.

"Oh, I need plenty," he said. He stood in the middle of the

living room, hands stuffed in pockets. His grin was large and goofy, but it did not match the fiery glint in his eye. "But we'll get to that later. I wanted to talk to you about this silly idea of yours of filing a lawsuit. In fact, I was so anxious you'd leave before I got home that I came back as fast as I could."

"Excuse me?" Linda frowned. Maybe a show of anger would stop this silly charade in its tracks. As it was, Stewart was making her very nervous.

His hand shot out. Linda flinched.

It stroked her hair.

"What are you doing?" Linda backed away like a scalded cat.

He held up his hand, grinning broadly. "Spider web. Your hair's chock full of them."

Linda touched her hair self-consciously.

Did he know she'd been in his house?

"Ye… yes," Linda stammered, trying to find a good excuse. "I was cleaning out the corners in the upper hall. The place is infested with them. You should do something about the rats as well."

"Rats?" Stewart lifted a sardonic brow.

"You have an infestation on your hands."

"Oh, you don't know the half of it." If it were possible his grin widened. "I have far worse things than rats on my property."

The shrill ring of a cell phone interrupted them. Linda nearly jumped out of her skin. Stewart checked his phone, but it was silent. Linda walked to the kitchen, where the sound was coming from.

The phone from the attic was ringing. Its screen glowed. It screamed for attention.

"It's Ashley's girlfriend," Linda lied. "I'd better get this. Excuse me."

Linda took the phone off the charging device and answered the call. It was still deathly cold and stung her hands.

"Hello?" she whispered, still in shock that the phone could receive calls.

"Help me..." The soft female voice was familiar. It was the voice she'd heard in the basement calling her name.

"Mom?" Linda yelped.

"No one will help you now, Shannon. I'll get away with this. Again." Stewart's voice came from the phone.

Linda reeled from shock. She took the phone away from her ear and looked at the screen. It was completely blank once again. She glanced back in the living room. Stewart sat sprawled on the sofa grinning at her. How could that be possible?

She placed the phone back by her ear.

"Somebody will find her body in the mine shaft like I did," the woman was saying. "You can't hide what you did to Tara forever."

"Are you threatening me, Shannon?" Stewart's voice growled in the phone. "You don't have to worry about Tara. You can keep her company."

Shannon screamed. The sound of something heavy crashing down steep stairs echoed through the receiver, then stopped. A gurgling choking cough punctuated the silence, then a whisper, soft as pigeon down.

"Trapped. Lost. Free me..."

The phone vibrated once and then became perfectly still.

CHAPTER 34

Licking her chapped lips, Linda turned back to the living room.

She pocketed the phone. So that was it. The phone belonged to Shannon. Stewart killed her in the attic by pushing her down the stairs; that was Shannon's influence in the haunting. She'd need it later if what Shannon had said was true.

It didn't occur to her to doubt the experience she had just had, because it was clear now that her world was thinner around the edges. She could see things, hear things others couldn't. She was more vulnerable and receptive to voices from the other side.

So it hadn't been her mother warning her in the basement after all; it was Shannon. It was no surprise she had been mistaken; she dreamed those voices more than she really heard them.

How else had Shannon tried to help her?

But what about the miners?

It begged the question who the source of the manifestation was. Which source was she looking for? How malevolent were they?

And Tara, poor murdered Tara? How much of the haunting was her?

Linda remembered the pictures she found in Stewart's apartment, the bright green eyes of Tara Walsh and the equally green pendant at her throat. The pictures were quite damning. Stewart had conducted an affair with a guest, a massive breach of conduct. Linda recalled Stewart asking her out to dinner and only now realized how unethical that suggestion was. She shuddered.

Shannon had mentioned Tara was buried in the mine shaft, and Stewart had promised Shannon would join her there. Linda's assumption had been correct, the mine shaft was where the source was, but what was the source?

Walking back into the living room, Linda couldn't help but feel a pulsing rage at the man sitting on her sofa. It was the same feeling that had erupted on the fateful day Jackson had driven her too far over the edge, and she had lashed out with a knife. But this feeling was less erratic, it was cautious like the pointed edge of a sword. There was fear there too, of course there was. She'd be stupid not to be scared.

"I'm glad you came by, Stewart," Linda said, voice quivering. "This way I can say goodbye."

Stewart's smile stiffened. "What do you mean?"

"I told you yesterday that I will not be continuing on as a guest," she said. She went over to the window and twitched the curtains aside. The house across the street was still. No one stood on the porch. Grady wasn't staring out the window. The sky grew darker as the second bout of rain lashed across the earth. "Ashley and I are willing to work here but live off-site."

Stewart chuckled. "You look so hot when you're angry."

"What?" Linda turned around, and the curtains closed behind her. Linda was perturbed by his casual smile.

He held out a hand for her to take, but she backed away. That made him laugh harder.

"I know what this is really about." He nodded. "You've had enough of me pretending this thing between us is platonic." He got up and stood tall. Red lines were streaked along his neck. "I know you like me. And oh, Linda, I like you too."

"What are you talking about?" Linda took another step back towards the kitchen. "You're crazy!"

"Crazy in love." Stewart lunged forward.

Linda cried out and sidestepped him. She ran for the front door, but strong hands gripped her arms, hindering her progress.

"No, you don't," he growled in her ear, his hot breath on her neck.

"Let go of me!" Linda screamed.

"I've waited too long for this." He licked her neck. Linda squirmed, nausea building in her stomach in waves. His hands ran up her waist, creeping fingers inching closer to her breasts.

Linda cried, her chest heaving with panicked sobs. "Please, let go of me!"

Stewart laughed like a greedy child who had gotten his hands on a bag of chocolates. Linda felt bile rise up her throat. Her own nails clawed at his hands, striking him to loosen his grip but to no avail.

"It's just so tempting seeing such pretty women move through the house." Stewart giggled. "But Stewart can't touch them; Stewart can't even talk to them because they're so damaged."

"Tara wasn't enough?" Linda shot back, hoping the name would distract him, make him cautious.

"So you know about Tara." His grip tightened. "Oh, you'll be a nice substitute. I knew you'd been inside the house. You left a trail of crumbs everywhere; just like that pesky Shannon. Good. Then you know what I'm capable of. Mother couldn't stand it though. It completely took her over the edge when she saw me strangling Tara to death."

Tara's pretty face loomed in front of Linda's eyes; how happy she had been with Stewart only for him to kill her.

"Don't worry," said Stewart with a smirk. "You'll get to know Tara soon. I'll bury you in the cave along with her and Shannon."

He hiked up her shirt. Linda yelped in surprise, shaken out of her roiling thoughts, her mind pulsing red. All thoughts abandoned her, as what was happening to her seared itself on the forefront of her mind.

He was going to assault her. He was going to kill her.

Someone came screaming from behind them.

Stewart's grip didn't slacken; it tightened and twisted as he turned. It was instinct for Linda to turn, as well to avoid his hands pinching her skin too hard. She saw Ashley bearing down on Stewart with a frying pan in hand, her face a mask of feral rage.

The metal hit bone with a sickening thwack.

Stewart went reeling to the floor, taking Linda with him.

Linda's jaw hit the floor. She cried out as searing pain shot up her jaw and nestled in her head, but it was drowned in Stewart's yowling curses. Pushing his hands away, she rolled away from him to crouch by the front door.

Ashley was breathing hard. Her teeth were bared. She kicked and punched Stewart, the frying pan discarded after the first blow. Blood smeared the floor. A shallow cut bled across Stewart's forehead.

Linda hardly had time to register what was happening in front of her when the front door burst open.

Scott stood in the doorframe, his gun held out in front of him.

He looked rooted to the spot, taking in the scene.

"He murdered them," Linda screamed. "He murdered Shannon and Tara!"

Whatever shock Scott was under, it finally broke. He strode into the apartment, stuffing his gun back in its holster. Linda got back up on unsteady feet. Mrs. Grady was climbing the porch steps beyond the open door.

"Are we too late?" Mrs. Grady asked, her green eyes sharp and alert. "I called Scott as soon as I saw Stewart enter your apartment."

"No." Linda grabbed Grady's hand, the urge to laugh aloud only mitigated by the need to cry. "You're just in time."

"Back up, Ashley," Scott was advising. "I've got it from here."

But Ashley wouldn't stop. She started a new assault, spit flying from her mouth, her face red, eyes focused on Stewart.

"Okay, that's enough now." Scott restrained her, placing both arms around her. She struggled, screaming in frustration. Spittle flew out of her sneering mouth, and her red-rimmed eyes were bulging out of her head.

Scott inched her towards the kitchen, struggling to keep on his feet.

Stewart groaned on the floor. A whooping cough racked his body, and he spat out blood. Linda saw fragments of broken teeth glisten in the crimson spit. He lolled from side to side humming a strange gurgling moan. Linda realized he was laughing. "You think you've won?" he said haltingly. "Ha!" Blood sprayed from his mouth. "She won't let you go that easy."

"You have the right to remain silent," Scott spat. "God! Ashley, what's gotten into you?"

Ashley had bitten his forearm. Linda sprinted forward to help Scott.

"Ashley, hey." Linda hugged her sister. "It's okay. I'm okay."

Ashley stiffened. She stopped struggling. Linda managed to extract her from Scott's restrictive grasp. All the frantic energy drained out of Ashley. Linda guided her to a kitchen chair.

"Now to arrest this moron." Scott turned back to the living room.

He stopped.

Linda saw Stewart standing across from Scott, Ashley's discarded frying pan in hand. Scott pulled his gun out of its holster and pointed it at Stewart. The manic smile had only intensified and looked far worse in the middle of Stewart's bleeding face. "None of you can escape. Only I could ever hope to control her. I don't know what exactly she became, but Tara loved me… madly. To death. And she was jealous; extremely jealous. The thing she became is bitter, and obsessive. And you can bet she hates any young woman here… any potential rival. She'll drain you all like she did Marisa. Oh, stupid, pathetic Marisa was a hoot to watch, eh, Linda?"

"No it wasn't, you psycho!" Linda shouted.

"She wanted me." Stewart twirled the frying pan in his hand. Grady was inching closer behind him. Scott had one hand on the butt of his gun. "The sad cow. Too bad she's dead."

"You sick bastard," Mrs. Grady snarled.

Stewart jumped and turned. He hadn't seen Grady at all.

Scott took that moment to lunge forward, but he hadn't banked on Stewart's speed.

Stewart swung the pan, striking Scott's fingers.

He bellowed. The gun went flying across the room.

Linda saw Stewart head for it.

All sense of preservation had gone out the window since she had broken into the other apartment. She was completely running on instinct. Instinct made her dive for the gun, hand outstretched.

Her fingers grazed the metal barrel but her momentum carried her too far away. She went sprawling across the floor. Stewart wasn't so unlucky. He managed to grab the gun.

With a triumphant cry he vaulted himself on top of Linda. "There's no point resisting. I'm the master of everything in the manor."

Linda slapped him.

Stewart's face changed from manic cheer to hateful wrath in seconds. "You think you're better than me?" He slapped her so hard that her face whiplashed the other way.

Her cheek stung, but the fear of being killed didn't manifest. The rage of years of oppression and abuse roared inside her like an angry sea. Adrenaline coursed through her veins fueled by the rage at all the men in her life: her no-good father, her abusive fiancé, and now Stewart.

Ashley came screaming at them, eyes wide, teeth bared.

Stewart swung the gun at her.

"No!" Linda screamed.

She bucked her hips, dislodging Stewart from on top of her.

The gun exploded in the small space, its screaming echo tearing though the madness, but the chaos did not end. Ashley kept coming. Scott ran towards Stewart, holding his injured hand. Linda scrambled out from underneath Stewart's shifted weight, forcing him to topple.

Stewart roared, the gun pointing directly in Linda's face.

Her whole life flashed before her eyes, every miserable minute of it. Bitter regret was immediately displaced by the sense of rage at being treated like dirt all her life.

Linda lunged at his gun-wielding hand, forcing the gun away at the last minute.

The second gunshot wasn't as jarring as before, but it was the fatal one.

Blood mixed with pieces of flesh and bone splattered across the floor.

Linda stared at Stewart and he stared back.

"You... bitch," he wheezed.

The bullet had hit the juncture between his throat and collarbone, shattering it completely. He wheezed and gurgled, drowning in his own blood. Strong hands grasped at Linda's front, pulling her forward and onto him.

Linda cried and slapped his hands away.

"Tara... won't let you escape." Stewart coughed blood. "You're... prisoners now."

"What is he talking about?" Scott was leaning down by Stewart. He had retrieved his gun and holstered it but his hands were shaking badly as he reached for his radio. Linda guessed nothing like this had ever happened in a small town like Keystone and the sight of so much blood was jarring.

Linda knew what Stewart had meant. He had just revealed that Tara was the main source of the manifestation.

"Necklace," Stewart laughed, his mouth a crimson slash. Blood sloshed out of his mouth. He coughed, and spluttered choking on his own blood. He propped his head up again and swallowed. "Won't... ever... find it. This..." He swung one pointed finger around the living room. "Our... playground. We'll start with you." He grinned a bloody smile at Linda. "Look forward to hearing... your screams."

"I won't let that happen." Linda wiped the tears from her cheeks.

Stewart chuckled. The blood around his face was a small pool. It had seeped through his clothes and Linda had the distinct image of blood dripping down the basement ceiling. His erratic, roaming eyes grew dimmer. He was losing his grip on life.

"Imagine all the women who will go through this house, Linda," Stewart said, his voice now as clear as a bell, surprisingly. "I'll join Tara, and you can see us torture them all for an eternity to come."

Despite his fatal wound, he laughed, loud and hysterical. Linda's nails dug into her palms. Stewart kept hooting with laughter, the sound grating on her shot nerves.

"Shut up!" Linda screamed. "Shut up, shut up!"

"Who are you talking to?" Scott placed a hand on her shoulder.

"Him of course," Linda gestured towards Stewart. "He just won't stop laughing."

"He's not laughing, Linda." Scott was looking at her strangely.

"Of course he is." Linda wanted to press her hands on her

ears to muffle the gloating sound. "Didn't you hear him gloat about the women he will torture in this house?"

"No." Scott shook his head. "He's dead."

Linda did a double take. She looked down at Stewart's relaxed body, his glassy, staring eyes. His mouth was indeed stuck in a grotesque smile, but he wasn't laughing. He was as dead as a doornail.

PART VI
ASHES TO ASHES

CHAPTER 35

Ashley was sitting on the living room sofa. Her skin was pale and had a clammy sheen like she was suffering from a fluctuating fever. She stared at Stewart's face.

"I did that?" she asked faintly. "Lin, did I do that?" Panic was paramount in her voice.

Linda hugged her sister. "He was attacking me," she soothed. "I would have done the same for you."

"But—" Ashley stammered.

"You're going to have to come down to the station with me," Scott said. "I need your statements."

"He's right." Grady nodded. "You should leave as soon as possible. This place isn't safe for you."

"It isn't safe for anyone." Linda shook her head. She got up to face Scott. "But no, I can't leave."

"Yes, you can, and you will." Scott turned on her. "I have to call a coroner and explain what happened here. We'll need the whole department down here."

"None of that matters right now," Linda said. "We need to find the receptacle and destroy it. I won't have this happening to anyone else. I just won't!"

"Commendable as that is," Grady said," how do you propose to do it? We have no leads, no idea where it is, and I'm still confused by Stewart's involvement in it all."

"Your theory about a haunting was correct," Linda said. "Only it wasn't the miners driving it. I've had phenomena from the miners, but it was limited and wasn't malicious. The book you gave me pointed me towards the legend of the banshee. There were similarities with that but it isn't exactly the same."

Scott scoffed. He looked between Grady's serious face and Linda's.

"Then who is behind it?" Grady asked.

"Tara Walsh," Linda said. "Stewart was having an affair with her. He murdered her around the time of her disappearance. It's her pendant I've been seeing in dreams, a peridot clover, and now I'm sure she's the one singing in that recording. After her death, the haunting began. I think his dog was the first victim. You said it acted strangely and threw itself down the porch."

"Are you insane?" Scott finally broke his silence. "You're crazy."

"No, I'm not," Linda said. "But you don't have to believe me. You want to know what happened to Tara Walsh and Shannon Dorothy? I know where their bodies are."

Scott's eyes widened. "Where?"

"There in the secret mine shaft that the miners were tunneling to Blackburn Manor."

"It makes sense," said Grady after a few seconds. "So you mean that Tara was buried in the mines where the Irish miners had been shot dead. There would be some Irish influence in the unconsecrated ground after hosting the Catholic Irish victims for a century. It probably helped turned the tortured soul of Tara into a sort of banshee."

Linda looked at Grady and then Scott's bewildered face. "That's why I asked you to take me through the mine to the speakeasy."

"We went there, Linda," Scott snapped. "It was inaccessible."

"It opens up in the basement from the other apartment." She ran a hand through her hair. "It's a horrible place, and I don't want to go alone, but we have to do this. We have to destroy the receptacle Tara was attached to, and Shannon's phone. Poor Shannon is part of the haunting too. I suspect she tried to warn me through dreams, but Tara's influence probably prevented her from getting through. Shannon's soul is a prisoner of the thing that Tara became."

She retrieved the device from her pocket.

Scott's eyes widened. "Where did you find it?"

"In Stewart's attic." Linda shuddered. "He pushed her down the attic stairs."

"I'm going to need that." Two points of color rose in Scott's cheeks. "It's evidence." He held out his hand.

Linda put the phone back in her pocket. "I can't give it to you. I need to destroy it to release Shannon's spirit."

Scott rolled his eyes. "Really? You expect me to buy this?"

"You don't have to buy it," Linda snapped. "Look, the bodies should be enough evidence to prove Stewart's guilt. If the bodies aren't there, I'll give you the phone." She crossed her fingers behind her back.

"No," Scott said. He took out his phone. "I'll find them anyway. I'll call Carter and get a team down here."

"And what?" Linda said trying a new tack. "Last time something big happened in Keystone, the Hackridge department stomped all over it. You said it yourself, they always make a mess of things. You can be sure if they hear of a high profile murder case, they will want to be in the thick of it, pushing you to the back where you won't even get credit."

Scott looked appalled.

Grady nodded. "I'm with Linda."

Scott shrugged. "Okay, but I call the shots here. You two," he pointed at Grady and Ashley, "will stay out of the house. I don't want anyone contaminating the crime scene. Linda, you will guide me to the basement, and then you must get out of there as well. I won't have any of you coming to harm on my watch."

"Good." Linda nodded. "Come on, we should go. Ashley?"

"Hmm?" Ashley looked worse than she had a minute ago. Her eyelids drooped, and she looked dead on her feet.

Linda walked over to her sister, and touched her forehead. It was cool. She wasn't running a fever. She figured the sudden exertion in her fight with Stewart had exhausted her. The bags under her eyes were purple bruises and she looked listless. Linda was painfully reminded of Marisa.

"Do you think you're up for it?" Linda asked. "You don't look so good."

"Still better than you," Ashley joked, but she still looked haggard. "I'll be fine. You should worry about Scott's hand. I think it's broken."

"It's not broken," Scott protested. "Just a little bruised. Let's go. I'm going to call Milo for backup."

"Stewart's front door might be locked," Linda said walking towards the kitchen. "The back door was open when I went in there earlier. We'll also need digging supplies from the shed."

"I'll get those," Ashley grumbled.

"I don't know how accessible the tunnel is from the basement, so you should also get a crowbar," Linda added. She held the screen door open. Everyone filed out onto the porch. She also looked a little pale, but her eyes were steady and determined. Once Scott ensured that everybody was out, he closed the door. Taking out his phone, he walked out into the back garden to call the police.

Linda watched Ashley enter the shed and a thought occurred to her. She made sure Scott's back was turned before she opened the back door to her apartment gently. "Wait right here," she whispered to Grady. "I'll be right back."

Linda slipped quickly into the house. Stewart's body was an eyesore. It both attracted and repulsed attention at the same time. Linda ignored it as best she could and climbed the stairs taking them two at a time.

The portraits were more animated than ever, their occupants twisting in horrific pain, but Linda kept her eyes averted. She now knew that the portraits on the landing were part of the manifestation, that if she looked at even one of them she would be ensnared and taken into a hallucination once again.

She came to a screeching halt in her room. She walked over to where she had dropped her handbag earlier and retrieved Grady's book, *Lore of the Land – A Concise History of Irish Folklore, Legends, and Myth*.

She opened it and went through the pages to reach Colin Prim's diary. Her finger slipped on the page, then stopped.

"*She is dead, we must bury her.*"

I told them that was nonsense; the girl looked dead, I granted them that, but there was something alive about her nonetheless.

They surged forward to take her. "We will break the curse; we will release her!"

Linda closed the book, and took it. She went briskly down the stairs and would have immediately headed out the back door had she not glanced in the living room. Stewart's body had moved.

CHAPTER 36

Linda stared at the sprawled corpse intently.

She wasn't mistaken. The body was several inches away from the pool of blood; drag marks swept across the floor.

Heart beating wildly in her chest, Linda tiptoed closer, watching his chest carefully to detect any movement.

Trembling from head to toe, Linda bent down; the phone in her pocket was a cold spot against her hip. She placed one finger along Stewart's neck. He was still warm but cooling rapidly. She stared at the drag marks. Someone, or something, had moved Stewart's body. There was no mistaking it.

The hair on the back of her neck was standing painfully on end. Her gut was a tight knot of fear. She physically cringed away from the sight and what it implied but it was as if it was beckoning her. Linda tilted her head up and looked at the painting on the wall. At first glance it was the same, but then she saw the trail of small black figures emerging from the woods along the hill, coming closer and closer.

She got up and backtracked to the kitchen and out the back door to join the others on the back porch. On the outside she was calm but on the inside she was holding back a petrified scream.

Scott was still making calls in the back garden, his back to the house. He hadn't noticed her go back in or out. Ashley had a crowbar, a shovel, and a small trowel leaning against the porch railing. Linda gave Grady the book for safekeeping.

As she had done the day she had first arrived in the house, Linda got a sense of being in an old decrepit castle, vast and hiding many dangerous secrets behind its walls.

Scott ended up the last call, and moved to the house. He tried to open the door, but it didn't move. "We can't. It's locked," Scott snapped. He turned to look back to Linda. "You said it wouldn't be."

"It wasn't earlier."

Scott turned the doorknob again, but it didn't budge. "See? Locked."

Linda tried it herself.

The knob twisted with ease and the door creaked open.

All of them stared at each other.

"Are you sure your hand's not broken?" Linda asked.

"My hand is fine." Scott pushed past her into the manor. "Everyone else stay out."

"Wait," Linda warned. "Be careful."

Evelyn was still in the living room with her back to the kitchen. Scott walked over to the old woman and Linda was suddenly full of anxious regret. How could she tell Evelyn that her son had been killed?

"Dr. Blackburn, I'm so sorry," Scott said, coming around the chair to face Evelyn but the remainder of the sentence vanished from his mouth, which was now open in an "o" of disgust. "Oh, my God!"

Evelyn whimpered.

Linda strode inside the house, as did Grady and Ashley. They congregated around Evelyn and a collective gasp slipped out of their throats.

A great red welt bloomed across her cheek. Blood trickled from her slack mouth, but it was her hand that caught their eyes. The only limb she had been in control of was twisted at a painful angle, clearly broken.

"I'll call the paramedics," Scott said. "God, that sick bastard. His own mother. Everyone else out!" He motioned them out of the manor.

They all complied.

Scott went to the front of the house from the gallery porch, his phone to his ear.

Grady opened up the passage on banshee lore and began to read.

"I think Tara's influence is increasing," Linda said. "She must have unlocked the door for me. I've felt her pushing and shoving me before."

"You are right about the influence increasing," Grady said, pushing her lower lip out as she scanned the page. "You're wrong about it being Tara."

Ashley leaned forward, her eyes clear and curious. Her face was still pasty but it wasn't listless and wan. She listened with rapt attention.

"What?" Linda was surprised. "You heard Stewart. Tara is driving this."

"You misunderstand me," Grady said. "Tara originated the ghostly manifestation, yes, but it would be wrong to think the influence on this house is her. The evil presence has metamorphic qualities and was formed out of Tara's death. The evil was always here. It just gained traction through Tara's rage. Whatever it is, isn't Tara anymore. None of that girl's goodness is in this, only the worst aspects of rage and jealousy."

Ashley licked her lips. Linda chewed her lower lip. What Grady said made sense. Her own dreams and visions had been torn and confusing, as if the messages were distorted, and they had never been about Tara or Shannon only, but a mix of things.

"Yes, I need it ASAP." Scott strode around the porch, a first aid kit in his hand. "And come in fast."

He went inside the apartment. Linda stood at the doorframe and watched him open the kit in front of him. She could feel her own body shutting down slowly. Sleep was always at the edge of her eyes. She needed to finish this now if she had any chance of surviving.

She entered the apartment.

"Hey! I told you to stay out," Scott said.

"You need help," Linda said briskly. She began to clean up a cut on Evelyn's chin. "If you don't do this fast, the city police will be here before you even make it to the basement landing."

Scott saw the sense in that.

Suddenly, heavy footsteps stomped overhead.

Linda and Scott stopped what they were doing. They stared at each other. Scott removed his gun and angled himself slowly towards the stairs.

Another crash and bang.

Footsteps, slow and measured, came down the stairs.

Scott cocked his gun.

Linda gasped. "Scott, no!"

It was Grady. She was huffing down the stairs, the heavy book stuffed under one hand. Ashley was close behind her.

"What in heaven's name is wrong with you?" Scott bellowed. "I could have shot you! I told you to stay out. I can arrest you for tampering with a crime scene!"

"I just needed to check something," Grady said. "I was wrong, so it doesn't matter."

Ashley swayed on her feet. She looked more exhausted than Linda felt.

Linda wished they could have left the Manor as soon as Stewart had been injured, but that was no longer an option; the incident at the motel last night had proven that. There had been no chance of avoiding this situation; not since the moment they stepped across the threshold five days ago. It would always have ended like this. The door opening only for her? It was a sign. Tara wanted Linda in the house and would have made sure she never left.

And even if Linda ran, she didn't think she'd escape the presence. Marisa didn't; neither did Colin Prim. All Linda could hope for was making it long enough so the curse ended with her.

"Scott," she said. "It's okay. Grady can wheel Evelyn out onto the porch and patch her up. We need to do this fast before the police arrive. Let's go," and she motioned to Scott.

He looked reluctant but saw the merit in her words. He followed her into the kitchen.

Linda grabbed the tools from the porch, and joined Scott by the basement door. She beckoned Ashley and Grady to wheel Evelyn out then turned her attention back to the task at hand.

She stood a moment before the basement door, preparing herself for what waited inside. "I really don't want to go in there," she confessed to Scott. "But I will."

"I'll be by your side, okay?" Scott said. "Besides, it's only the dark."

"You still don't believe there are supernatural forces at work here." It wasn't a question. Linda was stating a fact.

"Nope." Scott hefted the crowbar and shovel, leaving her with the trowel. His boyish grin made him look years younger.

"I guess that's a good thing." Linda smiled. "Your skepticism might just be what we need."

Taking a deep breath, she opened the door she knew would open only for her.

A large block of endless black met them, hazy tendrils of it seemed to be radiating out of the doorframe.

Sighing deeply, Linda set her shoulders.

"God, have mercy."

She stepped down into the dark.

CHAPTER 37

The first step was the hardest.

Scott had charged ahead, taking the lead. His flashlight illuminated the viscous dark with a beam of light. Even with his strong shoulders ahead of her, she wanted to flee. She steeled herself and followed him. At least, she wasn't alone.

"The light switch is halfway down," Linda whispered. She didn't know why, but speaking in normal tones in that prickly silence felt like a bad idea.

Scott scanned the wall with his flashlight. It started to rain outside. The heavy drops sounded like dirt on a wooden coffin. Scott found the switch and flipped it on.

Bright light flooded the darkness.

As if sensing them in its guts, the manor groaned as if the whirling wind was uprooting it right from its foundations. Linda screamed and nearly knocked Scott over the banister.

"What happened?" Scott clutched her shoulder.

"I thought I saw someone at the bottom of the stairs," Linda stammered. "A shadow."

Not just any shadow, the shadow she had seen push Marisa down the stairs.

"There's nothing there," Scott said.

Linda didn't answer. The only time Linda had seen the shadow was before something terrible was about to happen. What was going to happen now? Part of her wanted to turn tail and run, but the other part knew that the entity was getting under her skin.

The cold intensified as they went lower. Scott shivered beside her as they reached the landing.

Linda looked back up the stairs, at the rectangle of light that was a symbol of freedom. Grady and Ashley were framed in it, looking down at her. They had crept back into the house without her noticing. Grady pressed a finger against her lips, asking for Linda's silence. Linda nodded and turned her attention to Scott.

"It's under the stairs," Linda said, touching Scott's arm.

He followed her to the side of the stairs. The layout was much like the basement in the other apartment though wider. Linda looked down at the dirt around her feet. Maggots writhed in the piles of dirt. Spiders scuttled across the walls. She shuddered, and pulled her arms closer around herself to ward off the cold.

"Why is it so cold?" Scott's teeth chattered. "It's summer."

"You tell me," Linda murmured. "You're the one who doesn't believe."

She waded through the dirt and reached the hollow under the stairs. It was a large space covered with an oil tarp. The tarp had been hastily nailed to the base of the stairs. Scott flicked it aside with his good hand and whistled.

"The wall's been torn down," he said. "Look."

He pulled at the tarp so a few nails were dislodged and pinged against the floor. The whole thing hung by a single nail, draped to one side of the wall. The rest was revealed as a small crevice under the stairs.

The exposed brick wall had been busted in the middle to make an uneven opening that a tall man could enter by stooping down. Beyond the wall were torn wooden slats. Pieces of brick and wood littered the crevice both inside and out.

The hole was a yawning mouth, beckoning Linda to enter. She felt the pull like a cold hook lodged in her gut. Goosebumps broke out painfully all over her arms. She desperately wanted to look away, to run back up the stairs, but she was ensnared by the darkness and what it held within.

Scott flashed a strong beam into the hole.

The light shone off the dark dirt walls that glistened with buried minerals and parted to make way for anyone willing to pass through. Linda could hear the same sound of slowly moving air within that she had heard in the mines.

"The secret tunnel," Linda whispered.

Scott stepped inside.

Linda followed.

"Hey, we didn't need so many tools," he said. "There are several shovels here, and a wheelbarrow too. They must have been part of the distillery."

"It might even be tools of the miners," Linda said. She pointed at the bloom of green and bronze rust on the metal. "Grady would have a better clue." She glanced back at the room. "Maybe we should call her in?"

A thundering crash made them whirl around to face the basement.

The sound of a door creaking open reached them. It was muffled but unmistakable.

Scott stared at Linda. "I thought I told them to get out with Evelyn!"

"I'll go see what's up."

Linda picked her way carefully through the rubble. *Grady should know better than to make so much noise. Maybe she's fallen and hurt herself?* Thought Linda.

A loud bang made her jump, heart thudding a mile a minute in her eardrums.

She ran pell-mell to the base of the stairs.

The sound of the storm was a muted whistle, like a kettle sounds just before it screams.

Mrs. Grady hadn't fallen down the stairs like Linda had feared, nor had Ashley.

The book on Irish legends lay at the bottom step, torn in places; the spine was completely broken.

"You guys need to leave now," Scott warned, poking his head from the hole under the stairs.

Grady was standing halfway down the stairs but Ashley had only progressed beyond the second step from the top. She was looking down at her feet, but her eyes were unfocused. Her lips were curled into a grimace.

"I came to warn you. You need to hurry," Grady warned. "It doesn't need you to sleep anymore. It's got Ash—"

Ashley screamed and lunged at Grady. She wrapped her hands around Grady's neck, squeezing the life out of her. Grady was turning blue, but she kept protecting something with both hands, and made no effort to dislodge Ashley's hands. She was clutching the urn from Stewart's room.

"Ashley!" Linda cried, vaulting up the stairs.

Ashley's head snapped up. Linda stopped in her tracks.

Malevolence and utter hatred was etched in every line of Ashley's face. She licked her lips slowly, like a hungry cat savoring the thought of eating a nest of birds. Linda felt the oppressive influence of Tara; she felt her own resolve crack and fear seep in the folds.

How had she been so blind?

She had been so convinced that the monstrosity was focused on her that she had ignored the signs with Ashley. Marisa had been the same, tired, fatigued, and ill before every possession. And the frenzy of violence against Stewart: that had been the manifestation as well.

"Let her go, Tara." Linda said with as much authority as she could muster.

Ashley laughed. Grady spluttered and choked.

Then with an almighty cry, Ashley shoved Grady down the stairs. The old woman's body struck the stairs at an angle. The sound of bones breaking cracked in the silent basement.

Linda screamed.

Scott scrambled across the debris-ridden basement floor.

Grady lay sprawled at the foot of the stairs.

She wasn't moving.

CHAPTER 38

"What the hell?" Scott cried from under the stairs. He came sprinting to the base of them, nearly tripping on scattered rocks. "What's going on?"

"I'm fine," Grady wheezed. She tried to lift herself up but winced and gave up.

Linda came forward to help. "What happened?"

"I suspected Ashley was under the influence of that thing," Grady hissed against the pain. "Then Evelyn's wheelchair got stuck... in the kitchen and... none of the doors would open... only the basement door opened and... Oh God, I've broken a rib." She wheezed and allowed herself to be propped against the wall.

"Come down with your hands behind your head." Scott was inching towards the stairs, one hand on the butt of his gun.

"No!" Linda cried. "She doesn't know what she's doing."

"She just pushed Grady down the stairs!" Scott snapped.

"She's being possessed," Grady said.

Ashley laughed on the stairs, clearly enjoying the bickering she had caused.

"Let her go." Linda walked towards the stairs. Scott tried to stop her but she pushed him away. "You won't pull a gun on my sister, so help me God." She turned back to Ashley. "Hey, Ash. I know you're listening. I'm sorry I brought you here. This whole mess is my fault. I should never have dragged you all the way here."

The manic grin on Ashley's face eased a little. Her eyes lost the glint of steel.

"We'll leave," Linda went on. "Right now. You don't have to stop this monstrous ghost. We just need to get you away from here. I promise, you can wait for us outside, with the paramedics that are coming. Just fight back."

She knew there was no truth in her words. There was no way they could leave, but if lying was the only means to give Ashley some hope, she was willing to lie through her teeth to get her sister back.

Color returned to Ashley's face. She looked confused, as if she had woken from a long strange dream and was disoriented. Hope bloomed in Linda. She would get Ashley back, and then they would leave.

"Linda?" Ashley's face crumpled into tears. "I'm so confused. What's happening to me?"

"Nothing." Linda put her foot on the first step. "You're fine now."

She climbed the stairs, and took Ashley's hand. She guided her sister slowly up the stairs. She heard a muffled sound coming from the kitchen. Slowly, the kitchen came into view. Ashley's hand was cold and still in hers.

They had just reached the door when Linda saw Evelyn on

the back porch through the back door. Her eyes were wide with fear. The back door slammed and a rack of knives was upturned, and shaking. A handful of cooking utensils came zooming across the kitchen towards them.

"Look out!" Linda cried and shoved Ashley aside. "Aaah!" A knife point lodged itself in her arm.

She stumbled down a step. Knives and forks clattered on the stairs.

The basement door slammed shut. The light flickered, plunging them into sudden darkness and light.

Linda heard the groaning of heavy furniture flying across the kitchen and slamming against the basement door.

Not only were they locked in, now there was no means of escape.

"No," Linda moaned. She stumbled down the stairs, hope completely abandoning her.

"Linda!" Grady called up. "Come down. We're stuck."

The knives and forks shuffled beneath her, rolling down the stairs. She lost her footing, and went crashing down.

A gray shadow rose behind Ashley, tall and mighty.

"No!" Linda screamed, heart in throat, her guts twisting painfully. She came to a stop on the landing.

She looked up. Miraculously, Ashley had escaped harm. "Ashley, watch out!"

The shadow rose high and swung down, landing hard on Ashley's bewildered head.

But as she watched, Ashley's eyes rolled back. Her body went limp, and she keeled over. She would have hit her head on the stairs if Linda hadn't reached her in time.

She was a dead weight in Linda's arms, porcelain white, and just as cold.

CHAPTER 39

"Ashley, wake up." Linda slapped her sister's face hard. Her arm throbbed with pain and warm blood ran slick down to her wrist but she didn't care. "Wake up!"

"Stop that, Linda," Grady hissed. "You know she won't respond. You've read the book. You know about false corpses. It's what happened to the girl in the Irish village, it's what happened to Marisa that first night."

Linda was breathing hard. Her hands were shaking, but she kept slapping Ashley to make her wake. Sobs were choking her throat. How could she have let this happen to Ashley?

Scott's color resembled that of curdled milk. He walked up to Linda, and touched her injured arm gingerly. The gash wasn't deep but there was too much blood. "What just happened? I've never seen anything like it."

"I have." Linda winced as Scott brought out a handkerchief and tied it around the wound in her arm, staunching the flow of blood. "I've seen too much in this house. And now Ashley... I could have prevented this if I'd only been brave enough to end this sooner."

"You still can," Grady moaned. "There is very little time. You have to destroy the receptacle before this Thing gains full strength! If you don't, Ashley will die. Like Marisa."

Little time...

Linda thought back to the night Marisa fell, how she had been in a semi-dream state when hearing the recordings with Scott, and the one message that kept recurring in that state.

The soil is nourishing. We should put Marisa in the earth.

The priest wanted to bury the girl...

Linda sat up straighter. "The book mentioned resurrecting burials," she said to no one in particular. "That's what we have to do. We have to bury Ashley, but..." Linda bit her lip as uncertainty rocked her. "It will work, won't it, Grady?"

"Whatever you must do, do it fast." Grady's breath hitched.

"What are you talking about?" Scott became green.

"We have to bury Ashley before we break the receptacle," Linda said. Scott stared at her in horror. "I know how that sounds but that's what the book said. It's some sort of break from the curse, as if the malignant spirit has to remove its hold on the body it's possessing once it's buried or something. I'm not too clear on the whys, only that I need to do it if I have any chance of saving Ashley."

"That's crazy, Linda," Scott said.

Annoyed that they were losing time, Linda picked up the broken book from the floor and shifted through the papers that dropped out of the covers till she found the one she needed.

"Once a manifestation begins," she read out loud, "it is very hard to control if the receptacle is not identified. The more time that passes between the initiation of a curse and the investigation for its source, the more likely it is that it will never be identified. Unfortunately, it is the only resource that is foolproof in ending a banshee and its curse. The receptacle is anything that the deceased placed great value on, or had emotional attachment to. Once the receptacle is destroyed the manifestation can end."

She lowered the tattered remains of the book and looked Scott in the eyes.

"I know it looks insane, but we didn't bury Marisa and look what happened to her." She shifted Ashley off her lap and got up. "If we don't bury Ashley she will surely have another possession and..." She swallowed a sob as the memory of Marisa came back, her eyes haunted with terror as she warned Linda that "she" was coming back. How lost she sounded. "It won't be the last possession. This will keep happening again and again. If I bury Ashley, I can save her from the same fate. Her soul might not be trapped like Marisa's if I can break the receptacle in time. It's a small chance, but it's the only one I have. And if I fail to destroy Tara's receptacle in time, at least Ashley's soul will rest in peace and won't be tormented forever." She paused. "You said there was a wheelbarrow in the tunnel?"

"Yeah." Scott still looked like he thought Linda had lost a screw or two.

"Bring it." She eased Ashley off the stairs. Scott ran back to the tunnel. Linda let Ashley lie at the bottom of the steps and turned to Grady. "Let me see your rib."

Grady slapped her hand away. "I'll live with a broken rib. I won't survive a malicious entity hell-bent on choking me to death. Go now!"

Rusty wheels echoed down the tunnel. Scott emerged from under the stairs with an ancient wheelbarrow. He came as quickly as he could. Linda helped him lift Ashley up and into the barrow. It was hard with Scott's broken fingers and Linda's injured arm. Ashley fell out of their grasp twice, but they finally managed.

Linda checked Ashley's jeans pocket and was relieved to find the Polly Pocket in there. She placed it in her own pocket and turned to Scott, who was holding his broken fingers like a little boy.

"Why didn't you tape your fingers?" Linda complained as she huffed to catch her breath.

"I thought this would be a routine perimeter check of the house." H winced at the pain in his fingers. "I didn't think I'd be locked down here for hours."

"I don't want to leave you behind," Linda said to Grady. "What if the shadow comes back? Are you sure you can't walk?"

"I'll only slow you down." Grady waved them off. "Go… I can feel something starting… It's buzzing in my teeth fillings."

Linda didn't need to be told twice. Holding Ashley's limp hand, she helped Scott push the wheelbarrow into the black void.

She prayed they would make it out of there alive, but she knew better than to expect it to happen; not after what had happened to Marisa and what she had read in the book.

CHAPTER 40

It was unnerving how the sound of the storm outside completely cut out when they entered the tunnel. The silence here was predatory. Linda felt like a sheep being led to slaughter.

"So, it's true?" Scott murmured. "All this paranormal business."

"I know it's hard to believe. I tried to convince myself otherwise most of my childhood by believing I was suffering from sleep paralysis and hallucinations induced by anxiety." Linda took the flashlight from him and illuminated the way. "But the events here made me realize I've been seeing the departed my whole life. That's why I got the visions of Shannon's ghost. I also think that's one of the factors driving this Thing's power to such height now: having a conduit that is sensitive to its existence. It was weak with only Shannon to feed on, but when I arrived it grew stronger and fed on Marisa and Stewart, and it's been feeding off Ashley and me. The phenomenon is getting stronger as we get closer to the nexus of the haunting. See how cold it is?"

Her breath plumed in front of her. Icicles glistened along the ceiling of the tunnel.

"The portion of the attic where Shannon was killed and the bathroom beneath it have always been freezing cold, no matter how hot it is outside," Linda commented, her voice barely above a whisper.

Faint rustling sounds picked up as they progressed in the tunnel. Linda darted the beam of the flashlight around the black shaft. The path was littered with bits and pieces of broken rock, nails, and even glass where liquor bottles had been smashed.

Linda watched as a twisted rusty nail twitched slowly as if sensing a magnet nearby. Glass tinkled as shards rubbed against each other. The light beam arced along the ceiling; Linda swallowed as she saw spiders scuttling down the walls or dangling from the ceilings.

Worms burst their slimy blind heads from the earth, testing the air as they approached. The skittering of tiny rodent feet filled the tunnel. Linda was surprised there were so many insects and rodents here despite the supernatural cold. She could imagine sharp teeth clicking. Something brushed close by her feet. Linda screamed and jumped, knocking her glasses off her face.

Panic clutched at her throat as she bent down to retrieve them, the flashlight hitting her in the face, burning into her corneas. She blinked a few times trying to dislodge the imprint of the bright light from her vision, one hand patting the ground around her, fingers brushing over sharp objects.

Linda whimpered with fear.

Her hand slid across something clammy, cold, and coiled up

in a tense pile.

She snatched her hand away. "Snake!" she screamed.

"Linda, watch out!" Scott cried.

"I can't watch." She wanted to scream. "I'm blind without my glasses!"

She stumbled back and her hands grazed reliable plastic. She snatched the glasses up from the dirt and jammed them on her face, not caring that the lenses were streaked with grime.

The flashlight was still in her hand. She angled it in front and saw a dusty coil of rope, frayed and tattered at the edges. It was slinking back and forth like a snake trying to wrap around Scott's boots like a python. With a mighty cry of frustration Scott kicked the rope to the other side of the tunnel.

Linda was still breathing loudly. Scott was doing the same.

The objects didn't stop moving. The phenomenon was only going to get more intense from here on out.

The surroundings were getting to her. All the confidence and courage that had surged up in her apartment during Stewart's attack had evaporated.

"We have to hurry," she said.

Ashley's head lolled from side to side; her hands and feet jerked every time the wheelbarrow encountered a rut in the path.

No wonder this Thing is so pissed. I would be too if I had to spend all of eternity in this damp hellhole.

She trained Scott's flashlight on the ceiling so the whole area would be illuminated. It wasn't very large. The ceiling was low, nearly brushing Scott's head as he was already bent down to push the wheelbarrow. The sides were only far apart enough to allow two people to walk abreast uncomfortably.

The sound of trickling water came from all around them.

The ground wasn't hard-packed earth, but powdery, like cold wet sand. Spider webs hung from the walls. Linda wondered how many rats were down here, and she shuddered at the thought.

They walked in silence for a few minutes, the squeaking of the wheels the only sound. The air was thick and stale. The tunnel kept going, but a small opening in the right wall made them stop.

Linda swallowed audibly and flashed the light within the small opening. It was big enough to allow one person to go through at a time. She exchanged a look with Scott. His face mirrored her own anticipation and dread.

She approached the opening, clenching her teeth so they wouldn't chatter. A baleful cold, more intense than any they had experienced in the basement, bathed them. Linda inhaled sharply; every breath hurt like a knife to her chest.

"It's freezing in there," she murmured. Her body shivered of its own accord, as she hovered outside the notch of darkness. Scott gasped behind her, no doubt just getting the full force of the frigid air.

Linda lifted the torch up so its beam would bounce off the ceiling and illuminate a larger area.

A gasp escaped her blue lips.

It was an open area. The ceiling was vaulted and high; stalactites ranged across it, like the teeth of some sleeping monster. The light reflected off the ground up ahead and Linda realized it was a small body of water, a black underground pond.

The earth at their feet was disturbed. Linda was now used to the uneven nature of the ground but this was much more chaotic. Dirt was piled in places, and dug up in some; there were clear impressions of where the earth had been stacked on top of hidden things. The crosses from the police picture were also there, most erect and somber. One, however, was nearly falling over.

It was the place from her dreams. She had swum and stared at the ceiling before nearly drowning in that pond; she had choked on dirt in a shallow grave. This was the same mineshaft she had blundered through before being confronted by the mob of miners.

Linda tried to swallow but her throat was completely dry.

"This is the place," she said, her voice barely above a whisper, but Scott heard her. "This is where the miners were murdered. We'll find Tara and her necklace with the peridot here."

"How can you be so sure?" Scott asked. He picked the wheelbarrow up again and went inside. The flashlight shimmered on the still water, making eerie shapes, giving it the illusion of bodies swimming just beneath the surface.

"I've been seeing this place in my nightmares since I arrived." Linda's eyes filled with tears. Overwhelming fear climbed up her back, threatening to jam her throat. "Those were the visions Shannon's ghost sent to me, but It spoiled them somehow, distorting the truth so I was confused about what was happening and who was the source. Yet, it always started in this place. And Stewart admitted he buried Tara and Shannon here. I think this is where we'll find them."

She walked into the cave, and it was as if a button had been pressed. Strong winds began to roar through the cavern. Silt and rocks came flying at them. Linda covered her head. Scott crouched down by the wheelbarrow and lifted his jacket for Linda to hide under.

"It's in the water?" Scott asked.

"No." Linda pointed to the mounds of earth near the entrance to the tunnel and the crosses standing sentinel over the Irish miners. "She was buried, as was Shannon. We have to find the receptacle and destroy them both at the same time. It will be her necklace. I'm sure of it. She was fond of it, and Stewart confirmed it unwittingly."

Scott nodded and set his shoulders. He heaved up a shovel and handed her the crowbar. "So which one is it?"

Wind and dirt flying made their discussion difficult. They had to shout, and shield their eyes to avoid dirt.

It was a good question. Where were the bodies buried? Linda was sure Stewart had buried them and not dumped them in the lake. It was much more personal, and Stewart seemed like the person who liked to visit his trophies from time to time.

Linda looked at the graves intently. Which one of the twelve could it be? They had no time or energy to dig up all twelve. And the way the wind was howling, throwing small pieces of stone and glass their way, the monster that reigned here wouldn't let them.

How to distinguish between the miners and the new graves?

Linda pulled out the picture from her back pocket. The edges twitched in the wind but she held them firm. She squinted down at the photocopy, her eyes watering.

She shielded her eyes from the wind. Earth entered her eyes, her mouth and nose till she felt like her tongue was covered in mud.

"How many graves are there?" she yelled at Scott, the wind threatening to snatch the words from her mouth and spirit them away.

"Twelve!" he yelled back.

Linda counted the ones in the picture and then the ones in the graveyard, and she found the difference. "There are two extra graves at that end of the pool," she yelled in Scott's ear. "The crosses are the markers."

Scott's face cleared, and he gave her a thumbs-up indicating he understood. He helped drag the wheelbarrow over to the two new graves and began shoveling at one of them. Linda shoveled at the other with her trowel.

Bones emerged, wrapped under tattered dirty clothes. Scott made a retching noise as the shovel scraped over bone. Linda shoveled faster till she was looking down at a skull, head adorned with brittle blonde hair.

She sat back. The wind howled around her, but inside everything had frozen.

The hair was long and the tattered shirt was pink, with fat cats printed on it.

She had found Shannon.

"I think I've found Tara," Scott yelled, getting Linda's attention.

Linda glanced at his grave and saw he was right. The skeleton was swathed in clothes Linda recognized from the picture she had seen in Stewart's apartment.

"We have to bury Ashley first." Linda's voice sounded hollow to her own ears, like she was speaking from a great distance.

The wind howled louder.

Scott paled considerably in the weak light. "I still think you're wrong about that."

"No." Linda shook her head vehemently. She didn't have the time or energy to argue with Scott. "I know what I'm doing. The book detailed resurrection burials to rid the body of the banshee's influence. It's a risk, yes, but it's a risk I must take. You saw what happened to Marisa." Linda sank to her knees and crawled forward. She then dragged the wheelbarrow closer to the graves. "I'm not going to let Ashley go like that. I have to try."

Metal clanged on metal as rusty pipes came hurtling towards them. Linda ducked and Scott sidestepped away in time.

The pipes crashed against the far wall, chipping away rock.

"We need to hurry up!" Linda screamed, eyes wide with fear.

Linda stepped away from the wheelbarrow. Ashley's head lolled at one end, and her legs stuck out the other. Linda pressed a finger on her cold neck. There wasn't even a suggestion of a heartbeat.

Seeing her sister like that tore at her.

Linda went down on her knees and used her shaking hands to dig the grave because she felt the enormity of her guilt by doing it with her hands. Scott joined her in digging.

Once the grave was shallow enough for a ceremonial burial, Scott and Linda tried to get Ashley inside. Tiny stones flew up in the wind and struck them in the face, scratching their skin until their blood flowed in beads. Struggling, they managed to get Ashley's cold and lifeless body in the grave.

Linda bit on hysterical sobs of grief, as she brushed her fingers over Ashley's cold face. She willed herself not to break down crying. Ashley needed her to be strong right now.

"Linda, are you sure?" Scott sounded queasy.

Linda's heart constricted. Either this would work or it would go horribly wrong, and she wasn't ready for it to go wrong. Nothing had prepared her for the loss of her mother, and now she was standing at the same crossroads and she couldn't face losing her sister. Ashley was all the family she had left.

Linda pulled out the Polly Pocket from her pocket. She had been so sure this piece of a happy memory would be used by Ashley to release her once the monster's receptacle had been destroyed, but now the tables had turned. She placed the toy on top of Ashley's chest. If Shannon had made sure her phone was retrieved for release, then it only made sense that something Ashley was attached to should be sacrificed as well. The Polly Pocket. This was consistent with what she read in Colin's diary from Grady's book. She just hoped there was enough time.

"We'll bury her once we have the necklace in our hands," Linda said and looked up, steeling herself for the final act of rummaging through the graves of two dead girls. Her eyes bulged at the sight before her.

A soft mist was rising from the pond, gray and evil. The wind seemed to have no effect on it. They were two separate weather phenomena coexisting independently within the same cavern. In their preoccupation, the two people had missed the creeping fog and the sound of shuffling feet. It was barely audible, but Linda could hear the hum of many voices singing some slow lonesome song.

"Yes," she said brushing the dirt from her hands. "We have to hurry."

Scott had noticed the mist as well.

She scrambled back from the grave, holding Scott's arm to keep her balance. The sounds were getting louder. The icy mist crept around their feet, biting at their ankles. The song soared; the mourning voices were the long-dead miners at work in the bowels of the earth. Then the sounds stopped. The wind stilled, cut off as if a switch had been turned off.

An oppressive silence surrounded them. Scott and Linda stood with their backs to each other, flashlight aimed at the ceiling, eyes darting around the cavern.

Had the wailing spirit finally retreated?

Linda took a deep breath to calm her jangling nerves.

She licked her lips. "I think—"

A sudden wind whipped through the cavern, nearly knocking Linda off her feet. The flashlight went skittering away by the edge of the cavern where it stopped against the far wall, illuminating a jagged edge of rock and nothing else. Scott cursed and had to hold on to the shovel to keep his balance. Earth shifted on the grave, dislodging small stones and pebbles to hit them in the chest and legs.

Linda cried out against the unexpected assault. A fairly large stone came zooming at Scott and hit him squarely between the eyes. He stumbled and fell. Linda screamed. She struggled against the wind to reach him. He was still breathing but there was a bloody gash on his forehead.

"Scott!" Linda shook him, but his eyes rolled up in his head.

The wind persisted, dislodging clods of earth that manifested in the shape of a dirt storm obscuring her vision. Ashley's face and torso were rapidly swallowed under a mound of dirt as the earth shifted and sucked her in deeper.

"No!" Linda screamed.

Then, the wind died as swiftly as it had started.

Something wet and heavy sloshed out of the pond. Linda saw a hulking figure in the suspended dirt at the very edge of her vision. The sound of dragging feet came next from both in front of her and from behind her. It was everywhere, attacking her from all sides.

CHAPTER 41

Linda whimpered.

She was back in her old skin, petrified of every shadow and sound. The sound of sloshing feet came from the pond; the sound of dragging feet came from the passage they had just come from.

Sweat pooled under Linda's arms, even though she was shivering from the cold.

"Scott." She tried one more time to rouse him, but he just groaned and was still.

Letting him fall off her lap, Linda stood up and backed away from the pond.

The footsteps behind her stopped.

The ones coming towards her increased their pace.

Linda cried out and tried to run, but she tripped over the handle of the shovel and went sprawling into Tara's partially dug grave.

White teeth grinned up at her.

Linda screamed and scrambled back, displacing more dirt around the grave, revealing the skull and the brown bones of the neck. She stopped struggling and bent forward. Her shaking hands began to dig further, clearing the clavicle and breastbone.

Fragments of rotting cloth stuck to the bones, but there was no sign of a peridot necklace.

A shrill howl resounded in the cavern, bouncing off the walls, attacking her from every corner. The wind began again; a gale of water from the pond got into her eyes. The flashlight flickered on and off, plunging the cavern from pitch dark to partial gloom, obscuring Linda's senses.

Linda pressed her hands on her ears, clenching her teeth against the battering noise. Struggling against the sound, she dug further around the body, hoping to find the necklace dislodged in the dirt.

Her fingers got cut against sharp stones and bled freely but she ignored it. The footsteps behind her resumed, getting closer and closer. Her body shook with terror, Linda wanted to turn and face her assailant, but she knew nothing would change unless she had the receptacle. Forcing herself to focus on finding the necklace, Linda ignored the beads of cold sweat that trailed like grasping fingers down her spine.

A sharp wailing wheezed underneath the shrill screaming wind.

"I can't find it!" Linda bawled. She was crying freely now, her senses heightened, her fear knowing no bounds. "It's not here! It's not here!"

A hand clasped her shoulder.

Linda screamed.

CHAPTER 42

Cold hands clutched Linda's shoulders, bony fingers digging into her flesh.

Linda cried and tried to get out of the deathly grip but the hands were too strong. A hollow wheezing breath, warm and moist, cascaded down the back of her neck. Linda struggled, pushing her elbows back to hit her attacker in the ribs.

The attacker cursed aloud, and gasped as if the breath had been knocked out of them.

The curse was all too human, the wheezing cry much too surprised and agitated.

Linda grabbed at the flashlight, which had skidded against the far wall in the wind. Small stones flew across the cavern and scratched against her face, cutting at her skin, making her bleed. Her hands shook as she focused on the hulking figure in the supernatural misty wind.

"Linda," the figure moaned.

"Grady?"

"The urn…" she croaked. Blood trickled down the side of her mouth. Her face was blue, and not just from the cold in the cavern. Purple bruises lined her throat, bulging in an effort to pull in air to her lungs.

"Grady, it's too late," Linda sobbed. "It wasn't in the grave. I was wrong."

"The urn!" Grady said. "I kept it safe… Possessed Ashley wanted it… I had to stay silent not to attract attention from It… it's in here."

"How can you be so sure?" Linda asked.

"Stewart… loved his dog more than he loved anyone else," Grady wheezed, blood spilling out of her mouth. "I was sure he… he must have hidden it in the urn… When you all entered the tunnel, you got all the attention from It… I could open the urn, and I checked inside… but I didn't touch it, so as not to draw Its attention to myself." With the last of her strength, she threw the urn at Linda.

Linda sidestepped just in time.

The urn went arcing through the air and crashed against the wall behind Linda.

Wood cracked.

The wind halted.

Blood gushing out of her mouth in a scarlet vomit, Grady collapsed where she stood. She'd clearly pretended she only had a broken rib to avoid slowing down Linda and Scott, but she had been seriously hurt, and probably attacked in the tunnel too.

Linda made to go to her, but a glint of silver caught the light and she halted.

The silence had a keen edge to it. An expectant waiting pressed down on Linda's ear, worse than the howling screams from a few seconds ago. Linda bent down again. The urn had a large crack on one side. Ash spilled out from the crack and the dangling end of a silver chain.

Excitement and hope rekindled Linda's frozen extremities.

She tried to pry the top off, but it was sealed shut by some adhesive.

Scrambling closer to the wall, her knees slipping in the dirt, Linda lunged, striking the crack on the urn at the ragged wall.

The boom resounded around the cavern.

The silence shifted.

The crack opened wide enough for the necklace to spill out on to her palm.

The green peridot shone with a light of its own.

A low groan echoed behind her.

Linda whipped around.

Scott moaned and sat up. Blood trickled down his forehead, dripping off his nose. "Whass happin?" he slurred.

"I found it!" she cried. "I found the necklace! I—"

It had crept up on her without her sensing anything amiss. The shadow flitted against the wall, towering above her. The necklace slipped out of her fingers.

The shadow swooped down like a hawk.

Linda was paralyzed.

It hit her like a frigid ocean wave.

CHAPTER 43

Linda was paralyzed.

Her eyes saw the cavern; saw Scott stumble towards her; saw Grady wheezing, her lung obviously punctured by the broken rib; yet her body wouldn't move. A malicious entity was fighting her instincts of control. It was taking over.

"What are you waiting for?" Scott asked. "Destroy it!"

Linda tried to speak, but her jaw was clenched shut. The entity was breaking through her defenses, relentlessly attacking any strength Linda had.

Her eyelids fluttered. She was tired. Her limbs were heavy and her spine ached. Maybe she should just lie down. It couldn't hurt to take a little rest.

"Linda!" Scott shouted. He snatched the necklace from the ground. "Ashley doesn't have much time!"

Ashley!

Linda's eyes opened wide. She struggled against the possession. The writhing gray shadow whirled in and out of her vision, painting the world in its muted colors. Scott scrabbled in the dirt for the crowbar. His eyes widened as he looked at Linda. He must have seen the shadow.

"I'll destroy it!" he screamed. "Leave her, or I'll destroy you!"

Linda gasped as the evil influence lifted off her shoulder like discarding sodden clothes. The wind howled worse than before. Linda was buffeted back into the wall, hitting her head against a sharp edge. The rocks dug into her spine, making her cry out.

The shadow moved with fluid grace forging a path of destruction as it went. The wheelbarrow squeaked in the wind and struck Grady's head, again and again, till the bright red of blood bloomed at the back of her head.

Scott saw it coming. He feinted to the right then ran left towards the pond. The shadow didn't buy it for one second. The crowbar hurtled through the air, spinning end on end.

Scott twisted and threw the necklace at Linda.

Linda watched mesmerized as the silver chain caught the light as it spun across the cavern towards her, and a few feet away the crowbar came crashing down with immense force.

Linda watched in horror as Scott tried to dive away from under the sharp projectile but in vain. The crowbar caught him in his side, sinking all the way through. Blood and bits of flesh littered the floor.

Scott screamed.

"Scott!" Linda yelled, hysteria bursting inside her making everything else unimportant.

Scott fell to his knees at the foot of Ashley's grave. Ropes came coiling out of the darkness and looped around his legs, pinning him down. The sharp end of the crowbar stuck out of Scott's side. Blood bloomed across his shirt.

All hope leached out of Linda's toes. Ashley lay in a

makeshift grave. Grady was collapsed by the graves of Tara and Shannon, her face a pale moon in the gloom. Scott lay by the pool impaled on a crowbar. What chance did she have against an entity that could wreak so much havoc?

Amidst the howling wind and grit something glittered by her knee.

The peridot necklace was swiftly getting buried under the moving earth.

There was something so surreptitious about that small detail, the eager way the earth was devouring the necklace, the cockiness of the monster behind all of this sure that it had won.

Anger and rage bloomed inside Linda.

She snatched the necklace, her eyes barely opening in the strong wind.

The clang of metal rang in the cavern. Linda saw the shovel rise in the air. The entity was making its last assault.

Teeth bared in a feral grin, Linda whipped out Shannon's phone and Ashley's Polly Pocket from her jeans.

"This ends now!" she screamed, smashing her childhood toy against the wall. It shattered into pieces.

Placing the necklace so the peridot pendant, her childhood toy, and the phone screen were stacked on top of each other, Linda grabbed a stone. She smashed it on the pile, again, and again.

The peridot and the Polly Pocket broke into pieces, and the phone screen crunched.

The wind whipped up in an erratic frenzy.

The shovel whizzed through the air to hit her on her right arm.

Linda yowled and nearly loosened her grip on the phone.

She gritted her teeth and lifted her hand again. She let it drop and picked up a rock. She brought it crashing down.

The phone disintegrated into pieces.

The chain broke but the pendant still remained.

Tara howled in rage all around her.

Linda shouted back.

She picked up the trowel from the foot of the grave and placed the pendant on top of Tara's skull.

With a feral cry she brought the trowel down, smashing the pendant to pieces.

CHAPTER 44

The wind petered out.

One last sharp stone sliced across Linda's forehead. Blood trickled down her grimy face.

She sat back, breathing hard. Every limb ached, her body screamed for rest but there was none to be had. She had to be quick.

Stumbling up and across the cavern Linda fell twice. She struggled on her knees, and finally crawled to Ashley's shallow grave.

The wind had stirred dirt up till Ashley was almost covered; only bits of her pale face were visible underneath the dark soil.

"No! Please," was all Linda could manage to say. "Please!"

She raked the dirt away with her bare fingers, her hands frantically searching for her sister.

The earth was dislodged and Ashley's face emerged. Maggots wriggled across her sister's closed eyes. Linda moaned and wiped them away.

"Please," she whimpered.

She felt Ashley's neck for a heartbeat.

Seconds ticked by.

She felt nothing. Ashley wasn't breathing. There was no trace of a heartbeat.

Darkness threatened to overcome her again.

"Ash!" she moaned, and she burst into tears. "No, please!"

Guilt and remorse mingled with her overwhelming sense of loss. It was hard to breathe, hard to imagine the meaning of life without her sister. Crying like a child who has lost their mother, Linda laid her head down on Ashley's stationary chest, letting the weariness take her over. She wouldn't mind dying down here now.

A sonorous rumble came from Ashley's chest.

Linda sat back.

Coughing and spluttering, Ashley wheezed and sat up. Color was returning to her ashen face. She stared around at their surroundings, eyes wide.

Like the maggots, an insidious thought wormed its way through Linda's brain.

What if she was too late? What if Ashley was so far gone she had sustained brain damage?

She crept forward, her hands grazed by sharp stones, looking into her sister's eyes, not breaking contact.

"A-Ash?" Linda stammered.

Ashley stared, her expression blank, her face slack-jawed.

Linda sobbed. "Ashley!" She threw her head down on the ground, prostrated with grief. "No!"

"Linda, you buried me?" Ashley said, her voice a hoarse whisper.

Linda shot up, and stared at her sister.

Her cheeks were still pale, but her eyes were no longer blank slates. There was life in them: fright, terror, and confusion, but discernible emotions.

"Linda, am I back?" Ashley asked, her lips quivering. "Am I? I was so horribly lost! I didn't think I could ever get out. It was so dark. Am I back?"

"Ashley!" Linda threw herself at her sister. "I'm so sorry! I'm so sorry!" She rocked back and forth letting her tears fall freely. "You're okay! I'm sorry."

Ashley swallowed, then patted Linda's back. "I'm okay. I think. Oh my God," she gasped. "Scott? Grady?"

Linda looked back at the prone bodies of Grady and Scott.

Grady had given her life to ensure Linda could stop the haunting. It was a debt Linda could never repay.

And Scott...

Leave her or I'll destroy you.

Scott hadn't thought about himself. He had believed in Linda's possession and he had used the necklace as a bargaining chip to save her, risking himself. Linda let the fresh tears stream down her face. If it hadn't been for him, Linda would have failed and they would all be dead... or worse.

Guilt hit her. She had survived because there had been two people willing to risk their lives for her. At no other time had she felt this worthless or impotent.

"Can you walk?" Linda asked. "We should get out. The police must be there by now."

"Yeah." Ashley stepped out of the grave. Her knees looked wobbly, but she managed to stand. "I don't want to leave them down here like this."

"We won't," Linda said. "We'll call the police and show them.

They will bring them out. No one will be left behind in this hell-hole."

Ashley limped towards Linda and held her arm. Linda yowled.

"What is it?" Ashley gasped.

Linda peeled back the sleeve on her right arm to reveal a gash angling along her upper arm. The shovel had cut her skin open and it ran with blood.

"Paramedics should be here by now," Ashley said. "Come on."

Linda followed to the center of the cavern. The mist had parted and the cold was lessening, but Linda couldn't help but wonder if the terrorizing reign of Tara was truly over or not.

It sounded too good to be true that destroying the phone, the Polly Pocket, and the necklace had completely snuffed out the malevolent energy.

They had just reached the mouth of the opening when an eerie moan resounded in the cavern like a wounded animal's howl.

Linda froze.

The hair on the back of her neck stood on end.

"What was that?" Ashley clutched her hand.

Linda trained the flashlight within the cavern, picking out rocks and shadows.

A figure stirred on the ground.

"Linda?"

"Scott?"

Linda rushed back inside. Scott writhed on the ground, his wound bleeding profusely. His skin was as white as a sheet and he was losing blood fast.

"No!" Linda cried. She ripped her soiled sleeve and wound it around Scott's waist. She pulled it taut to staunch the bleeding. "We're getting you out of here," she promised. "We'll get you help! Ashley, check Grady."

Ashley scurried over to the old woman. She bent down, and felt her pulse. Linda helped Scott sit up, making him lean on her shoulder. She watched Ashley expectantly.

Ashley's face fell. She shook her head.

Linda swallowed her disappointment and grief. There would be time for that later. Grady would have told her not to dawdle and to get the job done.

"Help me with Scott," Linda instructed Ashley.

Together they helped Scott to the wheelbarrow and sat him inside.

They wheeled him out, both pushing.

As they left the cavern, Linda turned back once to take in the place of horror.

The mist had completely evaporated from the cavern. The pond was dark and lifeless. The frost was melting slowly as the temperature increased by small degrees.

At the very back of the cavern, a host of faint ghosts flitted in and out of existence like winking stars watching her leave.

I'll get you proper burials in consecrated ground, she thought, hoping the miners would get the message. *I promise.*

As if in response to her promise, the ethereal lights winked out one by one.

CHAPTER 45

The storm was still going strong, but the cold wind was nothing compared to what they had encountered inside.

A host of police officers and paramedics came to their aid, lifting Linda off her limping feet to deposit her in the back of an ambulance. Scott needed immediate medical attention so he was sped away to the hospital, leaving behind a disgruntled Hackridge Chief of Police and a grinning Milo, who was plying him with coffee and sandwiches. Cindy, mystified, stood next to the porch steps. She'd come back from her lunch break to find the house surrounded by police cars.

Ashley was lying down in the ambulance behind her, having her heart rate monitored.

Evelyn had been taken to the hospital before they had emerged from the basement.

The police officers had had a tough time removing furniture from the basement door.

Linda shuddered. She watched the house. It was still as malicious and brooding as before, but the edge to it had gone.

"Meow."

Linda looked down the road. Cats, at least ten of them, had converged in the middle of the street. They stood looking at the manor. Fear pulled at Linda, and she followed their gaze.

Men emerged from Blackburn Manor, their faces somber. They were wheeling a gurney between them. A black body bag rested on top.

Grady.

Linda's lower lip quivered.

She had escaped the jaws of death, but some hadn't.

Grady, Tara, and Shannon. They had all died.

Deep sorrow and the enormity of her experience crashed down on her, and all of her adrenaline left her body. She began to weep, letting the realization that she had survived sink in, and that the guilt would never go away.

EPILOGUE

"You nearly got me killed," Scott complained.

Monitors beeped. A tiny TV groaned in the corner. Nurses went about their business in the halls. Scott sat up in his hospital bed, eating green Jell-O.

"Oh, please." Ashley rolled her eyes. "You love the attention you're getting."

"And a promotion." Scott grinned.

"That's great," Linda said.

She was truly happy for Scott, but her mind was still at Grady's funeral. Her two daughters had come, and it had been hard to explain to them what had happened. Linda could still feel the skeptical, angry gazes of Grady's loved ones.

They had returned to their room at the local motel because the manor was now a crime scene. She had dreamt of nothing, no moaning lament, no bodies in underground lakes, no disturbing portraits, and certainly no blonde or brunette girls haunting her dreams.

That, more than anything else, had convinced her that it was all over. When they destroyed the creature, Shannon's ghost ceased to exist as well. Her soul was now at peace somewhere in the Beyond.

"So, did you manage to convince the mayor?" Scott asked. "You said you were going to talk to him yesterday."

"Yes." Linda nodded, grateful for a change of subject. "I told him it was the town's responsibility to recognize a great injustice done by one of the prominent figures in their history. Plus the church had no problem burying the miners in the graveyard."

"The mayor kept grousing about the town budget until his assistant reminded him it was an election year and it would look good on his campaign. He's even going to get a special plaque and all." Ashley stole a spoonful of mashed potatoes off Scott's tray.

"What about the girls?" Scott asked.

"Tara's stepfather came forward and claimed her body," Linda said, suppressing a shudder. "He wasn't very upset to learn what had happened to her. They didn't get along; hadn't spoken to each other in years."

"Yeah, I didn't like him much." Ashley nodded. "Marisa's brother signed out her body immediately after her death."

"Shannon's remains were claimed by a distant aunt," Linda said. "They have a family vault so she'll finally be with her loved ones."

"I'm glad," Scott said. "She was smart, wasn't she? Figuring out Stewart's diabolical nature?"

"She was very clever." Linda nodded. "More so than I would have been in that situation. There was no signal in the attic, but she didn't let that stop her. When Stewart found her she recorded their conversation and hid the phone."

"She would have made a great investigator." Scott sighed. "Speaking of investigations, the case has been closed. Milo told me this morning." He took a sip of water. "The coroner has ruled Stewart responsible for the murders of Tara, Shannon, and Grady. I told the Chief of Police in Hackridge that Stewart had drugged and trapped Ashley in the basement before he came for you. Things went south for him, and he was killed in self-defense; which explained his body in the apartment and why we were in the cavern under his house."

"Grady?" Linda asked. "He didn't kill Grady."

"Well," Scott grimaced, "I couldn't really say it was a gray shadow that pushed Grady down the stairs and have it pass muster, could I? They're more than willing to pin that on Stewart too."

"It isn't true though," Linda murmured.

"Whatever. It's much more honest than you thinking it's your fault," Scott scolded.

"Isn't it?" Linda snapped. "I forced us all to go on the 'witch hunt.' You guys could have just left."

"That's bullshit," Ashley said. "And you know it. That… ghostly *thing* wasn't going to let us go. And if anyone is responsible for Grady, it's me."

"No!" Linda said. "You can't be held responsible, you were possessed by the entity."

"And you didn't force Grady to be there," Scott said decisively. "She chose to be there. She chose to fight. If I know Grady, and I knew her pretty well, she would have wanted to die trying, rather than stick in her comfort zone, safe and secure."

Linda didn't press the point. No matter what anyone said, she would always feel deep regret about Grady's death.

"Speaking of old women," Ashley said breaking the awkward silence. "What about Evelyn? Is there anyone to care for her?"

"No known relatives." Scott shrugged then winced in pain. "Her lawyers will be instructed to sell the manor to pay for a care facility that Stewart designated in his will. She's in Pine Grove. It's a few miles away from Hackridge."

"I feel sorry for her. The poor woman had to witness so much and could do nothing about it."

Ashley shrugged. "I'm just glad we're getting out of here."

"Wait, what?" Scott asked. He let his spoonful of Jell-O drop back in its tray.

"We're leaving this afternoon." Linda smiled.

"My truck is fixed, and free of charge, thanks to Milo," Ashley said. "We had to stay for the purpose of investigation, but we are now free to leave. I can't wait to get back to civilization."

"I thought you were staying for a few months," Scott said to Linda. She could see the confused sparkle in his blue eyes, the dismay and the longing.

She blushed. "The retreat is the scene of a crime. I have nowhere to stay and no job to stay for. Plus, I decided to leave a few days ago, actually. But we'll keep in touch. I have your number."

"You'd better call," Scott warned. "Or I'll be forced to stalk you across the country like some psycho."

Ashley glared at him, but Linda only laughed.

"I'm sorry." Scott went red. "I wasn't trying to remind you of your ex."

"Actually," Linda said after a moment of reflection, "I haven't thought of Jackson in a while. And after what we've experienced here, I don't fear him as much as before. I'm ready to move on with my life."

"That's the best thing I've heard all day," Ashley said. "I guess this place did work for you after all."

It felt good to be rid of her old shackles. The trauma was still there, like the memory of an old bruise, but she was now well equipped to live her life in spite of it. It helped that she was no longer living a lie. She recognized that she didn't suffer from sleep paralysis or hallucinations, but her true potential was as a conduit for restless spirits bound to a place of trauma. It was heartening to know, finally, who she was, though it opened a whole door of uncertainties and she knew one day she'd have to deal with that.

"We'd better get going if we want to get home by sundown," Ashley said. "Bye, Scott. Be good." She shook hands with him. "I'll be outside," she said to Linda on her way out.

Linda gave him a sheepish smile.

"I wanted to thank you, Scott," she said, clasping his hand. It was warm, comforting, and dependable. "I haven't had many friends in life, but I count you as one of the best. You've done more than help me through this time. You've returned my faith in myself. Thank you."

"Any time, Linda," Scott said, placing his hand on top of hers. "Don't be a stranger now."

"I won't. I'll keep in touch. Goodbye," she said, pulling her hand back. She stepped away, but then on impulse lunged back and hugged him.

"Ouch," he said. "Watch the bandages!"

"Sorry." Linda laughed. Her insides roiled at her own bold

outburst. She whipped around and walked out of the room, blushing.

"You okay?" Ashley asked when she joined her. "You look like you're breaking out in hives."

"I'm great." Linda smiled. "Let's go, shall we?"

"I thought you'd never ask," Ashley grinned.

They walked down the hall, ready to put Blackwood County and its horrors behind them forever.

— ∞ § ∞ —

Thank you for reading the serialized novel. If you enjoyed it, please consider signing up to my Readers' Group mailing list. **You will receive a free copy of *The Abandoned House*,** a short spin-off of *The Haunting of Blackburn Manor* featuring Scott and Stewart some twenty years earlier. This story is not available anywhere else.

Click here to read *The Abandoned House*, and to get notification when the next book is available (or copy and paste this link into your browser: http://bit.ly/BCA-LP) . You will also hear occasionally about other good things we give to our readers.

FREE DOWNLOAD

EXCLUSIVE and FREE for all subscribers

CLICK HERE to get started!

amazon kindle

1995. On Halloween night, Scott just wants to go trick-or-treating, but his older brother has other plans. He is having a party in an abandoned house on the wrong side of town, and he insists Scott remains outside.

As the drinks flow so do the stories, until one of them starts to sound too familiar... and a night of fun turns into a night of terror.

Blake Croft & Ashley Raven
www.blakecroftauthor.com
www.facebook.com/BlakeCroftAuthor

NOTE FROM THE AUTHORS

Thank you for taking a chance on *the Haunting of Blackburn House*.

Did you enjoy the novel? We hope so, and we would really appreciate it if you would help others enjoy this story too and help spread the word.

Please consider leaving an honest review today telling other readers why you liked this book, wherever you purchased this book, or on Goodreads. **It doesn't need to be long**, just a few sentences can make a huge difference. **Your reviews go a long way in helping others discover what we are writing**, and decide if a book is for them.

We appreciate anything you can do to help, and if you do write a review, wherever it is, please send an email at croft.raven@blakecroftauthor.com, so we could thank you personally.

BLAKE CROFT

Thank you very much,

Blake Croft & Ashley Raven

OTHER BOOKS BY BLAKE CROFT & ASHLEY RAVEN

Click here to browse all Blake Croft's Books (or copy and paste this link into your browser: http://bit.ly/BCA-Books).

THE HAUNTING OF THE CREOLE HOUSE (EXCERPT)

Summary

A desperate move to secure their future becomes a descent into hell for a young family.

Abbie Coltrane and her husband Richard know their financial situation is dire, so when Richard decides to take the whole family on vacation in Louisiana, Abbie is baffled.

It doesn't take long for her apprehension to prove founded. Something dark lurks in the old Creole house.

Abbie and Richard's young sons are the first to witness this phenomenon. When Aiden, the youngest, treats the teddy bear he found in their room as a friend, his brother Dave senses something terrible. Constant nightmares and fighting take a toll on them all, and what begins as a strange occurrence takes an ugly turn that spurs them to run for their lives. However, the sinister entity has other plans.

Can the Coltranes bring an end to the madness before tragedy strikes?

There is something in the Creole house. Ever watching, always hungry… it waits.

>> **To get** *The Haunting of the Creole House,* type the title on Amazon.

Prologue

June 9th – 7:54 PM
Lakeshore Drive, Mandeville – Louisiana

The sun kissed the surface of the blue waters before it began its slow descent into Lake Pontchartrain. In the quiet old Creole house overlooking the creek, you could almost hear the hiss at the exact moment sun and water collided. The roar of an engine pierced the waiting quiet like a knife, stirring the stale air into the beginnings of energy. As suddenly as it had started, it stopped when the family car parked close to the colonial house. The quality of the stillness in the house changed from melancholia to anticipation. When the car doors opened, little children's voices mingled with their parents' and It knew that a serious change had come.

In the fast fading daylight, the sound of closing car doors echoed through the house, like thunder rolling across an immense empty plain. The floorboards creaked with expectation, and doors stood ajar with attention. The house braced itself for the new occupants. But in a room on the upper floor, It sat very still by the window, trying to make out the faces of the young children running about in the short driveway.

The windows were streaked with grime, blurring the children's faces. They were a neat family of four, a set of parents and two young boys. The perfect nuclear family. It hungered for a closer look, a whiff of scent, a snatch of song, and presently it was rewarded.

"*Bumble, bumble,*
My busy bee,
Buzzing around
The mulberry tree.
From hither to tither,
From blossom to bush,
Making up honey,
For Mummy and me!"

The giddy words were half chanted, half sung by the child with a head of yellow sunshine. His small legs pumped up and down as he ran around the garden, a tantalizing blur of yellow and green.

The elder of the two chased the little one, his arms outstretched. The squeals of delight rippled up to the window where the shadows shifted, and the glass fogged briefly under a splayed hand. It had to see their faces. It had to be sure.

The children ran closer to the house. The younger, no more than five, stopped to look up at the house. The older brother, twice his age, came to stop beside him. They shaded their eyes with their little hands, their faces twisted in concentration.

Two little boys. Finally returned.

It waited.

Chapter One

June 9th – 7:58 PM

Lakeshore Drive, Mandeville – Louisiana

"They're excited," said Richard.

Abbie Coltrane smiled and squeezed her husband's hand. The sand felt cool, wet, and alien beneath her toes. The foamy surf looked like aggressive fingers clawing ever nearer, to grasp unsuspecting passersby.

The laughter of her two boys pierced the air, competing with the shrill call of the seagulls. Dave, the elder at ten, with his mop of brown hair and his broad sloping shoulders, was running on ahead. Aiden, the baby of the family, tried his best to keep up, his yellow curls shining like a halo in the setting sun. He looked back often, his big blue eyes making sure Abbie and Richard were close by, then flitted behind them to the house they had just come from.

"This'll be good for our boys." Richard fished out a cigarette and lighter, and cupped his hand around the flame to protect it. "Two months on the beach, under the sun, and they'll be as brown and brawny as me."

"Hmm." Abbie bent down to pick up a seashell, letting her hair curtain her face.

"Two months is all I need, Abbie." Richard's voice was urgent, a precursor to an argument. "I have the perfect story. I just need to get most of it on paper, and this place is going to do wonders for my block. I'm sure of it."

"I just can't see why we couldn't have gone up to a cabin in Ridgeway." Her voice dropped lower. "Ali said she'd lend us the place free of charge for the summer." Abbie was still bent low, her fingers sifting aimlessly through the sand.

"This is not the same as Ridgeway."

She couldn't argue with that. The weather was warmer, the

houses had that tempered beauty you only get with really old places, the people were more colorful, and Lake Pontchartrain itself was mercurial. Maybe Richard was right. Maybe this was the place he needed to be to write his breakthrough novel. Goodness knew he was struggling back in Colorado. His agent was at his wit's end and had confessed to Abbie that the royalties were more of a drip than a steady trickle.

Standing up straight, Abbie brushed the sand off her hands and looked back at the beach house they had rented for the summer. It was built atop a narrow strip of rock that acted as a natural barrier to the beach and the lake, insuring the children would have a modest walk before they got anywhere near the water's edge. The house itself was built in classic French Creole style with wide porches and galleries, and several colonnettes that supported a wide roof. The main walls had been painted azure blue.

While the front garden was blooming with hibiscus and iris flowers, the inside was dreary. The furniture pieces were mismatched. Dirt choked the windows, and the whole place needed to be aired out. As for the owners, Abbie hadn't laid eyes on them at all. They had found the keys dangling by a hook next to the front door. The owner hadn't even bothered to leave a note.

As Abbie watched the house, the sun bled into the large body of water and the tall dark windows of the house stared out like blank brooding eyes. She had the acute sense that someone was watching her. A shiver ran up her spine, and she turned away to the lake. The children were playing at the water's edge, running away from the chasing waves. She was very aware of a sense of not belonging. Born and bred in land-locked Colorado, Abbie couldn't help but be aware of her location on the map, how New Orleans was right on the edge of a yawning abyss. The sight of the smoldering red waters of Lake Pontchartrain made her wonder how easy it would be to fall off the edge of the earth, swept away on one of the greedy waves, and disappear without a trace.

She shook her head, as if trying to dislodge the morbid thoughts that had made a nest in there.

This is all Richard's fault. Just because you write horror for a living doesn't mean your road trip stories need to be macabre.

"All right. Boys!" Abbie called out. "That's enough for today. You can come back to the beach in the morning."

"Pizza for dinner?" Richard asked, dropping his cigarette in the sand.

"I'm not sure any place will deliver."

"Why don't you and the boys take a shower and start settling in? I'll go into town and get us some dinner."

She smiled as he kissed her forehead and went off towards the house.

"Come on, boys! I'm going to count to ten."

They came running back at eight.

Chapter Two

June 10th – 12:31 PM

Beachfront, Lakeshore Drive, Mandeville – Louisiana

There was sand in his eyes. The more Aiden rubbed it, the more painful it became. He screamed, but not in pain. He was furious. He kicked in Dave's general direction, but his foot didn't make contact with anything.

"I hate you!" Aiden screamed. "I'm telling. That will teach you to bully me."

"I wasn't bullying you," Dave protested. "I just said you're too little to play with us, you'll get hurt. And you did, didn't you?"

"What a baby," one of the boys laughed.

Tears of frustration pooled in Aiden's eyes and dislodged some gritty sand; he could see better than he had a moment ago. He looked back at the boys that had ruined the day. They were taller than Dave, but not by much, and they had a beach ball. What wouldn't Aiden give to have a beach ball of his own? That'd teach stupid Dave, and his stupid new friends, that Aiden wasn't a baby, and he could play too.

"I'm not a baby! Dave's the baby. He cried last night for Mommy because he had a nightmare."

The boys laughed. Dave's face was red with embarrassment. He pushed Aiden in the sand.

"I'm telling!" Aiden stomped his little foot in the sand and made a mad dash for the beach house.

Filled with righteous fury, Aiden pushed the screen door open with a mighty bang. Abbie stood in the kitchen trying to sort through the boxes that the moving van had finally delivered that morning.

"Mom!"

"Hmm?" Abbie opened a box and rolled her eyes. "He's mislabeled another one."

"Mom!"

"What, Aiden?" Sharp tone. Not a good start to his righteous crusade against bullying older brothers, and the vagaries of their lofty stature. Yet Aiden persisted.

"Dave won't let me play volleyball with his new friends, and he pushed me so I got sand in my eyes, and I hurt my knee!" He tried not to sound too petulant, but he had learned that a few tears went a long way to soften his mother up, and gain the upper hand.

Not this time, though.

"That's all very sad, Aiden. Why don't you help me instead? It'll be fun. Take this box of your toys upstairs, and store it inside the wardrobe in there. And I mean inside, not scattered all over the floor."

"But Mom!"

"Thank you."

Puffing his cheeks in anger at the unfair conduct of adults, Aiden took the small box of toys and hauled it upstairs, step by step.

"Dad! Could you help me with the box?"

"I'm setting up my study, kiddo. Ask Mom," Richard called from the front of the house.

"I'm busy with the kitchen. Ask Dave." Abbie's distracted voice bobbed up the hall like a deflated balloon.

Aiden rolled his eyes. Mom had totally spaced out. She usually got this way when she was upset about something. He started dragging the box up one stair, then the next. It was so like his parents to completely ignore him at times. It felt like nothing he said was taken seriously, and that he was someone to be petted and cooed over. He hated being treated like a baby.

I'll show them. I'll take this box up and then dump it all on Dave's bed. Let him sort it out.

Evil plan in place, it became easier to tote the box up the unforgiving stairs and down the hall to the room with a view of the front drive. Aiden would have much preferred the room with the view of the beach, but his parents had laid claim to it. Another bit of unfairness notched against the adults.

Aiden kicked the box the last few feet into the room with twin beds. He hauled the box over to Dave's bed, the one closer to the bedroom door, the one Dave chose first even though it was Aiden's turn to do so. Aiden dumped the entire contents of the toy box onto the freshly made bed, giggling with glee.

"What are you doing?"

Aiden screamed and whirled around. His father stood in the door, a mug of coffee in his hands, and a stern frown on his brow.

"Are you trying to get your brother in trouble?"

"No." Aiden's voice was as small as he felt.

"Good. You should put those away in the wardrobe."

The wardrobe handles were wrought iron. Four slats spanned the wood, marking where the hinges were. It was a tatty old thing, dust nestled inside its carvings, and pushed against the far wall. Aiden made a show of collecting the toys back in the box and taking them up to the wardrobe till his father was satisfied and left. As soon as Richard's footsteps receded down the stairs, Aiden promptly dropped the box on the floor and kicked the wardrobe doors a few times for good measure. A splinter of wood felt from the bottom of the door.

Fuming, he paced the room and planned to run away to teach his family a lesson. Tantalizing images of his distraught parents and guilt-ridden brother made him smile.

The low creak of protesting wood made him stop in his tracks. The skin on the nape of his neck tickled, and he looked back. One wardrobe door had opened slightly, revealing a sliver of darkness. He must have unlatched it when he kicked it. Aiden peered a little closer, fancying he saw a smudge of red in the gloom. He stepped closer to get a better look. The sudden jangling of music made him jump back a few feet.

Music was coming from the wardrobe. It sounded scratchy and wobbly, like the old vinyl records his grandfather had in his study back home. Aiden tilted his head to hear the music better, taking a cautious step closer. It was a sweet melody, innocuous, yet engaging. Aiden placed his hand on the smooth edges of the wardrobe doors and opened them completely, letting in a shaft of light to dispel the darkness. The song seemed to swell in that moment.

A small teddy bear sat propped up in one dark corner of the wardrobe, a tartan red bow tied around its neck. It looked forlorn and lost. Aiden picked it up, his anger and frustration forgotten in the face of a surprising discovery.

The texture of the old toy was unlike any teddy bear Aiden had ever seen. It was rough, and it reminded him of the flour and grain sacks at the Whole Foods store. Layers of dust covered it, and the tartan bow was the color of moldy tomatoes.

Dodo tipititmanman
Manman-w ou pa la
L'alélarivyè
Si ou pa dodo djab la vamanjé-w
Dodo pititkrabnankalalou

The words sounded silly to Aiden, and meant nothing to him, yet he found the song soothing. He checked the teddy bear closely to find the source of the music, his back turned to the open wardrobe. The music stopped. Aiden searched more frantically, wanting to hear the song again, an unexplainable pressure building between his shoulders and the nape of his neck in the heavy silence.

"Aiden!"

Aiden looked up, his fingers going still. Dave stood just outside the bedroom door, one side of his face streaked with sand, his cheeks pallid as if all the blood had drained out of him.

"Aiden, come here." Dave waved him over frantically, standing absolutely still. "Aiden, get back! Hurry!"

But he wasn't looking at Aiden. He was looking directly behind him at the yawning dark mouth of the open wardrobe.

Copy and paste this link into your browser to read it now: bit.ly/hauntingcreole

THE WISHING BOX (EXCERPT)

Summary

When your secret dreams become real-life nightmares... there's no waking up.

Diana McCullough has been waiting. Watching. For the one thing that can change her life. The one thing that's always been just out of her reach. Until now.

When Diana McCullough comes into possession of a magic wishing box, she believes her luck has finally changed. But soon she'll discover that the distance between her expectations and a disturbing reality is rapidly narrowing.

She's unearthed something dangerous. And it wants more than Diana's life. But how do you outrun and outsmart what isn't really there?

The macabre comes to sinister life in this small Scottish village in October 1976. Gothic horror, suspense, and a haunted possession will leave you sleeping with the lights on until your own Wishing Box arrives. Then you won't be able to sleep at all.

>> **To get *The Wishing Box (a haunting)*,** type the title on Amazon.

Prologue

Forest Road, Marywell Village – Scotland
12th October 1976

Steven had to bury her to be sure nobody ever found her. He squinted through the fog, glancing surreptitiously in the rearview mirror to make sure he wasn't being followed. Steven drove slowly; the pea-souper made visibility poor, something he was banking on.

Deep into the forest, in a clearing, Steven stopped the stolen car. He sat a moment in the cold dark interior of the car, staring at the thick mist trailing out of the forest like reaching fingers. His breathing was shaky on each exhale, pregnant with unshed tears. It was exactly this weakness she had preyed on. The evil bitch.

Steven grabbed the shovel placed on the front passenger seat, and he stepped out into the fog. Condensation peppered his skin, and he felt soaked within minutes. A sudden cry from the forest made him drop the shovel with a clang. Heart hammering in chest, Steven swallowed.

"Must be an animal or something." He wiped the sweat off his forehead. Ignoring the chill, he picked up the shovel and his load, and trudged towards the forest.

It was strange how sound echoed in the mist. His footsteps resounded back, making the nape of his neck prickle as if he was being pursued. Straining his head forward, he hunched his shoulders, and ignored the instinct to keep looking behind him for any sign of the authorities rushing at him through the forest.

Steven stopped under an old oak tree, its trunk thick and the roots arching out of the ground like the backs of frightened cats. It was as good a spot as any to bury her. No one would find her here, and the horror would end.

With a grunt, Steven dug between a knot of roots. His arms ached, and his hands were raw by the time he stepped back from the neat hole. Getting down on his knees, Steven pulled a box out of his pocket. His jaw clenched tighter as he looked at the box. He stared down at *her*. Hateful, malevolent, spiteful *her*.

Steven had tried to burn her, to burn the bitch, but she didn't catch. The fire danced around her, producing noxious smoke. She had refused to burn.

That cursed box.

It, or rather *she*, wasn't a mere object. She was small enough to fit in the palm of his hand. The wood was carved with birds and flowers around a single command, "Make a Wish." He was convinced a malicious she-demon possessed the box, seducing unsuspecting owners into depravity and ruin. With an animal cry, Steven threw the box inside the hole. He had to make sure no one would find her.

Steven filled the hole in with his bare hands, his palms stinging, but he didn't pay them much attention. Once he had patted the earth down and scattered fallen leaves on top, he got back to his feet, knees creaking in pain.

Finding the way back to the car was harder than he had thought. Twice, he got lost and wondered if the evil box had the ability to trap him in the dark forest to die. He cursed himself for not leaving the car's headlights on as a marker, but he couldn't have the police finding him so soon. He finally stumbled on the forest road, the outline of the car dim in the mist that had crept out of the forest to consume it. He thought he saw something moving between the trees. His keys rattled together, scratching the side of the car as he tried to get to the lock. Steven's eyes darted to the tree line to make sure he hadn't been seen.

Sirens blared closer. The police were on the move again. He had to leave before they caught up with him. He couldn't get arrested here. Not so close to where he'd buried her.

Once the key found the lock, Steven rushed inside the car. He started the engine and tore down the road he had come from, not caring about the poor visibility, and his gaze continuously drawn to the rearview mirror.

Chapter One

Marywell Village – Scotland
7th October 1976 – Five days earlier

The McCullough cottage was small and remote, nestled in a hollow of land surrounded by spreading fields. A crow sat on the tiled roof, cawing at the passing of the few cars and people. No sounds came from the house. Smoke blew out from the chimney, the only sign that the cottage was occupied.

Inside, Diana couldn't take her eyes off the cake. It was the most expensive item of food she had ever seen. In comparison, her kitchen looked shabby and far worse for wear than it actually was. The cake had three layers, each put together with a mountain of icing, and topped with sugar flowers. Placing one last covetous finger on the cardboard box, Diana turned to the rest of the groceries Peter had brought from Arbroath.

There was more produce than Diana could ever afford: fresh raspberries, potatoes, peas and carrots, with a fine shank of lamb. She put away half to use later in the week. After placing the stale bread and cheese from the morning into the pigs' slop pail, she began preparing supper. The radio blasted the latest news on the American elections and President Gerald Ford's confidence at the lack of Soviet influence on Eastern Europe.

"Ma!" Peter's head popped in through the kitchen door. "Pa and I are going for a walk along the beach."

"You tell your Pa you get enough of the sea on that oil rig of yours."

Peter laughed, and Diana could see how much he had changed in the six months he had been on the job. His skin was several shades darker. The laugh lines around his eyes were deeper, and his lean frame had become broader. Her son had gone to the North Sea a boy, and he came back a man.

"I suspect he wants to show me off in the village along the way." Peter picked a handful of raspberries.

"And why would he nae?" Diana beamed with pride. "A son on the oil rig, that's something to boast of in this village."

"And I wouldnae rob you of such an opportunity. Did you know Adam Campbell is also applying for a place on the BP rig? Baldrick, the recruiter, told me of it in Arbroath this morning."

Diana sniffed. Her mouth pressed in a thin, disapproving line. "Aye, he's a capable enough lad, but he has no head for tricky situations. Best he doesn't get it for his own sake."

Footsteps shuffled behind Peter, and Steven's florid face poked in the doorframe.

"Smells grand!" He grinned.

"Now if only the kitchen were grander," Diana remarked. Steven's smile fell and his brow darkened. His eyes held reproach and he glanced at Peter, as if apologizing for Diana. A bolt of intense anger flared in Diana's chest.

Peter either didn't notice, or chose to ignore the exchange between his parents, and bent down to kiss Diana on the crown of her head where her brown hair was white and thinning. "Be back soon."

Diana waved them goodbye, then got back to cutting vegetables. Once the shank was in for roasting and the potatoes set to boil, Diana wiped her brow and stepped out in the back garden to have a smoke. It was a vegetable garden, where she tended her pumpkins. They were prized in all of Marywell. They were coming along well, and they would be ready to harvest in another week.

She took a long drag on her cigarette and looked skyward. The clouds were so low it seemed they would graze the top of the roof if they wished. The windows were dark and reflected the oppressive sky.

The taste of the tobacco was smooth, and she marveled at the luxury of a good cigarette. She looked at her yellowing nails, and then the patch of land in her backyard where she spent most of her day breaking her back to produce vegetables she could never eat, because the money they brought in was far more precious.

It had been a hard life for Diana, born between two World Wars. She spent her youth amidst food rations, and the spot of Blitz in Scotland, only to survive the ordeal to find the whole nation changed, and not for the better. But she was reaping the rewards now. Having a son on the oil rig meant a fortune in the bank, and goodness knew she deserved this good turn.

She had only one child, no thanks to Steven, who would have had a litter. It was Diana's foresight, her insistence that she could neither put in the work nor the money that more than one child would cost. So there was just Peter, and they had sacrificed every comfort and luxury for the future of their son.

"And lang may his lum reek." She puffed her wish up to the sky in tobacco smoke.

Diana inhaled deeply, as she watched a figure detach from the uniform shadows of the woods across the way, and hobble along the McNallys' wheat field.

For a moment Diana thought the woman was an acquaintance from the village, come to gossip about something trivial in the hopes of being invited to dinner; but then she saw the black skirt embroidered with large, gay flowers, a shawl in every color of the rainbow, and heard the tinkling of silver bangles.

"Bonnie day, aye?" The woman waved her hand in greeting, and Diana saw that she was very old and stooped, encumbered by a filthy bag on one of her shoulders. A mild wind would spirit her away.

"Aye." Diana wondered if she could simply scuff out her cigarette and get back inside, but she was loath to waste the smoke.

"Your house is it?"

"Aye."

"Smells dandy. Can you spare an old woman a *tattie*?"

>> **Copy and paste this link into your browser to read it now: bit.ly/wishingbox**

THE ABANDONED HOUSE

(EXCLUSIVE STORY FOR MEMBERS OF MY READERS' LIST)

On Halloween night, Scott just wants to go trick-or-treating but his older brother has other plans. He is having a party in an abandoned house on the wrong side of town, and he insists Scott remains outside.

As the drinks flow so do the stories, until one of them starts to sound too familiar… and a night of fun turns into a night of terror.

Note: this short story is a short spin-off of The Haunting of Blackburn Manor *featuring characters of the novel some twenty years earlier.*

Copy and paste this link into your browser to read it now: http://bit.ly/BCA-LP

COPYRIGHT

This book is a work of fiction. Names, characters and places are either products of the author's imagination or used fictitiously. Any resemblance to actual persons, living or dead, events or locales is entirely coincidental. The author has taken liberties with locales, including the creation of fictional towns and places, as a mean of creating the necessary circumstances for the story. This book is intended for fictional purposes only.

Copyright © 2019, 2021 by Blake Croft

All rights reserved. Without limiting the rights under copyright reserved above, no part of this publication may be reproduced, stored in or introduced into a retrieval system, or transmitted in any form, or by any means (electronic, mechanical, photocopying, recording, or otherwise), without the prior written permission of the copyright owner, except for the use of brief quotations in a book review.

ISBN: 979-8-6495-5016-1

Printed in Great Britain
by Amazon